P9-AQD-634

"I'm not hitting on you."

Brody grinned. "Not yet, anyway."

At the expression on his face Jillian's body responded, warming, as automatic as a reflex.

"The point is that this job kills relationships. We're on the road, out all night, always in a crowd, surrounded by people looking to get laid. It can get wild."

"It's a tough job, but someone has to do it?"

"You got it." His eyebrows rose as if her joke had surprised him. She was coming off too serious, she realized, no doubt a strike against her.

"I don't have a boyfriend, so that's no problem. Neither is the travel or the hours or whatever it takes. I'll work hard. I'll be what you need."

"And what do you think I need?"

There was heat in his words, something sexy and intimate that caught her short. Something that made her think of bodies entwining on twisted sheets.

"Me," she blurted. "You need me."

Blaze™

Dear Reader,

I used to be offended by men. Well, by how sexist they could be, crude and lewd and obsessed with women's bodies over their minds. I mellowed out—what choice did I have?—and now accept, even occasionally celebrate *la différence*. Men are visually stimulated and can't multitask, especially during sex, so we can't expect to hear how pretty our eyes are during the act, right? It's a brain thing. Who knew?

It's also true that we all have an angle on the world. We see it through the eyes of our past, our attitudes, our family roles, our life experiences. That's how it was for Jillian James in this story. She *believed* she was open to other viewpoints—crucial for a documentary filmmaker—but she learned through Brody that, well... maybe not so much.

Jillian taught Brody, aka Mr. Love 'Em and Leave 'Em Begging for More, a thing or two as well, such as how to stick around for love. They both saw the world through new eyes.

I hope their story opens your eyes a little, too. Oh, and warms your heart. Always that is my hope.

All my best,

Dawn Atkins

P.S. Please visit me at www.dawnatkins.com.

NO STOPPING NOW

Dawn Atkins

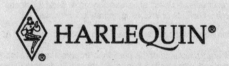

HARLEQUIN®

TORONTO • NEW YORK • LONDON
AMSTERDAM • PARIS • SYDNEY • HAMBURG
STOCKHOLM • ATHENS • TOKYO • MILAN • MADRID
PRAGUE • WARSAW • BUDAPEST • AUCKLAND

If you purchased this book without a cover you should be aware that this book is stolen property. It was reported as "unsold and destroyed" to the publisher, and neither the author nor the publisher has received any payment for this "stripped book."

ISBN-13: 978-0-373-79395-2
ISBN-10: 0-373-79395-2

NO STOPPING NOW

Copyright © 2008 by Daphne Atkeson.

All rights reserved. Except for use in any review, the reproduction or utilization of this work in whole or in part in any form by any electronic, mechanical or other means, now known or hereafter invented, including xerography, photocopying and recording, or in any information storage or retrieval system, is forbidden without the written permission of the publisher, Harlequin Enterprises Limited, 225 Duncan Mill Road, Don Mills, Ontario M3B 3K9, Canada.

This is a work of fiction. Names, characters, places and incidents are either the product of the author's imagination or are used fictitiously, and any resemblance to actual persons, living or dead, business establishments, events or locales is entirely coincidental.

This edition published by arrangement with Harlequin Books S.A.

® and TM are trademarks of the publisher. Trademarks indicated with ® are registered in the United States Patent and Trademark Office, the Canadian Trade Marks Office and in other countries.

www.eHarlequin.com

Printed in U.S.A.

ABOUT THE AUTHOR

Dawn Atkins started her writing career in the second grade, crafting stories that included every single spelling word her teacher gave her. Since then, she's expanded her vocabulary and her publishing credits. This is her twentieth published book. She won the 2005 Golden Quill Award for Best Sexy Romance and has been a *Romantic Times BOOKreviews* Reviewers Choice Award finalist for Best Flipside (2005) and Best Blaze (2006). She lives in Arizona with her husband, teenage son and a butterscotch-and-white cat.

Books by Dawn Atkins

HARLEQUIN BLAZE

93—FRIENDLY PERSUASION
155—VERY TRULY SEXY
176—GOING TO EXTREMES
205—SIMPLY SEX
214—TEASE ME
253—DON'T TEMPT ME*
294—WITH HIS TOUCH**
306—AT HER BECK AND CALL**
318—AT HIS FINGERTIPS**
348—SWEPT AWAY†

*Forbidden Fantasies
**Doing It...Better!
†Sex on the Beach

Don't miss any of our special offers. Write to us at the following address for information on our newest releases.

Harlequin Reader Service
U.S.: 3010 Walden Ave., P.O. Box 1325, Buffalo, NY 14269
Canadian: P.O. Box 609, Fort Erie, Ont. L2A 5X3

To David, my second set of eyes

Acknowledgments

A million thanks for a million answers to documentary filmmakers Suzanne Johnson and Penelope Price. I'm awestruck by your skill and dedication. Any film-related errors are strictly my own.

1

ON THE MONITOR, Brody Donegan, aka Doctor Nite, slid a five under the stripper's G-string and gave the knowing smirk that made his cable show must-see TV for every lounge lizard prowling the meat-market bars.

"I've got to get this guy," Jillian James said to her cousin Nate, in whose video-editing studio they sat. "For the documentary," she added quickly, hoping Nate hadn't noticed the edge in her voice. She tapped the Mute button so hard she snapped a nail.

Doctor Nite, Brody Donegan's show, featured sexy hot spots as the backdrop for advice on how to get laid and stay single. Donegan, who used women like tissues and taught his high-fiving, beer-guzzling fans to do the same, symbolized all that was wrong with a culture that exalted sex over love, external looks over inner beauty and self-involvement over emotional commitment.

Jillian *had* to get him.

She'd tried for weeks for an interview, but his network had stonewalled her and his agent had e-mailed that he was too busy. "For a no-name filmmaker" was implied, but Jillian got the message loud and clear.

That was where fate, through her cousin, had stepped in. Nate just happened to be good friends with Donegan's camera guy, who just happened to be out of commission for the upcoming shoot. Nate had recommended Jillian to fill in.

"So, you have the scoop for me?" she asked Nate now.

"Brody wants to meet you tonight." Nate handed her one of the show's business cards, which featured the star's face. Donegan was handsome enough if you liked the bad-boy look—square jaw…dangerous eyes…wicked grin.

Jillian could take or leave it.

"Time and place on the back," Nate said.

She flipped the card. *11 p.m., Score* was written in bold Sharpie. Score was a trendy bar in Santa Monica, she knew. "Eleven is late."

"Doctor Nite hours," Nate said. "Get used to it."

"I will. You bet. Whatever it takes." She flicked the card against her chin, her heart racing, her skin overheated, sole to scalp. This scrap of paper held the key to her future. Everything depended on this meeting. The job. Her documentary. Her career.

Well, maybe not everything, but this was big. In her pitch to the We Women Cable Network, she'd mentioned exclusive interviews with Doctor Nite, knowing that would pique the acquisitions manager's interest. Now she had to get the damn interviews.

"So this project you want him for is about dating?" Nate asked, looking doubtful. "Doesn't sound like you."

"I needed a change of pace after the foster care piece," she said. She'd devoted two years to the project, living on Top Ramen and dreams, begging favors from film school friends, selling her second camera, her extra computer and every spare piece of equipment to pay postproduction costs.

It had been her first major project since she left TV news. Her San Diego network had sponsored several small projects, all well received, but *Childhood Lost* took top honors at two prestigious film festivals. She'd floated on air.

Then slammed to the ground when she couldn't find a buyer. Everyone loved it, but it was "too local" for public television and "too dark" for commercial networks who seemed to be buying only lurid exposés or feel-good pieces. Without big-buck backers, *Childhood Lost* sank like a stone to the bottom of the sea of lost documentaries.

How could a movie change the world if the only people who saw it were her film school profs and die-hard fans?

She'd vowed her next project would be commercial from the get-go. Drinks out with her two best friends, Becca and Dana, had given her the idea for a movie about the dark side of the player lifestyle.

Becca had just broken up with her boyfriend of two years because, at thirty-seven, he claimed to be too young to get serious. Dana had lived through a similar scenario six months before. Jillian's own breakups had been amicable, but between the three friends, they knew a dozen other women who'd been victims of the Peter Pan syndrome—guys who refused to grow up and commit.

As they commiserated over margaritas, *Doctor Nite* had appeared on the bar's plasma and guys all over the place lifted their beer and woofed approval, and the idea was born.

Soon Jillian was frantically scribbling notes on napkins for *Peter Pan Prison: How Men Who Play Pay.*

Bare-bones grants from a social-psychology foundation and two women's groups had funded interviews with therapists, matchmakers and sociologists, along with women who'd dated Peter Pan boys and some longtime bachelors she'd snared outside a strip club. She'd obtained promotional footage from the *Doctor Nite* show, too. Now all she needed was in-depth interviews with the man himself to nail the sale to We Women.

On the screen in her cousin's studio, Donegan was flirting with a top-heavy blonde. "I love this bit," Nate said.

"You're a fan of the show?"

"Are you kidding? Doctor Nite is great." Nate was a good

person with a kind heart, but he was single and twenty-eight, exactly the show's demographic.

"You don't think marriage is a crime against men, though, do you? You want to settle down one day?"

"If I can't avoid it." He grinned.

Lord, if Nate bought the Doctor Nite philosophy, lots of other decent guys did, too, which made for a terrible trend.

She studied Doctor Nite. She could see why women liked him. Even with the sound muted, she picked up his strong masculine energy. He had expressive eyes, and a smile that *tugged* at you, invited you in. Infectious and appealing and—

"Oh, I get it," Nate said softly, "You're *into* the guy."

"God, no," she said, startled to feel her face flame.

"That's cool, JJ. Sometimes I forget you're a woman."

"Gee, thanks," she said, though she took pride in being one of the guys when she worked. In high school, when being overweight had rendered her sex-neutral, it had been hell. Fat girls were friends, not girlfriends.

Now being one of the guys served her well, kept any residual sexism at bay. She went by JJ and used the androgynous J. James as her credit line, and was as far from girlie as she could be. She carried her own equipment and never shied from intimidating shoots.

"Good luck with him," Nate said, studying her thoughtfully.

"Thanks. I'll need it." Getting the job was just the first step. She had to get Donegan to trust her enough to talk about his secret loneliness, the inner emptiness of his way of life.

She'd always been lucky getting honest answers to the boldest questions. She believed people responded to her bone-deep curiosity. Everyone longed to be understood, after all. Would Brody?

Watching him on the monitor, she felt a shiver of excitement. If her plan worked and she sold the movie, it would mean a big career leap. She'd have a name. Funding would fall into her lap. Not that fame or money was the point.

This piece was for Becca and Dana and all the women—and men, for that matter—crippled by the idea that just as a woman couldn't be too thin, a man couldn't be too single.

"You keep the DVD," Nate said with a wink. "Enjoy." Her cousin thought Jillian had a thing for Doctor Nite. Please. She took the DVD all the same. Research.

EVEN IF SHE HADN'T known what Brody Donegan looked like, Jillian would have known where he was by the crowd swarming his huge table in the raised central area of Score.

Designed to look like a bachelor pad from the Fifties, the club was furnished with zebra-striped chairs, low white and black leather couches, with a huge fire pit in the lounge and faux animal hides on the floor. The walls held framed nudes, the music was Sinatra and the signature drink a gin martini—shaken, not stirred. Perfect hangout for Doctor Nite.

Every seat at Donegan's long table was filled and people crowded around it, everyone talking at once. The women jutted their breasts forward, the men laughed boldly. Like mating birds, the males showed beak and claw, the females preened and flounced, hardwired to perform this primitive dance.

Jillian understood the drive, even if she didn't like it, and would use it to appeal to Brody. Instead of her usual jeans, chambray shirt and cargo vest, she'd worn a tailored white blouse that emphasized her tan and offered a sliver of cleavage, snug black slacks and heels high enough that her arches ached the instant she slid them on.

Why did women willingly endure this agony—not much better than ancient foot binding? Supposedly, spike heels enhanced a woman's sexual features—lifting her butt, lengthening her legs, tilting her breasts forward. Jillian had worn them so she could meet the six-foot Brody at eye level. If they made her more attractive to him, too, they were worth the temporary pain.

Instead of the usual ponytail under a ball cap, she'd let her curls fall wild to her shoulders. Sexier that way, she figured, though she wasn't much for the teasing hair toss.

She paused near the phone alcove to observe the scene. She liked to dip her toe into the social stream before getting swept into the current.

Donegan was clearly amusing the crowd, but she noticed that whenever someone addressed him, he made eye contact and turned his body toward them, giving full attention to the person. The man knew how to work a crowd, no question.

Jillian was prepared to be charmed. She hoped to charm him right back. At least enough to get hired. Then the real work began.

Abruptly, Donegan rose from the table and headed straight for her. Had he seen her, sensed her presence?

He's going to the men's room, you idiot. It was right behind her. She smiled at her foolishness. As he drew nearer, light hit his face and she was startled by his expression. He looked utterly weary. As if he were desperate to escape the noisy crowd and sleep for a week.

Wow. He was close and if she didn't speak soon, she'd seem like a bug-eyed gawker. She lurched forward. "Mr. Donegan? I'm Jillian James. JJ? Here to discuss filling in for Kirk Canter?"

He smiled and his expression warmed instantly. "Yes. JJ. That's right." He gave her an approving once-over. "Kirk didn't mention you were gorgeous."

"He's never seen me, actually. It's my cousin Nathan who recommended me. He went to film school with Kirk. Thank you, though." She tugged at her hair, uncomfortable with the compliment, but trying to look pleased.

"No, thank *you.*" Again his eyes traced her figure, making

her hot all over. She was flattered, of course, though years of being ignored by men because of her weight had given her a solid skepticism about superficial male attraction. In this case, she hoped it made Brody more amenable to hiring her.

Brody nodded toward his crowd at the table. "We're there if you want to head over."

"I'll just wait for you." She wondered how they would manage a meeting surrounded by the rowdy group now accepting a round of drinks. On Brody's tab, no doubt.

When Brody returned to her, his smile was so gracious she wondered if she'd imagined the naked exhaustion she'd seen in that unguarded moment.

"Shall we?" He put a hand to her back and led her to the table, fingertips light, the contact easy and natural on her body.

At the table, every head swiveled Brody's way, every pair of eyes turned to him. The king was back.

"I hate to break up the party, guys," Brody said, "but we need some alone time." His tone held a hint of sexual suggestion.

"Fo' sho," one guy said.

"Brody swings...he scores," said another, clinking beers with a third man. Two women cut Jillian glares, the message clear: *You're not that hot.*

Donegan's sexual pretense irritated her, but it worked. After a flurry of female kisses, male backslaps and handshakes, Brody and Jillian were suddenly alone.

Surveying the mess of abandoned martini glasses and beer steins, he sighed. "We'll be more comfortable in the lounge," he said and took her to a white leather couch in an alcove.

He sat just inside her personal space and studied her as if she were fragile or a work of art, his eyes a soulful brown that invited you in for a swim. If you had to drown, where better than warm chocolate?

Not Jillian's usual thoughts about men or their eyes, but Brody

Donegan was an unusual man. In person, she saw that he was more boy next door than bad boy. Maybe bad boy next door?

"Are you hungry?" he asked. "What would you like to drink?"

"I'm fine as far as food. Club soda to drink, please."

"Club soda?" He gave her look of mock disappointment. "Come on. You're out with Doctor Nite. You need something with a kick. Unless you're twelve-stepping it, JJ? Are you?"

"Twelve-stepping…? Oh. You mean, am I in recovery? No, no. I mean, I'm not an alcoholic—" She caught herself. "Not that that's bad. I mean, I know many people…" Her words trailed off.

"Some of your best friends are alcoholics?" He grinned.

"That came out wrong." She was falling on her first-impression face here.

"Don't be nervous, JJ. I don't bite. At least, not hard enough to leave a mark." He winked. "As to a drink, Andre mentioned this tricky little Australian Shiraz that I wanted to try. How's that sound? One glass? You're not driving, are you?"

"No. I came in a cab. One glass sounds fine."

The waiter appeared like a whispered breath and took Brody's order of the wine and an appetizer sampler. "Maybe you'll want a taste," he explained to her, throwing his arm across the back of the sofa and shifting his body her way.

She became aware of his broad shoulders and long legs, the expensive cologne he wore, the hint of stubble that on most men looked scruffy, but on him looked dead sexy.

Get a grip, Jillian.

She sat on the edge of the couch, her back straight, which was a technique she suggested for news interviews because it made you seem alert and prepared. "About the job…" she said, forging ahead. She intended to emphasize her experience, flexibility and the fact she was a quick study.

"Ever been here before?" he asked, his eyes full of mischief and fun. He didn't seem to be in any hurry to get to the point.

"No. I've heard of it, though." She forced herself to relax, take it easier, enjoy the conversation, despite how her heart thrummed and her brain pushed her to spit it out, get to the point, *get the job.* "It seems like a Doctor Nite kind of place."

"Exactly." He shot her a quick grin. "Tonight, though, I'm here for my agent. He's trolling for new clients and I knew we'd run into people he should know better."

"Did it work?"

"I think so. These things have to percolate."

"That was quite a crowd. Your agent and friends? Fans?" *Lovers?* The jealous daggers the women had zinged her way suggested they had been or intended to be.

"Friends, mostly. Some fans. Acquaintances. Industry people." He smiled. "The lines blur. Do you have friends you're close to?"

"Several, yes."

"You stay in touch…?"

"Sure. By phone and e-mail. Dinners and drinks. A movie or music somewhere when we can."

"The occasional slumber party? S'mores and pillow fights in your nighties?"

She laughed at the tease, despite her nervousness and urgency. "Sorry, no. Our schedules sometimes make it hard to find the time to get together in person."

"Does your work consume you, JJ? Are you like that?"

He'd batted her an easy lob she could direct toward the interview. "I do get so caught up in my work I forget everything else, yes." *My biggest flaw is perfectionism.* Which was true, but would sound like bragging.

Before she could say more, the runner arrived with their food—a tiered dish holding lobster ravioli, tenderloin satay and confit duck rolls that looked incredible.

"You forget to eat, too?" Brody asked.

"Sometimes," she said, her mouth watering madly. She'd

thought she was too nervous to eat. Brody had charmed her stomach, too.

The waiter appeared with the wine and poured it for Brody to sip. He nodded his approval, and when both glasses were full, held one out to her. "Now tell me what you think." His gaze stayed with her while she sipped the smoky blackberry wine with a bright finish. "Very nice," she said. "I like it."

"Andre never steers me wrong. Now for the food." He rubbed his hands together, then stabbed a ravioli with his fork and held it out to her. "Give it a try?"

She leaned forward and allowed Brody to feed her the square of pasta, his hand beneath her lips to catch any drips. The intimate gesture seemed completely normal coming from Brody.

The bite exploded in a lush blend of rich shellfish, creamy sauce and delicate pasta. "Oh, my God," she said.

"Heaven, huh?" He watched her closely as she chewed.

"Mmm-hmm." She licked her lips to catch a smear of sauce and Brody's gaze locked on.

She stilled, her tongue midlip.

"Hmm," he said, then cleared his throat and leaned for a satay stick. He dipped the meat into the sauce, then held it for her. "It's peanut-ginger, but light. Try it."

She tugged a bite of beef from the stick and savored the blend of meat and tangy sauce. "Incredible."

"I know." He seemed so happy about her pleasure. "The chef plays hard to get with the recipe. I've tried everything, even mentioned him on the show."

"So you cook?"

"When I have time."

"Does that mean you're consumed by your work, too?"

"In a way. The show's about what I do for fun, so I guess I'm always thinking about it, planning it, working. Like I said, the lines blur." He swirled his wine thoughtfully, then added, "But I wouldn't have it any other way." He smiled at her. "How about you? Would you want to be different?"

"Not really. No." He sat so close and the way they were talking made this feel like a date, not an interview. She had to stay on track. "It's late and I don't want to take up more of what free time you have. So, should we get to the reason I'm here?"

"Sure." Abruptly serious, Brody set down his wineglass with a firm click. "I've been wondering about that myself. Why are you here, JJ?"

"You need a cameraperson," she said, startled by his changed tone. "Obviously." She smiled.

"But why you? I looked you up. You do documentaries. You're absolutely serious and I'm absolutely not."

"You looked me up?" That surprised her.

He nodded. "I can't imagine why a woman who scored festival prizes for a film about foster kids would want to work on a cable show about men and beer and sex."

The blunt question made her stomach drop. She wasn't ready to mention her new documentary. "Well, *Doctor Nite* is a hit show and I'd love the credit. It's a challenge. I like variety. I did broadcast news for several years and—"

"Is it the money? I know documentary makers are always strapped for cash."

"The money's important, of course."

He watched her closely. The man was not nearly as laid-back as he let on.

"I'd value the experience," she said. "I enjoy learning." *Lame. So lame.* She hadn't expected to be grilled.

"Do you have a boyfriend, JJ?"

"Excuse me?"

"Relax, I'm making a point, not a pass." He grinned. "At least not yet, anyway."

Her body responded as if he were, though, warming as automatically as a reflex.

"This job is hell on couples. That's my point. We're on the road for days, out all night, surrounded by people looking to get laid. It gets wild."

"It's a tough job, but someone has to do it?"

"You got it." His eyebrows lifted, as if she'd surprised him by making a joke. She was coming off too serious, she realized. That had to be a strike against her with a man known for humor.

"I don't have a boyfriend, so that's no problem. Neither is the travel or the hours. I'll work hard. I'll be what you need."

"And what do you think I need?"

There was a beat of heat in his words, something sexy and intimate that caught her short.

"Me," she blurted. "You need me."

"Nice one," he said, tapping his wineglass against hers before turning serious. "It's a grind, JJ. There's no glamour. I'm picky and demanding and a pain in the ass. Kirk has the patience of a saint. Most people would want to throw me out a window after the first shoot."

"I'm very patient. And I'll shoot until I get it right. That's how I prefer to work. You can count on me. Not to brag, but I'm good."

"I have no doubt of that. But I have to say no. It's been nice meeting you and I appreciate your willingness to help, but I don't think this will work out."

"You're saying no? Just like that?"

A buzzing sound at the table drew her eye. Brody's cell had lit up and was vibrating against the laminate surface. He picked it up, glanced at the readout and said, "Sorry, I have to get this. My producer has issues with locations to talk about."

"No problem," she said, disappointment washing through her.

How could she reverse this? Be funnier, more insistent, more detailed? While she racked her brain, Brody talked to his producer about red tape in San Francisco, then something about Kirk Canter's surgery at Santa Monica Hospital.

Abruptly, he clicked his phone shut. "I hate to cut this short, but I've got to hit the road. They moved Kirk's surgery up a day and I need to go wish him luck. Let me get you a cab."

"But I—we—I mean—"

"You're too smart for this job, JJ," he said with a compassionate smile. "Wait for something that suits you. Never forget how good you are. Never sell yourself short." Somehow, he got her on her feet and hustled her out the door and into a cab, handing the driver money for her fare.

"Good luck to you," he said, leaning in the window. "I'll watch for your next piece."

"Wait," she said. "Is it because Kirk's a guy? Because it won't matter. I'll do whatever you need me to do. Whatever Kirk would do, I'll do."

"Score a hooker? Would you do that for me?"

She swallowed hard. "If I had to." The idea sounded awful, but her chance was slipping away and she couldn't bear it.

"Don't think I'm not tempted," he said, taking her in, dwelling on her mouth, "but this is better for both of us." He patted the taxi door and backed away.

Her head spun. She'd just been rejected so smoothly she hardly felt the sting. He'd teased her, poured her wine, fed her by his own hand, told her no, then paid her way home. She watched through the rear window as he climbed into a cab and left, taking her hopes and dreams with him.

2

DAMN, THAT WOMAN smelled good. Brody inhaled his fingers where he'd shaken her hand. What was the scent? Fresh laundry, a floral perfume, but also a homey spice that reminded him of something from childhood. What?

Barmbrack. Yeah. The Irish fruit bread his mother used to bake. JJ smelled like home. No wonder she'd caught his attention.

She was beautiful, too, in a way that snuck up on you. Like a young Julia Roberts with a soft mouth and big, intense eyes. Steady. Smart. Interested.

He'd liked that she didn't flirt. All the women he knew flirted. The head tilt, the teasing smile, the light touch on the arm or the pressure of a thigh…it was as common as breathing in his world.

J. James would be direct. Straightforward. *I want you.*

He could go that way. Sure. *You. Me. Naked. Now.* That would be just fine with him. In fact, it sounded damn good.

But he had enough on his plate at the moment. He didn't need an earnest filmmaker who smelled like childhood and looked like an actress. Even if he did have a thing for Julia Roberts.

He was sorry about the hooker remark, but he had to make the point that Jillian James was out of her league.

Maybe Brody was, too. Sometimes he believed his own hype. Worse, he feared that was all there was to him.

He was more than Doctor Nite. Jesus. He had to be.

He was weary of the role and the fame, tired of people always wanting something from him—to be with him, to be on his show or in his bed. He was actually sick of sex—or at least the one-night stands that served as his nightcap.

He watched L.A. traffic crawl by. Thudding music filled the cab from cars on either side. The night air was thick with the day's smog. This was his city, these were his hours and he loved it. But he was changing, moving on.

He was done with the show. He wanted to write. He'd started a book. The idea of it twisted him up inside. Writing alternately delighted and terrified him. When he was doing it, putting words on the screen, he felt like the Road Runner dashing over the gorge on thin air. He was good until he looked down.

His cell phone went off and he fished it out of his pocket, startled to see his parents' number in the readout. It was midnight. God. Had his father had another heart attack?

He answered the phone, fingers shaking. "Pop? You okay?" He held his breath.

"I'm fine, son. I can't sleep and you're the only night owl I know."

"Good. That's good." He blew out air, so relieved he wanted to laugh out loud. "So what's keeping you awake, Pop?"

"I get restless is all. Your mother kicks me out of bed when I get the jimmy legs."

"That's understandable." Brody scrambled for something to talk about. They'd only recently been having these conversations and it took a while to get a comfortable rhythm going. "How's the work on that Mustang coming?"

"Not too bad. Carburetor's giving me fits." He lapsed into a description of what he'd done so far and what he planned.

"You'll get it. I'm sure you will."

"Got to before your mother drags me on that cruise."

"You'll like it, Pop. There's bingo and dancing and the food never stops."

"That's no good for me, son. Gotta watch my ticker now."

"They have heart-healthy crap, don't worry."

"If it makes your ma happy, what choice do I have?"

He smiled, letting his dad's voice fill his head, listening as he talked about Ma's plans for the garden, how good her chiles were, how hard it was to get good help at his auto shop these days, and *why the hell was everything so computerized?*

Brody was just glad his pop was still around to complain about cruises and carburetors and computers. It had been his pop's heart attack six months ago that had made Brody decide to change his life.

After a bit, his father yawned.

"You getting sleepy?"

"Guess so. Good to hear your voice. Keep in touch now."

"I will, Pop." In fact, he'd put a reminder on his calendar so he'd make a call every two weeks.

When he'd heard the news about the heart attack, Brody had flown home and raced to the hospital, where he was startled to see his parents in a new light. He'd always thought they despised each other, but watching his mother pat Pop's hand, promising to hide the Jameson and bake only low-fat pasties, while tears rolled down Pop's cheeks, he knew he'd been wrong. They clearly adored each other. They'd changed or he'd been blind.

He realized something else. He wanted what they had—a life with one special someone and years and years together. The whole trip had been like that. He'd seen his old friend Cal Taylor differently, too. In his heart, a door opened to a world he'd almost missed.

His contract came due soon and he'd decided not to sign a new one. He'd been letting the idea sink in, become real. He'd made the mistake of confessing his discontent to Eve Gallen, his producer. Now she watched him like a hawk. *Are you okay? Happy? What else do you need? What can I do?* She'd pumped up the volume on everything, hunting up new show ideas, reminding him of the early days, poking at him constantly, driving him nuts.

With her hassling him and his plans to adjust to, he didn't need a complication like JJ, tempting as she was. What he needed now was focus and discipline, not temptation.

He would get Kirk's intern to fill in. Dave would slip easily into the groove of the shoot, leaving Brody's head clear and giving him plenty of time and energy to work on his book.

The cab was closing in on the hospital, so Brody had the guy pull over to a convenience store, so he could nab two *Playboys* and the latest *Gamer* magazine. Kirk's favorite pastimes were console games and naked women. Some of the newer games combined both, to Kirk's delight.

Brody grinned. He would miss the hell out of Kirk this trip. The accident had been weird. Kirk falling down stairs? Hurting himself badly enough to need surgery? The man knew how to hold his booze and he kept recreational chemistry to a minimum because of the side video work he did. What a drag.

They'd bumped the operation up to tomorrow—the surgeon probably had a golf game—so tonight was Brody's last chance to visit the guy, wish him well. He knew Kirk was superstitious about stuff like that, so he had to come. He wanted to talk to Kirk about an HBO project he'd heard about, too.

In the emergency driveway, Brody asked the driver to wait, then eased into the dim lobby. Eve had told him what floor Kirk was on, so he took the elevator up and sauntered to the nurse's station to coax Kirk's room number out of the short brunette with the stern face and tired eyes.

At the last second, he remembered to hide the *Playboys* behind the *Gamer* so as not to offend the woman, whose ID badge was hidden. He glanced at the duty board, then guessed. "Sue?"

"Yes?" She looked startled that he knew her.

"Sorry to bother you, but I'm here for Kirk Canter? He's expecting me. Brody Donegan?"

"Mr. Canter is sleeping."

"Oh, I doubt that. They're cutting him up at dawn."

"Which is why he needs his rest." She gave a prim smile.

"See, that's where I come in. I'm his security blanket."

"Oh, really?" She raised her eyebrows.

"Yeah, it's a superstitious deal. For luck?"

She stared at him and he could see recognition dawning. This happened a lot. People realized they'd seen him somewhere. "You look so familiar.... Aren't you...?"

"Doctor Nite? Guilty as charged."

"My brother loves your show." She smiled now, openly pleased, and stepped back, as if in the presence of someone important. He wanted to reverse that. *I'm an ordinary guy, sweetheart. I put my pants on one leg at a time like everyone else. Well, except I do it on TV for all the world to see.*

"I'd be happy to sign an autograph," he said, moving his finger as if with a pen.

"Oh, he'd love that." She seemed flustered, but handed him a square of hospital notepaper. "His name's Jordan."

He wrote, "Jordan, your sister is a dish," signed it and handed it over.

She read what he'd written and blushed.

"I won't be long, I promise," he said. "Kirk just needs to rub my beer gut for luck." He scrubbed his belly through his shirt. Sue's eyes followed his movement.

"But you don't have a gut," she said, a nurse observing his condition, though her cheeks held color and her eyes shone.

"It'll have to do." He winked.

"All right, I guess." She told him the number and pointed. "Down that hall. If he's asleep, don't wake him."

"Thanks, doll." He headed off, relieved she'd been agreeable. Women tended to like him. Of course, he liked them back. Was it a crime to use his gift to get what he wanted?

He'd begun to think so. Maybe that made things too easy, allowed him to glide, made him too lazy to work for what mattered. His pop, who'd been humbled out of his own wild ways, had always warned Brody against the easy road.

Brody had no real regrets about his life. It was just time to move on, try something different.

He tapped at the partially open door of the hospital room.

"What? Who is it?" Kirk nearly yelped.

"Just your wingman, buddy." He moved into the room, dark but for the bluish fluorescent light over Kirk's bed. "Relax."

Kirk flopped against his pillow in obvious relief.

"Were you having a nightmare or something?"

"Just freaked about the operation, I guess."

"Are you in pain? Need meds?"

"I'm okay."

"I stopped by to wish you good drugs and small scars. Sorry it's late. I just found out they changed your surgery."

"Better to get it over with, I figure."

"Here's something to kill the time." He handed over the magazines.

"Excellent," Kirk said, visibly cheered by the gift. "I don't have either one."

"So, listen, I need Dave's number. You have it?"

"My intern? What for?"

"To fill in for you on the shoot."

"But Eve said you were meeting with JJ tonight."

"I'd feel better with Dave."

"JJ's good, Brode."

"Oh, I'm sure she is. Just get me Dave's number, okay?"

"She's pretty hot. Are you sure?"

"I'm sure." That was part of the reason.

"His number's on my cell. In my bag." Kirk nodded at the bedside tray, grimacing, as if movement caused him pain.

Brody opened the messenger bag Eve had bought Kirk in an effort to organize the most laid-back guy on the planet.

"While you're at it, could you do me a favor?" Kirk asked. "There's a DVD in there I need dropped off."

The phone in his hand, Brody picked up a generic brown plastic case. "This one?"

"Yeah. Could you drop that off to a guy who'll be at the Xanadu? He'll be at a conference there on Thursday—that's your first night, right?"

He nodded. They launched each shoot with a couple nights at the Xanadu, a landmark resort popular for its proximity to LAX and its business amenities. Kicking off the run at the luxurious old place felt lucky to Brody.

"Freelance project?" Brody asked.

"More or less. I could courier it, but the guy will be at the hotel. His name's Lars Madden. I'll tell him to call you. I'd do it myself except for…" He raised his sling-covered arm.

"You just get better, my friend. I'm glad to do it."

Kirk fell back against the bed, looking exhausted. "I'm sorry to let you down on the taping, Brode."

"You fell. Not your fault. Just be more careful on the stairs."

"Yeah." A peculiar look crossed his face, then he shook it off. "I'll be back as soon as they'll let me."

"No rush. And, listen, I understand they're looking for an assistant director on that HBO project."

"I heard about that, yeah."

"So go for it." He leaned in so Kirk would know he was serious. "It'd be a great opportunity for you."

Kirk shook his head. "Too much pressure. Some good people already said no. I'd never leave you. I'm your cameraman."

"Don't get pigeonholed, that's what I'm saying."

"You know me, Brode." Yeah, he did. And when Brody left the show, Kirk would be thrown big-time.

"I'm sorry it didn't work with JJ," Kirk said. "What was it? She say something wrong?"

How could he put it? *She smells too good? She's too smart, too Julia Roberts?* "I didn't get the right vibe."

He said goodbye and backed from the room, thinking about JJ. She might have spiced up the shoot. Half his problem might be boredom. She had a great voice. Low and husky, but smooth, too. Like rough honey…

"Brody?"

He was startled to hear that rough honey voice say his name. He turned and there she was, as if he'd conjured her up. "JJ?" He was pleased to see her, no matter how strange it was. Had she told her driver, *Follow that cab?* "This isn't, like, a stalking thing, is it?" he said.

"No. Not at all." Even in the dim light, he saw she'd blushed. "You mentioned the hospital where you were going and I realized I could help with the red tape in San Francisco." She held out a business card, her fingers shaking a little, so he knew she was nervous.

"That's a woman in the city tourism office who's a wizard at making things happen. Mention my name. I hope it helps."

Her eyes moved across his face, her wavy hair quivered against her shoulders. She was breathing hard and her breasts rose and fell, appealing in a simple white blouse that looked as sexy as plunging silk.

"Thanks," he said. He liked her green eyes, her steady gaze. Her smell, of course. Her voice. Her body, chest, legs. She met him eye-to-eye. He liked that, too.

Keep it up, Brody, and you'll *be the stalker.*

"This job is really important to me." She met his gaze, standing solid and steady, telling him what she wanted.

"It must be. You chased me all the way here."

"There's another thing," she said, not even smiling at his joke. "I'm working on a documentary about…um…dating. I hoped we could fit in an interview."

"You want to interview me?"

She nodded. "You're something of an icon for single men."

"I like sex and I talk about it on the air. I'm hardly statue worthy."

"Men in bars all over the country play drinking games when you're on the air. How does it go? Every time you say 'The Doctor is *in'* they all drink shots?"

"So you've seen the show?"

"Seen it? I've studied it."

"I'll give you an interview for your movie, JJ. You don't have to work for me to get it."

"I need to. For the perspective. We'd have more time. Please. I'm…desperate."

"I'm not in the habit of turning down desperate women." She'd come all this way. For a woman as no-bullshit as she was to *beg* meant something. He would like having her around, he realized. Maybe he needed a woman's viewpoint—other than Eve's, who seemed devoted to keeping everything the same. JJ was so…interesting.

He went with his gut on big decisions, but it had been his head that had insisted he not hire her. Now his heart wanted a vote. His heart wanted to see what would happen.

Maybe he could handle his plan and JJ, too. She was looking at him with her eager, steady eyes, hope shining in her face. How could he turn her down?

"You won't bitch when I shift shots fifty times or drag you

out in the rain at one in the morning or make you run footage until you want to puke?"

"I won't. I swear." She made an *X* with her fingers across her chest. And what a nice chest it was.

He sighed and dragged his eyes up where they belonged. "Anything to keep you from stalking me, I guess. You're in."

Her smile was so bright it lit a fire in her green eyes. "Thank you, Brody. You won't regret this."

He sure as hell hoped not.

"Eve will call with the details. We start Thursday at the Xanadu. First meeting's around noon in my room."

"Great. See you there!" She danced off to her cab.

Watching her ride away, he had the feeling he'd be better off grabbing the first joker he could find with a digicam than hiring the woman, but it was too late now.

All the same, he grinned all the way home.

3

JILLIAN LET her room door close, tucked the key card into her wallet and checked her watch. Two minutes to noon. Just enough time to get to Brody's suite, where she was to meet with him and his producer, Eve Gallen, to go over the trip and plan the night's shoot.

She was on the twenty-fifth floor of the Xanadu, a big, bustling hotel with endless, poorly marked corridors she'd gotten lost in more than once already. Refurbished repeatedly, it was an odd mix of luxury and convenience—elegant deco furnishings with modern minioffices in spacious rooms.

She took a deep breath of the gardenia scent misting the hallways and headed for the elevator across the thick, silver-and-black, deco-style carpet, the only sound her slides slapping her bare soles.

Inside the elevator, she checked herself out in the mirrored walls. She looked decent in a red jersey top with spaghetti straps and khaki capris with plenty of stretch—she might not have time to change before they set off on the shoot and she needed to be able to bend and kneel with ease.

She couldn't believe how late they were starting. She usually put in five hours by noon, but she was on Doctor Nite time now. She would adapt to late hours and wild nights.

She still felt queasy about how she'd gotten the job. She'd practically stalked the man, then groveled. Begged. Hell, she'd offered to hire the man a hooker. On the other hand, too much was at stake to accept no. Doggedness and total focus had earned every success so far. Those traits would help her now.

She was nervous, she had to admit. She'd doubled her usual run to calm herself, but so many butterflies packed her stomach they could barely flutter a wing.

She'd called the We Women Network and left a voice mail with May Lee, the head of acquisitions, telling her she'd gotten the job and would score the "inside scoop, the real nitty-gritty" on Doctor Nite.

The real nitty-gritty? She couldn't believe those words had come out of her mouth, but that was how the game was played. She had to tantalize the network, get them hot for the project, then the caliber and substance of her work would make the final sale.

Outside Brody's door, she took a couple of settling breaths, determined to be cool and calm.

She'd have to contend with that snap-crackle of attraction, but Jillian knew how to manage that. She kept sex in its place, like everything else in her life. Weeks of twelve-hour workdays limited her free time. When she did connect with a man, she kept it friendly, not making any promises or expecting any back, and she had a serviceable vibrator for the in-between times.

Any flare-ups with Brody she would douse, no problem. She would be the consummate professional and hope he'd forget about the hooker request and her groveling. Oh, and the sexual sparks.

Composed and determined, she tapped at Brody's room. After a long pause, the door flew open to reveal Brody...*in his boxers.*

She took in rounded pecs, a flat belly, a thin, teasing trail of dark hair, black underwear. Silk, maybe? The fabric was shiny and slippery. Thick, almost like satin—

Whoops. She jerked her eyes up where they belonged.

"You're early," he said, his voice scratchy, his eyes at half-mast, leaning on the jamb, muscular arm extended upward.

"You said noon."

"I said *around* noon."

"Sorry. I just thought—"

"'Sokay. You're eager." He managed a slow spider-to-the-fly grin and waved her inside.

She entered the room, dim and intimate, with its unmade bed, tangled sheets, the bolsters tossed carelessly to the floor. So he was a wild sleeper. Or maybe he'd had company. Was there a woman? No, the bed was empty. Besides, that was none of her business. Again, she pulled her gaze to him.

Brody gave her his once-over, though the sleep crease in his cheeks softened the effect to sweet instead of predatory. "So you're perky in the morning," he said, scratching his hair with his knuckles, tousling it nicely.

"I like mornings. Is that bad?"

"And a health nut on top of it."

"Beg your pardon?"

"You've exercised. Your cheeks are flushed." He rubbed his knuckles against his own cheek, then ran his eyes down her length and around her body. "A runner, right? With those calves…absolutely."

"I do run, yes, but that doesn't make me a nut." He was as observant as a detective, and it made her uncomfortable. She decided to turn the tables. "You obviously exercise, too. Good pecs, flat abs, developed quads." She swallowed over a dry throat. "So you must lift weights. But with those shoulders and that tan, you swim, too." She stopped talking, not sure the hard-body inventory was helping her problem.

"It's all in my contract," he said, evidently not bothered by her exam. "If they can pinch an inch, I'm out." He grabbed a bit of skin beneath his rib cage. There was no fat to grab.

"You're joking."

"Not completely, no. Speaking of which, I'm starving. Let's order breakfast, huh? What would you like?"

"I already ate, thank you."

"But hours ago, right?" He put his finger to his chin. "Let me guess. Fruit, granola and yogurt."

"A smoothie," she said, annoyed at how close he was. "Aren't you going to guess the flavor?"

He moved in, startling her, and sniffed. "Too long ago. I'm just getting you." She felt a zing of unwanted electricity. "You smell great, by the way."

"Thank you." He seemed so aware, so *there.* She picked up his smell, too—warm skin, a trace of last night's cologne. His grin was lazy and knowing, and she found she was holding her breath.

"How about if I order a few things? Maybe you'll nibble, like the other night."

"Whatever you want," she said, deciding to be as cooperative as she could.

"And to drink? I'm having coffee, but I bet you're more of a hot-tea girl. Say, chai spice?"

Her favorite, dammit. "No one likes to feel predictable."

"How about noticed? Don't you like to be noticed?"

"Who wouldn't?" That was his secret, of course. Or one of them. All that attention was tough to resist in a world where it was all about me, me, me. Especially with men. A man who paid attention, really listened and remembered…was golden.

Brody moved to the phone and placed a lengthy order, turning to smile at her as if she were his room service conspirator.

It was unnerving to stand this close to a nearly naked Brody, looking at him over his bed, while he guessed her pleasures, his voice lazy with sex—er, sleep. Jeez. "Don't you want to put some clothes on?" she said, sounding more exasperated than she'd intended.

"Am I making you uncomfortable?" This seemed to delight him.

"Of course not. Get naked if you want. I'm ready to work."

"Mm-mm-mm. With lines like that, you're going to be a hell of a lot more fun than Kirk, that's for sure."

"He's not your type?" She was pleased to tease back, to reverse his impression of her as too serious.

He shook his head in mock sorrow. "Too much body hair."

"That makes sense. However, I doubt I'm your type, either." She was trying to joke, but it came out sounding defensive.

"What does that mean?" Brody moved to stand toe-to-toe with her. She didn't back up, despite how big and male he seemed, his bare chest gleaming in the shard of sunlight that sliced between the blackout curtains.

He was studying her. "You're not fishing for a compliment. That's not you. Ah…I get it. You were insulting my type, right? Which is, what, brainless sluts?"

"That's not what I meant at all." The reaction was deep and knee-jerk, from her past, but she could hardly get into that.

"Brainless sluts need love, too, you know."

"I'm sure they do. That wasn't what I was saying or what I meant. It's just me. Just old stuff popping out, God knows why."

"What old stuff?"

He acted honestly curious and he'd no doubt drag it out of her anyway, so she just told him. "I was overweight—a fat girl all through college, actually. So guys were my friends, not my boyfriends, okay? I wasn't any guy's type."

"You're thin now," he said simply.

"That happened by accident. I was working days at a news station in Fresno and making films at night—too busy to eat and jogging to boost my energy and all of a sudden, guys started looking *at* me instead of through me."

"You sure that was it?"

"Oh, yeah. I was the same lively, interesting person I'd always been, but no guy noticed until I got skinny."

"That must have pissed you off."

"Royally. I got over it, though."

"Not entirely, right? Hence, the comment?"

"I don't know. Maybe."

"The past colors the present, JJ."

"Ah, so this is why they call you doctor," she said, deflecting his analysis with a joke. "You're analyzing me."

"I charge $150 an hour and accept most insurance."

"Please. What kind of therapist practices in his underwear?"

He laughed. "My more traditional clients sometimes insist I wear pants." He sighed.

"I see," she said.

He smiled, moving close to her. "If it makes you feel better, JJ, I don't sleep with my crew. Even moral reprobates have some standards."

"Good to know," she said, startled by his frankness.

"So now can you drop your shoulders? They're up around your ears." He squeezed her muscles there with such perfect pressure that tension peeled away like the skin of an apple under the sharpest of knives.

"Oooh," she said.

"Turn around," he whispered.

She did and he began to rub in earnest.

"Wow. Oh, wow," she said. "That feels great." Not suggestive at all. It was pure physical relief. She let it go on entirely too long, but she couldn't remember the last time she'd had a massage and it was just *soooo* nice.

"That working for you?"

"Oh, yeah." She tried to collect her thoughts, say something funny or sensible. "You give shoulder rubs to all your crew?"

"Only the cute ones."

"Kirk? Never mind. Too hairy, right?"

"You're catching on." He patted her shoulders, signifying he was finished. "Now what was I doing? Oh, yeah, putting on my pants." He went to the side of the bed, whistling softly.

There was a knock at the door. Figuring it was room service, Jillian answered, but instead she found a short woman holding a stack of multicolored file folders in the hall. Eve Gallen, Brody's producer, no doubt.

Her eyes widened when she saw Jillian, but when she looked past her to where Brody was *pulling up his pants,* they narrowed, along with her lips, and her face took on an ah-ha expression. She thought that Jillian and Brody had been…oh, damn.

Jillian reached out a hand. "I'm JJ. Filling in for Kirk on this shoot?" She hoped her tone cleared up the false impression.

"I know who you are," Eve said, with a businesslike handshake and a brief smile.

"I got here early. I thought noon meant noon."

"Then you don't know Brody."

"She's learning," Brody said. "I answered the door in my shorts and shocked the shit out of her." He was clearly trying to show that nothing sexual was going on.

Eve paused, seemed to accept that, then strode to the window to fling open the curtains. "You live like a vampire, Brody," she said, dusting off her hands. She had bird-bright eyes and a restless energy, and she took over the room, putting a third chair at the table, shifting Brody's laptop to one side, taking legal pads and stapled pages from her messenger bag and laying items at each place.

Jillian raised her gaze to Brody, who shrugged. "Eve's the boss. I'm just the hired help."

When the food arrived, Eve signed the check, too, then lifted off the cover plates and stacked them. She looked over the omelets, sausage, granola, yogurt and pastry Brody had ordered, then grabbed a bear claw and bit into it. She made a face. "This isn't blackberry, Brode."

"They were out. It's fig. Sorry." Brody poured orange juice into a glass of cranberry juice and handed it to her.

"Thanks," she said.

Jillian was impressed. Brody had ordered his producer's favorite foods, including a juice combo he'd prepared for her.

Eve sipped the juice, nibbled on the pastry, then nodded slowly. "Goes good with the juice." She scooped ice from the water glass into Brody's coffee, taking care of him, too.

"The tea yours?" she asked Jillian, sounding almost offended by the presence of an alien beverage at the table.

"Yes," she said, preparing her cup.

"Brody guess what you liked to drink and eat?" Eve asked.

"He did, as a matter of fact."

"That's the Brody Treatment. You'll get used to it." Her words felt like a subtle jab. *He does this for everyone. You're not special.*

Brody circled the food cart, moving with an athlete's grace in bare feet, loading his plate with an omelet and sausage and fruit. He looked like a Calvin Klein ad, his chest still bare, his jeans low on his hips, his boxers peeking out.

A sigh escaped Jillian.

"You okay?" Eve shot her a look.

"Fine." *Stop staring at the man.* Her cup rattled in its saucer as she took her place at the table with Eve.

"Top sheet is the itinerary," Eve said, then flipped to the next page. "The second is a shot list for tonight and tomorrow."

"Looks good," Jillian said. Eve was clearly organized. Her folders were color-coded by city, Jillian noticed, reading the tabs. They would be on the road for nearly a week—spending two days in L.A., two in San Francisco and two in San Diego, before returning to L.A. for postproduction work.

Jillian wouldn't be needed for that.

Brody joined them, but he didn't look at Eve's pages, just dug into his food.

"I don't know how familiar you are with *Doctor Nite,* JJ," Eve said, "but men watch our show for the hottest clubs, the sexiest events and the wildest women. When you're looking for shots, you're going to have to think like a man. Maximum skin is what we're after. Short skirts, serious cleavage, all the tongue kissing you can score. Think Mardi Gras. Think spring break."

Think vulgar, woman-hating, exploitive. "I get it," she said, Eve's condescension annoying her. "I've watched the show."

"Studied it, you mean," Brody said, shooting her a wink.

"Then let's dig in," Eve said. "First I wanted to show you some new stuff I've got going, Brody." She whipped a paper from a red folder and gave it to him.

He read down the list. "You've been a busy girl."

"I've barely begun. Most of this can wait for Kirk, though." She shot Jillian a patronizing look.

"You don't need to do extra stuff. We're fine." There seemed to be tension between them. Had Eve disappointed him?

"We can't dial it in, Brody." She glanced at Jillian, almost as if she wished she were gone, then back at Brody. "Your fans count on you. We can't take anything for granted. It's good to shake things up." The two watched each other for a moment.

Jillian shifted and her leg jarred the table, making Eve sit straight, then tap her folders straight. "So! Moving on. Today's shoot." She flipped to the second stapled page.

Jillian was watching her, wondering what was really up.

With an impatient huff, Eve flipped Jillian's papers to the correct page. "You'll get used to how we work," she said, her tone suggesting Jillian was already hopelessly behind.

"School of Bondage?" Jillian read from the page.

"We're filming the dominatrix class," Eve said, as if it were an everyday thing to do. "Then we'll hang in the bar where the students and teachers mingle and practice."

"I've planned out the Top Ten S&M Tips," Brody said.

"Good. We need to save time if we want to get footage at the condom factory before they stop the machines for the day."

"Will I be able to scout these places?" Jillian asked.

Eve's gaze shot to her. "Traffic's brutal and we have lots to discuss. Kirk always wings it."

"I'm sure JJ can wing it, too," Brody said. "Speaking of Kirk, have you talked to him today?"

Eve's face softened. "He's great. They're releasing him this afternoon."

"He was higher than a kite when I called last night."

"He's already doing physical therapy." She smiled. "I'm so glad that's over. Kirk was so flipped out." She paused, lost in thought for a second. "Oh, yeah, he wanted me to remind you about some DVD. The guy's supposed to call you tonight?"

"Sure. Yeah. I'll drop it off for him."

"Anyway, okay, so let's see.... Back to San Francisco."

"Did that tip from JJ work out with the tourism office?" Brody asked, shooting Jillian a wink.

"Yes, actually, it did." She lifted her gaze to Jillian and said a quick, begrudging, "Thank you."

"No problem. I'm happy to help." *Even if I'm not Kirk.*

Eve hunkered over her notes. "Turns out we have to revise the San Francisco segments, since the show will run on Valentine's Day. We'll use 'Raunchy Romance' as the theme. All we have to do is add some V-Day bits. I hate Valentine's Day."

"Why is that?" Jillian asked.

"It's death for single guys," Eve said. "Girls get all gooey and want promises, and guys get stuck with the bill."

"It's a racket," Brody added. "Guys forking over a fortune for a fat diamond floating in Cristal, flaming dishes in restaurants where even the busboys are snots, and for what? If that's what love is, save your money."

"Good stuff, Brody," Eve said. "Use all that. Also, how is a single guy supposed to get laid on Valentine's Day? Do a riff on that. You know, how all the available chicks are home moping, eating Chunky Monkey from the carton, watching sappy movies in their sweats, wishing they had a boyfriend."

Jillian needed to contribute something to the brainstorming. "Why not hang out at the video store where the women are renting their sappy movies?"

Brody and Eve stared at her, blinking.

"Say, fiveish, after work," she continued. "Stand in the romantic comedy aisle, holding *When Harry Met Sally* or *Sleepless in Seattle*."

"Too gay," Brody said. "Maybe *American Pie II* or *There's Something About Mary*."

"I guess the movies don't matter, as long as you look harmless and lonely. Oh, and buy snacks. Popcorn and M&M's?"

"The doctor is *in*," Brody said. "Good one, JJ. So, Eve, score us a video store we can haunt? We can get opinions on our theories, too, while we're there."

"Video stores are chains. I'll have to deal with corporate permissions. It'll take time."

"You're the queen of pulling rabbits from hats."

Eve sighed, but a smile teased her lips. She grabbed Brody's laptop and began clicking away.

Brody leaned close to Jillian. "You *are* good," he said.

She was glad she'd impressed him. Now she had to get through to Eve. While they worked, Jillian complimented the woman's planning, her filing system, hell, her acrylic nails, but the producer remained distant with her.

Two hours later, Eve looked at her watch. "The crew will be here soon, Brody, so let's wrap up."

"Time for Red Stripe and beer nuts," he declared, picking up the phone to call room service.

"I'd like a club soda, please," Jillian said.

"Do you believe this woman, Eve? Club soda?"

"Brody hates health nuts," Eve said matter-of-factly.

"Sorry. But would you also add a fruit and veggie tray?"

"If I have to," Brody said, grinning. "As long as you keep it away from the good food."

The rest of the crew arrived and went over technical details about the upcoming shoot, while drinking beer and wolfing nuts. Jillian liked that the show worked with a bare-bones staff in an informal atmosphere. Brody asked about kids and pets and planned vacations, and she could see the crew loved him. She liked Brian and Bob, the light and sound guys she'd work most closely with, and felt good about their skills.

The crew left, Eve ran down one last checklist with Brody, then declared them set. It was nearly 4 p.m.

"The vans will be out front in exactly two hours, so don't be late," Eve said to Jillian, messenger bag over her arm.

"I won't," she said, fighting the urge to defend herself. *I'm a professional and as prompt as sunrise.* Instead, she gathered up her papers and purse.

Lounging on the couch, Brody took a long swallow of beer, his throat muscles sliding, forearm muscles twining, legs stretched out. He was still half-naked and all male. Even his toes looked sexy.

Jillian could hardly take her eyes off him.

"What are you up to now?" Brody asked her.

"I'm going to check my equipment, think through the shots, plan things out a bit."

"Don't get too locked down," Eve said. "Brody always shakes things up. Kirk goes with the flow. That's the best way."

"I understand," she said. "I'm sure it will be fine." *Grr.*

"You should take a nap," Eve said to Brody with an affectionate smile. "We'll be out late. After the taping, I thought we'd check out that new bar near the W."

"I'm making it an early night, Eve."

"On our launch? We always party."

"Not this time. Not me."

"But I already rounded up the crowd."

"You'll have fun."

"It's not the same without you."

"Take my credit card and it will be."

Eve stared at him. "Aren't you feeling well?"

"I'm fine. Just taking it easy for a change. Thanks, ladies. Here's to a great tour." He tilted his beer at them.

"Looking forward to it," Jillian said, but she noticed Eve was watching Brody and chewing her nail.

The two women moved outside Brody's room.

"So, you and Brody seem to be close," she said, thinking that if she could get Eve talk to her about Brody she might learn some interesting tidbits. She wondered if they'd ever been an item, back before he made that rule about crew.

"We've worked together a long time, sure." Eve paused, then looked at Jillian dead-on. "Brody's a friendly guy, open and easy to talk to, but he's really a very private person." *Don't even think you'll get close.*

Jillian had to try. Maybe he was happy to be a playboy forever. Or maybe that weary look she'd seen meant something. Maybe that was what had Eve worried, too.

Jillian had a week to find out.

4

IT WASN'T BONDAGE SCHOOL that surprised Brody—he'd expected the place to be decorated like a torture chamber, with displays of menacing devices and all the students in leather and latex and spikes—it was Jillian's reaction to the place that amazed him.

She was *relaxed,* as calm and easy as if she were filming a field of wheat, a sunny meadow or a small-town park. She focused on the best angle to view a whipping, the right lighting for black leather, how to capture shiny spikes without glare.

He almost laughed when she shifted furniture and climbed a ladder to get the perfect shot of a paddling. Kirk would never have gone to that much trouble.

She put up with a bunch of Brody's reshoots without complaint, too, just as she'd promised. When Brody blew off the shot list, instead of going along like Kirk would have done, she'd do the new stuff, then go back to what they'd planned and do that, too. She missed *nothing.*

He was behaving differently, too. Showing off, for one thing. When the head dominatrix, Mistress Mona, tried out the cat-o'-nine-tails on him, it stung like a bitch, but he'd refused to wince.

Now they were in the bar, which was raking in cash with overpriced liquor. The whole school was a moneymaker with brutal tuition fees and criminally expensive paraphernalia. A hundred bucks for a rubber hood? Come on. All part of the punishment, he guessed.

In the bar, the students and teachers mingled, leather and rubber clothes squeaking, chains clanking. It was like some weird costume party with everyone in black and metal.

Whatever stuffed your jeans, he guessed. Not his thing.

They had tons of footage, but he still had that restless, unfinished feeling, so he motioned JJ over, hoping for some ideas. Between shots, he'd noticed how busy she was, scoping the place, talking to the instructors, the patrons, the bartender.

"I need something more from the Queen of Pain," he told her, nodding toward Mistress Mona, holding court at the bar. "Any ideas?"

She didn't miss a beat, just leaned close to talk low in his ear, giving him a delicious blast of her spicy scent. "See the guy in the Girls Gone Wild ball cap at the back table?"

He looked, spotting the guy with his frat-boy buds. They'd stumbled into the place, not knowing what it was, then stuck around to gawk and joke.

"He's laughing like his friends, but his eyes never leave Mona. I think we should bring her to his table."

"You don't miss much, do you?" he asked her.

"I try not to. No."

"I'll have to remember that," he said, thinking about the interviews he'd promised her and all he had to hide.

"I'll go talk up the college boys," she said. "You tell Mona."

He headed for the bar and sat beside the dominatrix. "A minute more of your time, Mistress Mona?"

"Yes?" she purred, pursing bright red lips. Her hair was teased platinum and her eyes were heavy with black gunk—pure drama, but he'd seen she had humor about herself, unlike the students who were hyper about the rules of their sexual roles.

"I think we know someone who could use a touch of your lash," he said.

"Tell me more," she said in the German accent that ebbed and flowed. While he explained the plan, he glanced over to see how much more time JJ needed. He was surprised to find her waiting for him, ready, and she'd gotten the frat boys primed, too.

She was fast, moving like smoke, subtle and smooth, never drawing attention to herself, almost invisible, efficient and effortless and always there. She'd even gotten Brian and Bob to pick up the pace. The lights and boom mic were ready, too.

She'd told him she often did her own lights and sound on documentaries because it lessened the intimidation factor. The fewer people and equipment, the more relaxed her subjects were.

He and Mistress Mona moved toward the frat-boy table and JJ signaled she was rolling tape.

Mona loomed over the boys, silencing them, and the kid in question blinked up at her. "I'm not really into all this," he said, looking utterly enthralled. JJ had been right about him.

"Come on," Brody coaxed. "We all need the occasional smack on the behind, don't we, Mistress Mona?"

"You vill gif your mistress respect," Mistress Mona snapped. "Take off zat ridiculous cap."

The kid jerked the hat from his head, grinning, his face pink. Oh, he was into this, all right.

"Wipe zat smile off your face." Mona whipped her crop onto the table so that it slapped his fingers.

The kid stared at his hand, then at Mona, utterly thrilled.

"I'll leave you two alone." Brody patted him on the back and stood. "Enjoy. The cat-o'-nine-tails is intense."

JJ backed up, keeping the camera on Brody as he left the table. She was waiting for his wrap-up. He liked that she'd picked up on their system.

"Whatever polishes your jewels, guys," he said into the lens, walking slowly enough that JJ and Bob could keep their equipment steady. "You like rubber hoods or get off on wearing pink panties under your Dockers? As long as no one gets hurt—well, sent to the hospital—go for it."

He needed something else...a final comment.

JJ pointed him toward a student practicing her riding crop moves on a guy's backside.

"My turn?" Brody said to the girl, then turned and bent over. She smacked him lightly.

"Oooh, the Doctor is *in,*" he said with a wink, holding his pose until JJ took the camera away from her eye.

"You got what you needed?" he asked her.

"I did. Yes." Her voice was low and throaty. There was that spark again, flying between them, unexpectedly strong. She felt it, too, he could tell, but backed away fast. He couldn't figure out if she was scared of it or irritated by the distraction. Interesting...

"We've got to *move,*" Eve said, bustling up, her messenger bag tugging her shoulder down. It amazed him how much junk she hauled around—energy drinks, files, notebooks, forms, batteries, cosmetics, even a flashlight and, for some reason, latex gloves. "They're waiting for us at the condom factory."

"I'd like to look over the footage before we go," JJ said.

"You'll have to check it in the van," Eve said. "We don't have time for a reshoot anyway."

Why was Eve so bristly with JJ? She was always a steamroller, but she was particularly pushy with JJ. Had Eve picked up on the attraction? Maybe she missed Kirk. The two of them bickered like an old married couple and they talked daily.

At the van, JJ let him help her into the seat, then set up the computer and external drive for a playback, quick and efficient, resting the laptop on both their knees. He liked the slide of her thigh against his own.

Eve sat up front where she could more comfortably boss the

driver. Eve made him grin. She had the tenacity of a terrier, a great eye for detail and was utterly competent. Sometimes over the top, but that was part of the package.

He was determined his crew would make a soft landing when he left the show. He'd take care of them all—Eve and Kirk; Brian and Bob; the assistant producers who helped Eve from time to time; Chloe, his editor.

Maybe *Doctor Nite* would get a new host. His network had done that with that car mechanic show. Talk shows did it all the time. Maybe they'd hardly notice he was gone.

"Brody?"

He drew his attention back to JJ, who nodded at the screen. "Does this B-roll work, do you think?" Never wasting a minute, she'd grabbed charming background shots of bondage students in class while he talked to the instructor. Kirk needed to step it up. He'd been dialing it in as much as Brody had begun to do.

"I'm thinking we could cut this piece—" she shuttled the video further "—and shift to here. Do you agree?"

She sat so close he could smell the strawberry scent of her clear lip gloss. JJ wore little makeup. She didn't need it, as far as he could see.

"Uh, yes," he finally said, realizing she was waiting for his reply. "Looks good."

"I don't want to push you into shots you don't want, so tell me to back off when I'm out of line."

"I'm always up for a better idea. You didn't mind the multiple takes?"

"Not at all. I want to do this right. Like I said."

"Yeah." He paused, lost in her steady, green eyes. "Like you said."

"So, am I giving you what you need?"

Not yet, but I have some ideas.... He cleared his throat. "You're doing great."

"Except that extra interview threw us off," Eve said, evidently listening in. "We have to keep on schedule or the shoot spirals out of control, JJ."

"You're so tough, Eve. Mistress Mona could take lessons," Brody said, trying to tease away his producer's edginess.

"What's the deal with Eve and me?" JJ muttered very low.

"Later," he said softly, then raised his tone to a conversational level. "So now on to condoms, right? I'll ask the guy about what's new—materials, shapes, colors, textures—and find out what's popular these days."

"Here's an idea," JJ said. "What if we also interview women about the features? Cut back and forth from the factory guy describing the item to the users' take on the feature."

"That's pretty arty for Doctor Nite." He shook his head in mock disapproval. "But we want to stay fresh, right, Eve?" He leaned forward to involve her in the conversation.

"We'd need samples from the factory. And what women would we use?" Eve asked, then answered her own question, clearly intrigued by the challenge. "Privilege has tons of models. It could work. I just wish you'd think of these things earlier."

"Come on. You know you love to perform last-minute miracles, Eve." She'd do anything to make the show better. He winked at JJ, who shot him a thumbs-up.

He liked that. It felt like the old days, when the nutty chaos and crazy energy of location shoots had energized rather than exhausted him. It was all due to JJ—her skill, ideas and liveliness. At the moment, despite how distracting she was, he was glad he'd hired her.

BY THE TIME they pulled into the driveway of the Xanadu at close to midnight, JJ was physically and emotionally wiped out. Physically, her shoulders throbbed from all the handheld work and schlepping her heavy tripod—it had better fluid heads for panning.

Emotionally, she'd been on a roller coaster. Bondage School had been surreal, but she'd maintained her professionalism. The condom factory had been fascinating. Then they'd hit the bars and started on the typical *Doctor Nite* segments, which had bothered her. She'd shot women pretending to be turned on as they unrolled condoms onto bananas from the bartender's daiquiri supply or onto Brody's fingers, while Brody made suggestive remarks. All night, women rubbed against him. Two of them flashed boobs at him, nearby men howling like jackals.

Jillian gritted her teeth the whole time. It was her *job* to go along with the exploitive, offensive aspects of the show. Hell, she was making the show *better.* She couldn't help herself.

She vowed to get in the woman's view wherever she could. Getting women's opinions of condoms had been a start. Though each conversation deteriorated into flirting with Brody.

That didn't surprise her. Despite his offensive on-camera persona, Brody charmed her more and more, adding to her confusion. He seemed untouched by fame. Everywhere they went, people demanded autographs, hugs, handshakes, kisses, sometimes full-body humps, depending on the sex and drunkenness of the fan. Brody remained patient and gracious, smiling at the hero worship, signing his name on whatever he was offered—a sodden napkin, tattered bar menu, a bare back or a naked breast.

Plus, she approved of how he worked. He was demanding, quick to dump a setup for something better, no matter how long it had taken to arrange. That was how she worked, too. He asked for her feedback and retook every shot she had doubts about.

The physical closeness was wearisome, too. Man-woman electricity hummed and snapped constantly. But these moments of mind-reading teamwork were the worst, shooting ever more powerful jolts of attraction straight through her.

Shaky from the emotional whiplash of the day—loving her work and hating it, fighting her attraction to Brody and being drawn deeper into it—Jillian was relieved they were done for the night. A tension headache raged behind her eyes.

Brody led the way into the crowded lobby of the Xanadu, decorated everywhere with patriotic-hued bunting in honor of the political convention being held there, and Jillian couldn't wait to get upstairs and fall into bed.

"I see more condom opinions dead ahead," Brody said, motioning toward the lobby bar, packed with people wearing convention name tags. He turned to her, took in her face and hesitated. "Unless you're too tired?"

"Of course not." JJ managed a smile, determined to be a trouper. "Lead the way." She hefted her camera onto her shoulder and followed Brody to a table of four women who turned out to be just tipsy enough to say yes to interviews.

Brian and Bob set up lights and sound while Eve nabbed releases, and in minutes they were rolling.

"Condoms prevent disease and pregnancy. Period," a blonde in glasses said. "They're like brushing your teeth to prevent cavities. A necessary pain in the ass."

"What's with the ribs and colors?" added a brunette in a chignon. "You can't feel those teensy bumps and who cares what color it is?"

"And the flavored ones? Forget it," added a black woman with cornrows, shaking her head so the beads rattled. "They taste like the rubber dams my dentist uses."

"Plus, they're like thirty calories each," added a rail-thin redhead.

"No!" said the blonde. "Not thirty? Aren't they sugarless?"

"Don't get fancy, I say," declared the redhead. "Just make them with *no holes*. Functional. And, for God's sake, men, *practice*. The fumbling has got to *go*."

They wrapped the shoot, which she'd enjoyed despite her headache, and the crew disappeared. She noticed one of the women slipping Brody a business card with what looked like a room number on it. Ah, her cue to escape. She was relieved, since she'd planned to ask Brody for an interview after the shoot, but was entirely too tired to try for it. Now it was impossible.

"I'll head upstairs," she said, backing away.

"Me, too," Brody said, half-rising, as if he were leaving, but the women made disappointed noises and she knew they'd keep him longer.

At the gift shop, Jillian had to wait for the sleepy clerk to find her an aspirin packet she could buy, but finally she was in the elevator, relieved to be away from Brody and her growing attraction to the man.

It was ridiculous, she told herself. The man was probably a sociopath. Certainly his TV character was, treating women like enemies to be conquered, sex objects to be preyed upon. The show's message was "Screw anything in skirts, then run like hell." She hated that attitude. Meanwhile, she kept reliving the pleasure of his eyes on hers, his hand at her back, his thigh rubbing against hers in the van. What a *girl* she was.

On her floor, she took the wrong corridor first, but finally found the arrow to her hall. Just around the bend was blessed peace. She would take the aspirin, stretch out with some dull talk show and drift to dreamless sleep.

Except when she turned the corner, there was Brody again, leaning on her door, watching for her, a big grin on his face. He was such a male animal, strong and relaxed against the door, jeans low on his hips, easy in his skin, confident his body would do whatever he asked of it.

Whatever *she* asked of it. Her weary body went on full alert and she felt tight and wet in a secret place.

Stop that right now, she commanded, as if she could control her body's fluids and flows and reflexes.

When she got closer, she saw Brody had four liquor miniatures between his fingers and a DVD case under his arm. "What's up?" she asked, trying to smile in welcome.

"I thought we'd toast the shoot and check out the footage."

"How'd you get here so fast?"

"I left when you left." He nodded at the aspirin bottle. "You have a headache?"

"A bit of one, yes."

"That my fault? I work you too hard?"

"Of course not. It's my sinuses. Hotel air is so dry." She had to lie. No way could she let him know she was exhausted on her first shoot. "I thought you'd be busy. I saw that woman give you her room number."

"Not brainless enough for me." He grinned at her, his expression almost fond. She realized this was a perfect chance to get to know the man behind the persona, maybe get that interview. That was her reason for being here, after all.

"I'd love to," she said, steadying herself against the tingles and heat of her body's response to the man. "You want to watch that?" She nodded at the DVD under his arm.

"Nah. I've got to drop this off with a guy on your floor. It's a favor for Kirk. When he calls I'll take it over."

She waved him into her room, which had been neatened by the maid, scanning for anything she didn't want him to see. The bathroom mirror reflected her black bra on a hook from when she'd hand-washed it. Whoops. She hurried to snatch it down.

"Black lace…nice," he said.

"Not that it's any of your business."

"I'm interested. Curious. Aren't you a curious person? Being a documentary filmmaker and all? Don't you have to be nosy?"

"Yes, actually, I am a curious person." All her life she'd asked questions of everyone about everything. Her parents, especially her father, used to complain about her nonstop demands for answers. Which made sense, since he had all those affairs to hide. The last thing he wanted to do was say where he'd been and what he'd been doing.

"What is it?" Brody asked, leaning toward her.

"Just thinking," she said, wishing he weren't so observant.

"You're always analyzing. Figuring the angles, working things through in your mind."

"No more than most people, I don't think."

He just looked at her, telling her that she wasn't like most people and that he liked that about her. She felt warm all over, almost girlish. Ridiculous.

He studied her—hair, face, body—lingering over each feature as if she were a shiny toy he wanted to take apart and put together. Then he smiled, pleased with what he'd discovered.

"So, what will you have, miss?" He laid the small bottles against the back of his forearm like a sommelier presenting a wine for her approval.

"The Grand Marnier, please," she said. She loved the sweet citrus sting of the orange liqueur.

"Excellent choice." Brody twisted off the top and poured the drink into a water glass, pouring himself a neat scotch. "Here's to a great start." He tinked his glass against hers.

"So you're not sorry you hired me?"

"How could I be? You caught the rhythm of the show, but you added your signature, made us work harder, too."

She was inordinately pleased by his praise. "I'm glad. I had fun." She realized that was true, despite her doubts, despite the subject matter, despite the push-pull of her attraction and disgust with Brody.

"We make a good team," he said.

"We do." Her mind slipped to where else they might pair up and snapped off that thought at the root.

Brody's eyes stayed with her. God, was he reading her mind? She dipped her nose into her glass and sipped, letting the orange aroma fill her head, the alcohol burn gently down her throat and settle in a warm pool in her stomach, which did nothing to ease the heat she felt from Brody.

She looked up and he was still watching her with those riveting chocolate eyes. There was something so male about his face, with its bold nose, dark eyebrows and that strong, square jaw. His lips were nice, too. Full, always moving, ready to laugh or joke or smile or kiss—

Don't go there.

"Can I use your bathroom?" he asked, sounding like he wanted to break the tension, too. "Gotta check out that bra," he said, wiggling his eyebrows, joking away the moment.

"I'll off-load what we got," she said. Even better, with him out of the room, she could set up her camera to tape whatever conversation they had. Brody had signed her release, of course, and he'd urged her to nab footage on their shoots whenever she saw something she wanted, but she felt uncomfortable taping him secretly. But her watchwords had served her well: *Always be ready and film far more than you'll ever use.* She would consider this deep background. Once she saw what she had, she'd decide how to approach Brody about using it.

She tied her hair away from her face to get it out of the way and set to work, first moving the latest footage onto her external drive, then setting up her laptop on the table. She shifted the lamps to maximize the light where Brody would be.

Next, she placed her camera on the bureau, set it at a low resolution to maximize the card space and turned it on.

She'd disabled the red signal—all documentary filmmakers did that to prevent subjects from tensing when they thought the camera was on. The best stuff often came before and after the official interview, when people were relaxed.

Brody, meanwhile, was clunking around in her bathroom. Was he checking out her cosmetics? Strangely enough, the idea didn't bother her. He had an innocent curiosity that appealed to her. It was something they shared, actually.

She was waiting in her chair with the laptop cued for viewing, when he emerged, trailing wafts of her perfume and maybe her hair spray?

"Find anything you like?" Jillian asked.

He grinned, not seeming the least embarrassed that she'd been aware of his movements. "Just figuring out what makes you smell so good."

"My perfume."

"It's more than that," he said, heading straight for her.

"My shampoo?"

He got closer. "Nope. Tried those. You smell like my mother's kitchen when she baked."

"I smell like a kitchen?"

He took her upper arms and leaned in to sniff her neck, sending chills down her body. "It's your skin, I think. If you could bottle that…I'd buy."

"I'll have to see what I can do." He was so close and his voice had a low, sexy rumble to it.

"Why'd you tie your hair back?" he asked.

"It gets in my way."

"I like it better loose. Don't you?"

She found herself ripping off the band and shaking her hair free, warm against her shoulders. Her heart banged her ribs.

"Yeah, like that," he said. "It looks so soft. Natural curl? May I?"

"Yes." She felt uncomfortable under his scrutiny, with the

air tightening between them, his gaze so steady on her face, his fingers in her hair, a licking flame crackling in his dark eyes.

What was he thinking? Surely he wouldn't make a pass. He'd said that thing about not sleeping with crew. They were alone in a hotel room, very close to a bed, and it was very late at night.

What would she do if he kissed her? Kiss him back? Melt into his arms? She wanted to desperately. Her body was such a traitor. Where was her famous self-control when she needed it?

"You going to show me what you've got?" he asked softly.

"What I've got?" She had the impulse to open her shirt, fling off her bra. So outrageous and so not like her.

But no wonder. The atmosphere of the shoot had fairly dripped with sex. A dozen women had rubbed against Brody, kissed him, run their tongues along his ears, suggested what they'd do to him if he'd let them. Two *had* showed him their breasts. Watching that, filming it, thinking about it, would naturally make her more aware of her girl-gone-wild side…or give her one.

Get a grip, she told herself. *Settle down.* How could she be considering such a thing with a man whose entire purpose offended her to her core? The kind of guy who, back when she'd been a fat girl in high school, had made her feel so alone.

"You okay?" he asked, as if he were worried about her. "Are you too beat to do this now?"

"No, no. I'm fine." And her camera was running, by God, waiting for Brody's secrets. That was why she was here. "Sit," she said, indicating the chair where her camera secretly pointed. "Let's see what we got." *And what I can get.*

5

DETERMINED TO STAY in control, Jillian sank into her chair and grabbed the mouse, ready to click through the clips. She'd need to log them all when she had a chance. "Anything in particular you want to see?" *Like me naked?*

No. No. No.

"Just run through the stuff so I can get the feel of it."

She let the footage run, moving the Play head every few seconds, while Brody nodded and smiled, commenting here and there. She was pleased with her work, considering she was new.

"You were a good sport tonight," Brody said, looking at her instead of the footage. "You took it all in stride—the whips and chains, the condoms, the bare breasts."

"That happen a lot? Women showing you their goods?"

"Are you kidding? After midnight in a bar, all signs of civilization fade." He smiled, but his eyes seemed to empty out.

Here was her chance to find out if he really loved it as much as he pretended to. "Doesn't that get kind of…old?"

His lips twitched, but he forced a grin. "How could it? I've got women bribing the bellboys to let them into my room to wait for me. I'm a lucky, lucky man."

"That sounds like something Doctor Nite would say. What about Brody Donegan? What does he think about all that?"

"I *am* Doctor Nite, JJ. That's the point."

"I don't think it's that simple." she said. "I don't think you're that simple."

He just looked at her, but she felt him pull back. "This is starting to sound like an after-sex conversation, doll."

"And you never have sex with your crew, right?" Her heart pounded way too hard in her chest. She was holding her breath.

"You got it." He turned back to the laptop. "That's a great shot," he said, nodding at the screen, where a curly-haired brunette applied a condom to Brody's fingers with her mouth. "You got both of us without distortion."

On screen, Brody made a face that was both funny and sexy, with a Hugh Grant sweetness to it, and Jillian felt arousal burn through her, speeded by the Grand Marnier, which seemed to have reduced her ability to control her body.

"Do you think the sound is fuzzy?" she said to stay focused.

"With that on the screen, who cares about the sound?"

They both watched as the on-screen Brody left the table where they'd been filming and came toward Jillian's camera. "Does that do it for you, JJ?" He meant the shot, had they nailed what she needed, but his voice had a slowness to it and his eyes shone wickedly.

"Yes," she said, matching his tone, "it does." Watching the footage, Jillian could see that Brody wanted her. And her own voice betrayed the fact that she wanted him, too. It was in plain view on the monitor. Things always came clearer for her on screen. It wasn't until she looked at what she'd captured for her documentaries that she discovered the real story she had to tell.

Now, in her hotel room they both stared at the laptop. She heard Brody swallow hard as she did the same. In unison, they turned their heads and looked at each other, faces inches apart, the golden light making the moment cinematic.

They were so close, lips almost touching, breathing each other's breaths, holding each other's gaze, heat swelling between them, pulling them closer.

"You know, you're not really crew...." He ran a finger down her arm, sending a quiver down her body, then cupped her cheek.

"I'm guess I'm not," she breathed.

Their lips met. She wasn't sure whose mouth ate up that last inch, but she was relieved, as if someone had poured water on a fire that threatened to engulf her.

Except now it burned even hotter.

Brody took her mouth more completely, his lips firm and tasting of smoky whiskey. She leaned in and he put his other hand to her face and deepened the kiss.

She felt captured, overwhelmed, raging with desire, and she began to tremble. They breathed harshly, desperate for air, eating each other up with their mouths.

She should stop. So far it was just a kiss, easy enough to explain away and forget. Except everything in her wanted more of this man. His mouth, his lips, his fingers, his body.

She heard music and Barry White's low growl, something about taking it off...tonight, baby...can't get enough.... Brody had managed mood music?

"Damn." Brody reached into his pants pocket and pulled out a cell phone. Barry White got louder. The Walrus of Love was Brody's ring tone. "It's the guy for the DVD, no doubt," he said, putting the phone to his ear and leaning away.

"Yeah?" he said, then listened. "I'm just down the hall.... Sure.... Right.... I'll be there." He clicked off. "Jeez, where's the fire? Duty calls, I guess," he said, looking sheepish.

"You could come back," she said. They could have that after-sex conversation about the real Brody. She needed that, she told herself. She did.

"But you think that would be a mistake, huh?" He smiled.

She hadn't said that, hadn't thought it yet, would think it only when it was far too late.

He ran his knuckle down her jawline, pressed his lips against her forehead in soft farewell. "I'm glad one of us can be sensible." When he pulled away, she swore he looked... *relieved.* As if he'd dodged a bullet.

She followed him to the door on shaky legs, completely confused.

"See you tomorrow?" He chucked her chin. "Flight's at eleven."

"See you then." She closed the door, utterly mortified. She'd been overwhelmed by unimaginable lust, while Brody had been going through the motions, working his Doctor Nite mojo in a knee-jerk seduction. He probably couldn't help himself. It was a reflex and she was the handiest female.

That stung.

Her gaze fell on her camera, which she realized was still running. Hell, she'd filmed that kiss. She rushed to turn it off, then returned to the table to grab one of the bottles Brody had left. She drank all of it from its tiny top. Scotch, she realized afterward, because it tasted like Brody's kiss.

She undressed and donned her comforting blue chenille robe, trying to look on the bright side. She'd figured it out before she embarrassed herself, at least. To Brody, sex was no more intimate than a handshake. Even if she wasn't ready to settle down like Dana and Becca, sex meant more to her. It signified a deepening friendship, mutual comfort, an emotional connection. She certainly didn't want to sleep with a guy who'd likely check his watch in the middle of the act.

She'd dated and slept with a few guys, but had had only two real boyfriends. Ben, a producer at her news station, for six months, and Gary for a whole a year. He was a filmmaker, too, and they'd had long earnest conversations about film and their separate visions for their own work.

The sex had been...friendly. But when Gary got the chance to work on a film in Australia, she'd seen it as a natural break before either of them got carried away. She'd only been miserable for a week after he left and counted herself lucky to have escaped so easily.

She had hopes, of course. Surely there were serious, sincere men who wanted a solid life with a partner, men who were above Doctor Nite's shallow philosophy. Men who weren't players like her father. When she was ready, she'd look for one. Maybe have a family. Down the line, when she had her career squared away. Right now, her work was everything.

It was natural to respond to Brody, really. So much of sexual attraction was reflexive—biology's automatic On switch. But she was bigger than her urges. Even if Brody's kiss could melt cold steel.

She touched her lips, felt that spike of lust again. She wanted to chase him down for more. For enough. Brody would be a fantastic lover, after all. She deserved that experience, didn't she? Except she didn't want to be another notch on the belt of a guy who found naked women in his bed every night.

Nope. She could control this, she told herself, twisting off the cap of another scotch, planning to numb herself enough to sleep. She had it to her lips when she stopped.

No more alcohol. She was already woozy. What she needed was a cold, fuzzy soda to cool herself down. For that she'd need ice. Maybe she could dump some in her lap while she was at it.

She grabbed her ice bucket, braced her room door open and headed down the hall, wobbling, so she knew she was right to lay off the booze. She didn't need a hangover to make it harder to endure another day of the Brody Treatment.

JUST OUTSIDE JJ's door, Brody stopped, closed his eyes and relived that kiss. What a mouth. Soft as butter, but firm, too. She could use it to give him hell or kiss him into submission.

Either way, he'd enjoy it. He could still taste her. Orange from the drink and sweet—that lip gloss? Maybe just her lips. Mmm.

That was a bad idea, he told himself, setting off to deliver the DVD. He'd meant to work on *Night Crimes,* his thriller featuring Detective Trent Lager, the first of what he hoped would be a series. His life as Doctor Nite presented plenty of plots—late nights brought out vice, excess and stupidity, he'd found.

He'd been carving out the tale, page by painful page, for the past month. Until now. One hundred and twenty-three pages into it, he'd become stuck, stalled, blocked. He'd intended to work on in tonight, but he'd only glanced at his laptop before grabbing up the miniatures and hightailing it to JJ's room.

How could he resist? She was so smart, so quick, her mind ticking away every second. She had him pushing himself with the show, too, and that was good. He did want to talk about the show. Really.

He surely did not want to talk about himself. Not with someone so hard to resist. Her question about what Brody Donegan thought about Doctor Nite's life had hit him hard. He'd gotten so good at faking it, he wasn't sure he knew the answer, not without a shrink jabbing at him. Or Jillian.

Now that he was shaky about his book, doubts about his plans to change had seeped in. The crew would be devastated. Kirk wasn't willing to consider another job. His friends loved Doctor Nite. They'd think he was joking or crazy. He liked making people happy, hated to disappoint. He loved his show, too. He just wanted…more.

Maybe he was just burned out. Maybe he was fooling himself that he could change his life.

He wondered if JJ would think he was crazy to quit. She would have an opinion, for sure. The woman knew what she wanted and went after it, no doubts at all. She'd chased him down and demanded the job. He wished he could be that certain about what he wanted.

Madden's room was at the far end of the hall. Passing the ice machine, he made a decision. He would return to his room and open that blasted laptop and write one page, dammit. Two hundred and fifty words. He could handle that. How did that famous quote go? *Writing is easy. All you do is stare at a blank sheet of paper until drops of blood form on your forehead.*

No shit. Writing was hard. Writing a novel, anyway. Writing for his show was as easy as breathing. Fiction required the careful mix of back story and action, character and plot, sensual detail and narrative drive. It was tough. But when the words flowed, it was like flying, and Brody loved it. Craved it.

He'd just have to work at it. Stop being lazy. If it were easy, everyone would be published.

Finding Madden's room, Brody tapped on the door. There was a flick of light while the man checked the peephole, then the door opened, security bar in place. "Donegan?"

"That's me." He held up the DVD case.

The guy unlatched the bar and tried to open the door, but it snagged on something—a throw rug, Brody saw when Madden finally waved him inside. The suite smelled of cigars and the large bar held a row of half-empty liquor bottles. Baskets and trays of cheeses, chips and snacks littered the space.

Madden checked the hall, then shut the door fast, as if for privacy. He was tall and thin and wore a rumpled discount suit too short in the sleeves. His armpits were sweaty, his striped tie askew, and *Lars Madden* had been hastily scribbled on the patriotically trimmed name tag.

"You're at the shindig downstairs?" Brody nodded at the tag. The women he'd interviewed had preprinted names on theirs.

"I am indeed," he said, oddly emphatic. "It's all exciting...."

Politics is...amazing.... Just so...important...." He trailed off, looking as if he wanted to be finished.

"Here you go," Brody said, holding out the DVD.

The guy grabbed it, dropped it into an open briefcase on the bureau. He slammed it shut and latched the briefcase fast, as if the disc were on fire and he had to smother it out.

"Having a party?" Brody asked, nodding at the loaded bar.

"This is the hospitality suite," he said, going to hold the door for Brody. He was in a hurry, all right. "Thanks again."

"No prob—" He turned, but got the door in his face. *Okay. I know when I'm not wanted.* Where *was* the fire?

Brody headed for the elevator, wondering why he'd gotten the bum's rush. He'd gone down two hallways before he realized Madden hadn't given him a check or a receipt. Kirk hadn't said anything about money, but he tended to be casual with details and Brody knew a few clients had been slippery about payment.

He headed back to confirm. Turning the last corner, he saw a heavyset man at Madden's door. Turned away from Brody, the guy hitched up his jacket for a room key, revealing a holster clipped to his waistband. With a gun in it. Madden had a roommate. And he was *armed.*

The key card turned the lock green, but when the guy pushed at the door, it didn't give. He shoved harder, clearly fighting resistance. Madden was trying to keep him out?

Now the big guy slammed his bulk against the door and forced his way inside. What the hell...?

Brody moved closer. He could see the door was stuck partly open. The rug, no doubt. Skin prickling, he slid near enough to see inside, where the two men struggled over the briefcase, groaning and huffing as they dragged each other around the room. Banging into the bar, the big guy lost his balance and fell onto a chair.

When he stood, he reached back and grabbed the gun, which he extended, two-handed, at Madden, who froze, gasping in alarm.

Unwilling to get shot, Brody backed silently from the door, intending to get help, braced for action, the way he'd felt at tae kwan do meets, physically primed and mentally stoked. Reaching for his phone, though, he was horrified to see JJ toddling toward him with an ice bucket, wearing a god-awful robe.

"Brody!" She smiled a loopy smile and waved in a very un-JJ-like way. She was drunk?

He lunged for her, a finger to his lips, grabbed her arm and quickstepped her back toward her room. When he heard movement behind him, he slid her into the ice cubicle, fearing it was the gunman.

She opened her mouth, so he stopped her from speaking the quickest way he knew—with his mouth on hers. He kept his back to the hall to hide their faces. Making out was a reasonable excuse to be lurking in the alcove in the middle of the night should the guy look their way as he passed.

"Mmmmph," JJ said into his mouth. The ice bucket clanged to the linoleum as she let it go.

"Play along," he whispered, holding her close, listening with all his might as heavy footsteps approached, then passed. He managed to be aware of how good JJ tasted and the way she softened against him beneath the fuzzy fabric.

When he heard no more noise, he broke off the kiss to verify the coast was clear.

"What's going on?" she asked, dazed.

"I'll explain. Come on." He wrapped an arm around her waist and walked her quickly back to her door. He saw she'd propped it open with the lock bar. "This is a bad idea," he said, flipping it out of the way, then pushing her ahead of him.

When he turned to close the door, he caught sight of the

gunman standing at the end of the hall. He'd evidently gone the wrong way looking for the elevator, a mistake Brody had made himself. The guy looked right at him with cold, dead eyes in a red, meaty face. He knew Brody knew something. He hesitated, as if considering whether to go after Brody, then took off, briefcase banging against his thigh as he ran.

A finger of ice ran down Brody's spine. The gunman not only knew Brody had seen him, but he knew which room he was in. Except it was JJ's. Damn. "I've got to call hotel security," he said, going for the phone beside her bed.

"What happened?" she asked.

"I'll explain after I get some help." He got the security manager on the phone and explained that he'd seen a guy with a gun break into a room, scuffle over a briefcase, which he then ran off with. JJ's eyes went wide as she listened in. The security manager promised to handle the situation and asked Brody to stay put until he called back.

Brody set down the phone. How would they catch the guy? A man in a suit with a briefcase was in perfect camouflage for a convention hotel.

"Wow," she said. "You saw all that. The gun…the fight…and he stole the DVD you gave the guy?"

"Yeah. I'm sorry I had to grab you. I didn't want him to see you."

"You kissed me." She brought her fingers to her lips, as if in memory. Her robe gaped, revealing the swell of a breast. It was no more skin than he'd see at any singles bar, but with JJ it seemed somehow sexier, even in that funky robe she had on.

Adrenaline still poured through him, but lust hit head-on. "I needed to distract you," he said, moving closer.

"You did…very much." The robe was short and fuzzy and loose, tied by a fat belt that would come apart with the merest tug. He thought about getting his hands on those breasts. Would they taste as delicious as they looked. Would she moan? Throw her head back? Soften against him?

How the hell could he be thinking about getting naked with a gunman on the loose?

"It's the danger," JJ said, as if in reply. An answering fire burned in her eyes. "It makes me feel...odd." Aroused, she meant. She was breathing funny, she was flushed and her voice was husky and slow.

"That must be it," he said. "I, uh, need to make sure Madden's okay." He lurched forward to lap her robe more securely and yank the belt tighter, then backed away fast.

He got no answer on the room phone or Madden's cell, and when the cell voice mail gave only a number, not a name, Brody disconnected without leaving a message. Meathead might had taken Madden's phone, for all he knew.

He looked at JJ. "I have to check the room. The guy could be passed out on the floor, injured or dead." He hadn't heard a shot, but still...

"Let the hotel handle it, Brody."

"Who knows when they'll get there. They're looking for the guy with the gun. I have to see for myself. I'll be careful."

"I'm coming with you," she said, wobbling a little.

He smiled. "In your fuzzy robe? Got bunny slippers?"

"Why not?" She stuck her chin out, her eyes determined.

Because you're drunk. He knew better than to say that to a woman this stubborn. "Your reflexes might not be as lightning-quick as mine."

"Oh, please," she said, rolling her eyes, but she walked him to the door, gnawing her lower lip.

"I'll be right back," he said, feeling like Trent Lager. "Don't let anyone in. Make security show you ID if they knock."

"Be careful," she said and he felt her watching him all the way down the hall. It made him want to smile.

He found Madden's door open slightly, the room empty. No suitcase, no clothes in the closet, no toiletries in the bathroom. No sign the man had ever been in the room. Well, except for the hospitality leftovers. Both men had keys to the room. Maybe because hospitality suites often had several hosts.

When Brody left Madden's empty bathroom, he was startled to find JJ standing there. "You were supposed to wait." She'd put herself at risk following him here.

"You needed backup," she said, giving the cop show line her usual no-nonsense delivery. An insight hit him like lightning. Trent Lager needed a woman. A female sidekick. A P.I. maybe? Sure. Someone with corkscrew curls and intense green eyes and a no-bullshit way about her. A P.I. who charged too much and was worth every penny and refused to put up with an ounce of grief from him.

He felt a rush of pleasure at the prospect of writing about her. It was the adrenaline of the moment, no doubt, but it was also JJ, standing there looking a little bleary, but stubborn as hell. She just made him smile.

"He's gone?" she asked.

"There's no sign he was ever here. Maybe he packed up and left. Hard to say. Come on."

As he walked JJ to her room, his mind flicked through possibilities. What the hell was on that DVD that someone would use force to take it? He would call Kirk in the morning and find out. He was home from the hospital and would hopefully be clearheaded enough to fill Brody in.

Meanwhile, would the gunman come back looking for him? Was JJ in any danger? He'd protect her at all costs, though he hadn't used his black belt in more than a decade and what use was a roundhouse kick against a 9-millimeter anyway?

Back in the room, he checked again with security. They

hadn't found the guy, but the hotel was clear. Brody was free to return to his room.

"The guy's gone. The hotel's supposedly safe."

"You're going back to your room?"

"I should, don't you think?"

"Maybe not." She wore the steamy, woozy look of a woman who'd had a tad too much to drink to tamp down her lust. He knew that look. Loved it, actually. Had enjoyed many happy hours because of it. Did it get any better than hot sex with an eager, uninhibited partner?

Maybe. That was the point, wasn't it? There had to be more. You found one special person and built a connection. Sex was part of it, sure, but not the whole enchilada. Just the salsa, maybe.

"Will you be able to sleep?" he asked her.

She shook her head. "Not feeling like this." The room was dim and smelled of her, laced with the dangerous smoke of liquor. He had his own arousal to deal with.

He'd always had a big appetite. He'd been the Godzilla of sensation, stomping through life, taking big bites of everything. Giving back, too, of course. The women he took to bed wanted more from him, never less. But he needed to curb his cravings, hone in on what was valuable, what counted, what really mattered.

Her eyes shone, her color was high.

Did she have on panties under that goofy robe?

Forget it. That was the old Brody. The new Brody made good decisions, considered implications. The new Brody didn't screw his camerawoman just because he felt like it, and she felt like it, and they'd been through a dangerous adventure together.

If he tasted her heat, dipped into her warm body, he wouldn't be walking away soon, not without leaving something of himself behind. Something he needed to hang on to.

"Maybe we could…talk?" she said, blinking at him.

"Talk?" he said, thinking about her pink body underneath the blue fuzz. He wanted to touch and taste and explore. Need thickened the air between them.

"You can maybe tell me about the real Brody Donegan. How about that?" Her eyes pinned him to the wall, not letting go.

He swallowed hard. "Sure. I guess."

He'd been dying to find out what was under her robe, and she was hot for the contents of his brain. Great. He hadn't told his crew what was up; he certainly couldn't tell a virtual stranger, no matter how irresistible. He had the feeling the gunman was a kid with a water pistol compared to JJ on the hunt for a story.

He had to keep her from getting his.

6

THIS WAS PERFECT, Jillian realized, proud she'd resisted throwing herself at Brody. The thrill of the robbery and Brody's kiss had erased her exhaustion, and now she would get her interview after all. "Can I get you something to drink?"

"I'm good." Brody pulled a chair between the two beds and patted the mattress for her. "Get comfortable and let's see if we can put you to sleep."

While she fixed herself a Coke, she was able to reposition her camera to capture Brody. From this distance, the low light meant a grainy image, but she'd have decent sound.

Back at the bed, she leaned against the fat bolsters, one foot on the floor to stabilize herself, fighting what was left of the alcohol in her blood. And the lust. She couldn't forget that. "So, tell me," she said, tilting her head at a teasing angle, "does Brody Donegan think marriage is death for men the way Doctor Nite does?"

"I don't know," he said, clearly not wanting to say. "Most men feel that way, don't they?"

"Somebody's marrying all the women wearing wedding bands."

"Marriage is a girl thing. Why else are there dozens of bride magazines and not one called *Groom?*"

She had to laugh. "You make a good point. However, men are happier in marriage than women. Poll after poll says so."

"And you believe them?"

"Marriage is a good deal for a man. Even the women who hold full-time jobs handle all the domestic details. Face it, we all need a wife—someone to cook and shop and book the dentist."

"You've thought about this," he said, lifting an eyebrow.

"I've read a lot. For men, marriage has a great upside."

"Ah, but look at the downside. Stuck sleeping with the same woman for the rest of your days?" He pretended to shudder.

"So get creative," she said.

"You read about that, too?"

"I have ideas," she said, pleased that she was able to tease back, even as the exchange made her pulse race.

Brody hissed in an aroused gasp. Good. She'd had a sexual effect on him. "Men have a biological imperative to sleep around," he said, settling back into the argument. "It refreshes the gene pool. For a man, fidelity is unnatural."

"Oh, please," she said, realizing they'd strayed from Brody's story. "That sounds like Doctor Nite talking. What does Brody think?" Playfully, she tapped her toe against his knee.

He caught her foot in his hand, sending an explosion of heat up her leg, straight to her sex.

"What are you doing?" she breathed.

"Helping you relax," he said, and squeezed the top of her foot in a way that made her want to moan. "That okay?"

"I don't know…."

"Feels great, doesn't it?"

She could only nod. Yanking her foot away would be rude, right? It would make the physical gesture seem too big a deal.

"There are thousands of nerve endings in your feet. According to reflexology, I'm actually rubbing your organs."

"My…organs?" She'd moaned after all.

He laughed softly. "Sure. There's a whole reference chart. I believe this is your kidneys."

"My…mmm…kidneys?"

"And this is your stomach."

"I definitely feel it there." Butterflies were staging a riot in her belly, throwing chairs around and setting fires. "Where did you learn this?" she asked faintly.

"We did a show on massage once."

"Doctor Nite and massage? Had to be full release, right?"

"Now, now. It was *therapeutic* and very cool."

"Oooh." She tried to make that a comment, but it was obviously a reaction to what his fingers were doing. She needed to focus on her interview, get to the point, but this felt *soooo* good. "So, go on. You were telling me what you think…about what I said…." Whatever that was.

Luckily, Brody remembered. "Okay. I don't get why women want men in the first place. We're pigs. Scratching our balls in public, glued to the game all weekend, dropping Doritos down the couch cushions, leaving the toilet seat up."

"I'm with you so far. Why do we want you?" She paused. "Okay, I can think of one reason."

"There's that. Yeah." He sighed. "So have sex with us when you're in the mood—we always are—then live a satisfying life on your own, in peace. No barbells in the den, no pizza stains on the Persian, no thousand-dollar 900-number bills."

She could only laugh. "You're making more and more sense." He was digging in deliciously and she felt shivers move all along her body. "What organ is that?"

"Your heart, I think. And this is your…pancreas…and this—"

"*Oooooh.* I know what that is." An electric charge had turned her clitoris into an aching knot of need. Any second her hips would start moving on their own, seeking relief.

She should stop him, but if she ripped her foot away she'd

seem pathetic, as if she were so horny that someone rubbing her toes could make her come. Which was exactly what would happen any minute if he…didn't…stop…now.

Thankfully, he did, but only to grab the other foot from the bed and start on it, sliding his chair closer. She fell back against the pillows as a shivery wave of pleasure moved through her. She'd soon puddle on the bed and dribble to the floor at his feet. The man was that *good.*

She had to think, think, think. Instead, she moaned, sounding as close to ecstasy as she could get without his fingers on her spot. Worse, her camera was recording this moment. She would erase it, of course, as soon as she could *move.*

Brody Donegan clearly knew what he was doing on the human body. If he could turn her bones to jelly with a little foot massage, think what he could do to the rest of her.

It boggled the mind. And other parts.

"So, what do you have against men, JJ?" Brody asked her, dragging her from her haze.

Reluctantly, she blinked him into focus. "Nothing." Not at the moment anyway. Or at least not this man. "Some of my best friends are men."

He laughed and she liked it. She liked even more than he was now running his thumbs along the muscles at her shinbone, sending thrilling chills along her nerve endings, like a harpist stroking strings in a cascade of beautiful notes.

She forced herself to argue a point. "I'm not happy about the male fixation with youth, beauty and Double Ds, that's for sure."

"We can't help checking out the goods, JJ. Besides, plenty of flat-chested women with junk in the trunk convince guys to put rings on their fingers and SUVs in their garages."

He dug into her calf muscle now and it felt like easing into a hot bath, quivery and melty and deliciously sensual.

"Until the guy takes off with the secretary half his age,"

she inserted, "and leaves his wife with stretch marks and no child support."

"Men suffer, too. It's no fun to be judged by your bank account, the car you drive or your biceps."

"You poor, poor dears," she said, grateful that the debate managed to distract her a little. What he was doing to her muscles should be illegal.

"Society is easy on men," she continued. "Think of all the trophy wives. The breast implants, the BOTOX. The fixation on beauty in magazines, TV, movies. Look at the epidemic of anorexia among teen girls. Hell, they had to set weight rules to keep runway models from starving themselves to death."

"Is this about you being fat as a kid? Because I would have been all over you in high school."

"I doubt that." She tried to laugh, but she was abruptly yanked back to her teen self, when she'd felt trapped in her chubby body, fighting to shine her personality through her eyes, as if through the bars of a cage.

She'd been friendly and interesting and fun, but guys wanted her for a study partner or to play video games or shoot photos with. Being the only girl in her crowd without a boyfriend had stung, no matter how she pretended not to care. College hadn't been much better.

"You didn't know me then," Brody said, his eyes holding hers, looking so sincere. "I was weird. Class clown with odd hobbies. I collected vinyl records of obscure Jamaican artists and built an entire World War II battleground using toothpicks… Don't ask." He laughed, shaking his head at himself.

"Making friends with everyone was a self-defense move. I figured the more people liked me, the higher the odds that when I showed my loser colors, I'd still have crew left."

"It's hard to imagine you that way," she said.

"Everyone's insecure in high school, JJ. Whether you're fat

or skinny or have a twelve-inch dick or the original Toots and the Maytals' recording of '54-46 Was My Number.'"

"I guess that's true." She was startled that Brody had dredged up a long-ago misery in her life and made it seem not so bad. But they were talking about her again, not him. The foot massage made it so hard to think.

Her whole body was softening, loosening, feeling better and better. Hotter and hotter, too, of course. And Brody looked so appealing in the golden glow of lamplight. There was a beauty mark on his cheek, and he had impossibly long lashes over dark eyes that burned into her. She could see his pulse throb in his neck, could smell his cologne, hear the rustle of his shirt when he moved.

"Enough therapy for me, Doctor Nite," she said. "Let's talk about you. Doesn't the way you live make you feel…empty?"

He rubbed away, not answering for long seconds. "Doesn't everyone feel empty sometimes?"

She didn't answer, giving him a silence to fill.

"My life is full. I've got a great job…plenty of money…friends…fans…all the sex I could want…."

"So what are you doing here in my room?" That wasn't the question she meant to ask at all; it had just slipped out.

"Rubbing your feet?" he offered softly.

"That isn't my foot, Brody."

He looked at his hands, which now squeezed the muscles just above her left knee. "True." He raised his gaze to hers. "At the moment, I'd rather be here than anywhere else. This is fun, right? And I'm helping you relax."

"It's more than fun and I'm not a bit relaxed." Her tone showed how aroused she was, she knew. She wasn't even sorry.

"You want me to stop?"

The correct answer was yes, but her eager, aching body yelled, *Don't you dare.* If he moved his fingers upward a few inches, her body would tell him exactly what she wanted. She was wet and swollen and needy. She couldn't speak.

"Because I want to make you feel good," he said. He didn't look weary or bored, that was certain. He seemed as riveted by the moment as she was. That meant something, didn't it?

It meant enough, evidently, because her hips rocked upward in search of relief, desperate to scratch her inner itch.

In response, Brody slid his hands up both thighs, slowly, slowly, holding her gaze. He paused, nearly touching her, but not quite, waiting for the final word from her.

Please, her quivering body begged.

Couldn't they slip into this moment, escape into the physical need pulsing between them like a heartbeat? Why not?

Looking him straight in the eye, she opened her thighs.

Brody made a sound of pleasure and touched her clit with one finger. She gasped, electrified.

"You're so wet," he groaned, as if that caused him pain. He ran his finger down the length of her swollen place, back and forth, slow, then quick, catching her, making her surge, startling her with the rush of sensation.

Shamelessly, she pushed at him, wanting more, grateful when he slid a second finger to the other side of her clit. When he gently pressed it between his fingers, she was startled to feel her orgasm erupt, burst forth, like swollen fruit so ripe its skin split with relief. She cried out, almost yelped. Sensations rolled through her body and she rocked against Brody's fingers, panting, trembling, feeling as if she were burning to ash.

When it was over, she opened her eyes and saw he was smiling lazily down at her. He cupped her mound gently with his palm. "That was nice."

She managed a gasp and a nod.

"Been a while?"

"With a person, yeah." She'd taken care of herself often

enough, but hadn't been with a man in months. Somehow, saying that to him wasn't embarrassing at all.

"Wish I'd been inside to feel that," he said, running his palms along her thighs, massaging gently, reaching under to squeeze her bottom—softly, taking his time, making warmth lap away at her insides.

"Me, too," she said huskily. "That's where I want you now."

Brody was shaking, which surprised her, as if he hadn't been with someone in a while, either. Maybe that made this right.

As if being wrong would stop her now. She wanted more and she was going to get it. She leaned forward to start on Brody's shirt, but she'd only managed two buttons when he pulled it impatiently over his head.

She ran greedy fingers across his bare chest, his skin so warm it was like toasting her fingers before a friendly fire.

Brody pushed open her robe and cupped her breasts, then leaned down to touch each nipple with his tongue. Each tightened and ached, while heat pulsed along her nerves. Reading her reaction, he changed from tonguing to sucking her nipples deeply into his mouth.

She arched into the wet suction of his mouth, rocking her hips against his erection. She needed him naked so she could see him, hold him, get him inside. She reached for his fly.

"I got nothing," he breathed.

She gripped him through the thick cloth. "You have plenty."

"I mean condoms. Not on me."

"Condoms?" Damn. How had she skipped that step? She'd been derailed by the man and the moment. "I don't have any, either." Why hadn't she nabbed extras from the condom factory when she'd shot tape?

Shot tape? And her camera was on this minute! A stark reminder of how wrong this was. She fought to clear her head, to stop this before they'd gone too far.

"Who needs condoms?" Brody asked and slid his tongue down the middle of her trembling stomach.

Huh? Too dazed to move, she could only feel him moving down her body, slipping his hands over her ribs, cupping her hips....

Oh. My. Word. The man was going down on her. In her experience, oral sex came after the compulsories, after you knew each other better. Certainly not the first time.

She was paralyzed, though, unable to object, completely pinned by his body—and, heaven help her, his mouth. When his moist breath heated her pubic area, she moaned. He ran his tongue along the line where her curls began, teasing her, then digging in to where her flesh parted and her swollen clit waited, greedy for more, as if it hadn't just burst with pleasure moments before. She bucked into the wet pressure, her thighs trembling, her body shaking, her knees liquid.

Brody held her legs in place, taking charge, promising with his mouth that he would make it all better.

And he was making it better. *Waaaay* better.

Soon she was writhing and crying out as he slid his tongue up and down, edging deep, then attending to the hot knot gearing up to explode again.

"Oh, oh, oh." She made odd noises, jerking like a puppet, but she didn't care; she was so caught up in the hot glory, the surge of pleasure that rolled through her, swept her off a steep cliff into wild heaven.

Long seconds later, when she finally quieted, Brody slid up her body and kissed her mouth. Tasting herself on his lips was so intimate. But it felt right. Familiar. Despite the fact that Brody was nearly a stranger and her employer besides. Worse, a documentary subject. Somehow, none of that mattered.

"That was...amazing," she said.

"It was, wasn't it?" He smiled, then kissed her neck. "I had a great time." He was planning to leave? Without his own climax? No way.

"You're not going anywhere," she said. A man who had sent her to the moon twice in a few effortless minutes was not leaving her room without an erotic ride of his own.

Jillian pushed up and rolled Brody onto his back, then knelt on either side of his hips, naked, sitting tall, feeling supremely sexual.

She leaned forward to undo his fly, each button a sharp pop in the quiet room.

"Great idea," he said, folding his arms behind his head to watch her tug down his jeans and boxers, and reveal him, erect velvet, ready for whatever she wanted to do with him.

She took him in her hands. He felt good, warm, promising.

He reached up to cup her breasts, heavy and swollen, the nipples still tender. But that was too distracting, so she grabbed his wrists and pressed them against the mattress.

"What's this?" He grinned up at her.

"A little something I picked up in Bondage School."

"Mmm. Whatever you say, Mistress JJ."

She leaned forward, sliding against his penis, loving the thickness of him, wishing for a condom so she could take him inside her body and they could move as one.

Except maybe this was better. They were playing at sex. This wasn't the real deal, the physical union, the couple thing. Maybe, when the haze cleared, she wouldn't blame herself too terribly for succumbing to the moment.

She let go of his wrists and trailed her nails along his chest as she moved down his body, digging in so he would feel the slight stab. Reaching his groin area, she wrapped her fingers around his penis.

He sucked in a breath, and a smile of anticipated pleasure spread across his face and lit his eyes.

Moving herself into position, she closed her lips gently over the head of his cock, then tightened them, sliding down slow and careful, feeling him against the back of her throat.

He shuddered in appreciation. "Oh, yeah."

She moved up and down, experimenting with pace, with tongue pressure, making her lips tight, then loose. He tasted warm and lightly salty, and she pushed her tongue against the veins that curved around his shaft.

He brushed her hair away from her face. "I want to watch you move."

"Mmm." She ran her tongue around the head of his penis, giving him a show, enjoying acting sexy, knowing he liked this because of how he moved in her mouth. While she licked, she used her hands at the base of his shaft, squeezing gently, urging him closer and closer to climax.

He gripped her hair with both hands and groaned.

She loosened her throat to take him deeper.

He moved faster, in a rhythm that told her he was nearly there. She sped up, giving him steady suction, getting into the dance of it, coaxing him to the brink, closer, closer. Then over.

He came, a warm spurt in her mouth, and she swallowed it right down. This felt so human, so basic, so right. She let him slip from her mouth and rested her cheek on his chest, listening to the thud of his heart, licking the last of his essence from her lips.

Brody pushed his fingers into her hair. "Wow," he managed, his breathing ragged.

She smiled, running her fingers along his rib cage, noticing how great she felt, how happy, how relaxed.

Until regret hit like an icy wave in the face.

She felt Brody tense at the same moment. His breathing went so shallow she couldn't hear it. He was thinking so hard she could almost *feel* it. He was wondering if he could escape, no doubt, or whether she expected him to stay the night or, God forbid, cuddle.

She smiled, knowing that she could relieve his mind. She lifted her head and patted his chest. "You need to go."

"I do?" He looked startled.

"You need your sleep. We both do."

"But I don't want to leave you alone."

"I'm a big girl, Brody. And if you're worried about the guy with the gun, he's long gone. I won't let anyone in, I swear."

"Sure, but I…"

She reached down to grab his jeans and shirt from the floor and tossed them to him. "That was great, but it's almost two." She put on her robe, suddenly sad, wishing she'd lain in his arms a bit before proving this was no big deal to her. Sometimes she had too much discipline for her own good.

Brody stared.

"Go on. Get dressed. I sleep better alone."

"Are you sure?"

"It's better for you, too. I'd probably knee you in the nuts in my sleep. You know, payback for all womankind?"

Slowly, he stepped into his pants and pulled on his shirt, doing up the two buttons with those incredible fingers that had done amazing things to her body….

She could feel herself melting, so she decided to speed things up. She sat on the end of the bed and did up his fly. She patted him through the jeans, then looked up at him.

He still looked doubtful and a little nervous.

"You're afraid this is a trap? That I really want you to stay? I don't play those games, Brody."

"I know." He relaxed, let out his breath. "And I like that about you. You're honest and direct. No bullshit."

"Exactly." She pulled away from his fingers and tightened her robe to reinforce her point, wishing she were as serene as she was pretending to be. She led the way to the door, fighting a wobble in her legs.

"You sure you're okay?" he asked.

"I'm sure," she said. "And we won't let this affect our work, either. It was just...what?...tension relief?"

"It was a hell of a lot more than that."

That made her feel better. "But it was just a blip, a slip. We just erase the tape." Which she would do *immediately*, now that she thought about it. She hoped the card in her camera had filled up long ago. "Forget it ever happened."

He smiled, looking so sexy, smelling so good. "Can I just say that was amazing?"

"I guess that's allowed." Her own emotions were confused. Delight and worry and longing tumbled together like clothes in a dryer, sleeves and legs and socks and towels tangled in a warm and messy mass. By morning, when she saw him again, she'd have it straight in her mind.

He leaned in to kiss her, but she gave him her cheek. "Better start forgetting now," she said.

Brody sighed and she had the feeling he didn't really want to leave. "Throw the security bar and don't let anyone in, okay?" He pushed her hair from her cheek, one side at a time.

"I'll be fine," she said, liking his concern. That would be a cool thing about being in a relationship—knowing there was a person in the world who thought of you every day, worried about your well-being, cared about how you'd slept, how you felt, wanted you to keep your doors locked and not talk to strangers.

They said good-night and she closed the door behind him, regret returning like a wise old friend. She'd made one mistake after another tonight, starting with the ice room kiss, followed by the foot massage, then opening her thighs to his touch, then getting naked.... Bad decisions like a series of dominoes click, click, clicking away until they'd made love to each other with their mouths, the biggest mistake of all.

Now the bed seemed too empty and she could still feel his

fingers on her skin. Plus they'd only had an appetizer, not the full five-course meal of naked, sweaty, consuming sex.

What would *that* be like? Her heart pounded. She had to get over this. By morning for sure. By morning she'd be back to normal. She had to be.

7

OUTSIDE THE DOOR, Brody considered going back into JJ's room. He was still worried about the gunman, right?

Nope. He'd decided to be honest with himself. The truth was he just wanted to wrap his arms around her warm, spice-scented body and make love to her until they headed for the airport in the morning.

Bad idea. Very bad. Thank God JJ was a sensible person. One of them had to be. Brody headed back to his room, still feeling the silk of her skin on his fingers, the rough honey of her voice still in his head.

Maybe that wasn't a full screwup. Maybe it was merely the last hurrah of the old Brody out for a good time. JJ was not his usual bedmate, however. She had forever in her steady green eyes. And, to be honest again, he hadn't felt like the old Brody. He'd felt completely new. Different.

He plain liked her. He liked that she wasn't impressed by his celebrity, that she called him on his shit, that she didn't cater to him. He was sick of people always kissing his ass.

Speaking of kissing...did that woman know how. The memory of her mouth on his cock made him fall back against the elevator wall, the air completely gone from his lungs.

It wasn't technique. He was sick of that, too. He knew all the tricks and toys and turns of the tongue. So much of the sex he'd had lately had been a performance—both of them going through the motions. Enjoying it, but not fully *present.*

JJ had been so *there.* He'd been there, too. He'd felt young and new at it. Maybe he was making this up. It couldn't be *that* great….

He suddenly wanted to go back and find out. He was out of condoms, though—another sign he'd lost interest in sex. He could bribe the desk clerk to snag him some from the gift shop, then bang on JJ's door and really make love to her.

They'd just had a taste, after all. A *taste.* He'd loved hers. And he wanted more. His finger hovered over the *L* button.

Leave it alone. You got off easy, pal.

What had she called it? Tension relief? Lord. He'd gotten about as much relief as a sip of bicarbonate on a stomach full of jalapeños. He should be happy she was so easy about it.

With a sigh, he raised his fingers to the number for his floor and sailed upward.

Why the hell was he so fixated on her anyway? To prove himself to her? She didn't approve of his show or him, that was obvious. Which bothered him. He wanted everyone to love him, and he worked at it. Maybe that made him a bit of a chameleon, morphing into a shape that pleased the person he wanted to impress.

Worse, he'd wanted to *confide* in her. He'd almost told her he was sick of Doctor Nite, that he did feel empty, that he wanted to get back to who he was.

If he even knew anymore.

JJ wouldn't have laughed or jeered. He knew that about her. She would have listened hard, serious and aware, and encouraged him, rooted for him, wanted what he wanted for himself.

He wanted to know her story, too. She'd spilled that bit about being fat as a kid, but secrets percolated behind the deep green of her eyes and, suddenly, he wanted to know them all.

Inside his room, his message light was flashing, so he clicked into the message center, half expecting to hear from hotel security or, maybe, Lars Madden.

But it was Eve. *Just checking on you, Brode. We missed you tonight. But I scored cool places to hang in San Fran. Call me back. You know I'm here for you. Always.*

He should never have let Eve know he was bored. She was trying way too hard, hounding him, trying to keep him too busy to ponder his navel or his future. She was psyched about Europe, where they'd head next. He didn't dare stick around that long or he'd lose his nerve. He couldn't sign a new contract no matter what the network offered. Saying no to all that money would be tough. It was a hell of a lot easier to be rich than poor, and he hadn't socked away much in the past two years.

It was late, but he was too restless to sleep. So, he'd work on *Night Crimes* as he'd intended, make like he hadn't been weak and stupid. Erase the tape, like JJ said. God, she was sensible.

He sat down at his laptop, fired it up and scrolled to where he'd left Trent Lager—outside the warehouse on the pier, listening for the drug smugglers to make the deal.

What would Trent be hearing, feeling, seeing, smelling? Brady closed his eyes to imagine. Waves slapping the pier? Seagulls? At night? Did seagulls cry at night or did they sleep? What did it smell like? Fish, tar, old wood? He was lost.

Maybe he was too flipped out to write tonight.

Then he remembered the P.I. he'd decided to add and a shot of pleasure sent his fingers flying. What about this P.I.? What was her name? Not JJ. How about Jane? A simple name for a complicated woman—a smart-ass who rolled her big eyes, green as moss, at Trent and called him an arrogant SOB. He began to write: *I'd like to get her in the sack, Lager thought, as he'd thought many times about the curly-headed P.I. with the soulful eyes, the secrets in her heart and a right cross he never wanted to tempt his way.*

Brody woke with a start, his face pressed on the laptop keyboard, the screensaver fish scooting placidly across the screen. He rubbed his face, bumpy from the keyboard. He hoped to hell he hadn't shorted the wiring with drool. His watch said eight, and sun streamed across the bed from the open curtains. It was late enough to call Kirk about the DVD.

Moving the computer disturbed the screensaver and his document appeared. He'd only managed a few lines of text about Lager's lust for his P.I., who favored tight red dresses, before dropping off to sleep. He'd dreamt about the P.I., too, except in his dream, she'd worn a fluffy blue bathrobe.

He smiled, shook his head at himself, then decided to find out what had made that DVD worthy of armed robbery. It took three tries before Kirk finally picked up. "I wake you?"

"No. I'm good." Kirk sounded foggy. "I've got physical therapy soon. Crack of dawn. I hate that."

"You doing okay?"

"Everything's chill. Hoarding the Percocet." He suddenly got more alert. "You deliver the DVD okay to Madden?"

"Not exactly. That's why I called. Something weird happened. I gave the DVD to Madden and he shoved it into this briefcase and rushed me out of the room before I could ask about a receipt. Did he pay you, by the way?"

"Yeah. Up-front. Sorry I didn't mention that."

"So I went back to ask about it and I see this big guy forcing his way into Madden's room with a gun." He explained about the wrestling match he'd witnessed.

"No. Wow." Kirk took a harsh breath. "Shit."

"No kidding. So hotel security didn't catch the guy. I went to Madden's room to see if he was okay and he was gone."

"He checked out, probably." Kirk took a couple of nervous breaths. "But it's all good, right? We delivered the video. If he lost it, that's on him. We're out of it."

"What the hell was on that DVD, Kirk?" Brady tried to be patient, to coax out the truth. He could tell there was more to the story from Kirk's voice.

"Maybe he just wanted the briefcase?"

"Imitation leather? I doubt it. And the timing makes it obvious what he was after. What's the deal, Kirk? I could have got my ass capped here."

Kirk groaned. "There might be a problem, okay? But I had no idea it was a big deal or I would never have dragged you into it. You have to know that, Brode."

"What's on the tape, Kirk?"

"Remember the poker party last month? After the reshoot? You were playing chess with that stripper?"

"The one in the nurse costume? Candy Stripe? Yeah."

"She was topless, bro."

"Whatever. She was a damn good chess player." It was a measure of how jaded he'd become that he was more interested in her moves on the chess board than her lap dances at the party.

"Remember all the suits who were there?" Kirk asked.

"Sure." Brody's suite had been crowded with people he didn't know, but that was normal. The *Doctor Nite* blog posted where he was taping, and fans often located his hotel and tracked him around the city, eager to be on the show or buy him a shot.

The party Kirk mentioned had included some high-powered types—CEOs, politicos, Japanese and German businessmen, if he remembered right.

"I shot video for the dancers, remember? That was the freelance job. For their Web site. But, the thing is, I guess I also caught this political guy getting a lap dance. There was coke, too, I think. The guy's name is Jed…Bascom. Yeah. Bascom. He's in Congress or a judge or whatever."

"What does he have to do with Lars Madden?"

"Madden works for him. So Madden calls me up and says Bascom wants a copy of what I shot. As a souvenir. For grins, he says. I'd given the footage to the strippers, but luckily hadn't dumped the rest of the clip, so I said, sure, I'd burn a DVD. And the money was very, very good."

"And that didn't make you suspicious?"

"I'm in hock for the new camera and I was about to lose the Porsche. You know how it is."

"Yeah." Kirk tended to live on the razor's edge of financial viability. Brody wasn't that big on IRAs himself, but, unlike Kirk, he knew to look a gift horse in every relevant orifice. "All he wanted was a copy? As a souvenir? I'd think he'd want to destroy every inch of that footage."

"I didn't think about it that hard." He gave a nervous laugh. There was definitely more to this.

"What aren't you telling me?"

"Yeah…that. See, the thing is, when I got hurt? I didn't exactly fall."

"What do you mean?"

"I got thrown down the stairs. I interrupted a burglar and he kind of head-butted me off the landing."

"You're kidding."

"I didn't want Eve to worry, so I said I fell."

"Did you call the police?"

"I blacked out from the pain and my neighbor took me to a doc in the box. When I got back, it didn't look like anything was missing, so I let it go. The next day I noticed my external drives were gone and all my P2 cards, including the one in my camera."

"They left a 20K camera to steal a media card? *Then* did you call the cops?"

"Why? I don't have insurance. The drives and cards aren't worth much. They're backup or I reuse them. Besides, the cops would just get black dust all over everything."

"So there's no police report, and some guy took external drives and media cards and nothing else. Huh. You think maybe it was Bascom's people after the original footage?"

"If it was, they didn't get it. It's still in the drive I left at the studio where I get high-res output."

"You're kidding. So...what if they come back?" A chill went through Brody. He felt like some TV detective, except real-life crimes didn't get cleared up in sixty minutes, with a happy little epilogue at the end.

"That would be a bummer."

"Why would Bascom *buy* a copy from you if he was stealing the original tape? And who took it from Madden?"

"You got me, Brody. This makes my head hurt."

"Maybe they were working both ends. Or maybe your burglar was my gunman—Meathead. Did the guy who hit you have a red face and little beady eyes? Was he heavyset?"

"I didn't see much of him. He just rammed into me and kept running. I don't get it. I'd have wiped the drive if they'd asked me to. Shit. Why go to so much trouble?"

"Why does anybody commit a crime? For money, sex or power. To get more or protect what they have." He'd put those words in Trent Lager's mouth on paper already.

"I'm sorry I threw you into this, Brode. I was going to deliver the DVD myself, except the surgery. And I didn't put Madden and the burglary together."

"Maybe they're unrelated. We'll figure it out, though. First off, call the police and tell them what happened."

"If you think it'll help."

"It's a start. Give them my number because they'll want to talk to me about Madden and Meathead."

"I'll do that. Okay. Sure."

He had a bad thought. "You know, if they come back you could be in trouble. Maybe get out of your apartment for a while. Is there some place you can stay?"

"I have Eve's keys. When she's on vacation, I watch her stuff. She's got the best plasma."

"So stay there. Also, make another copy of the footage and put it and the drive somewhere safe—a safe-deposit box, maybe? See what the police suggest. It might be evidence."

"You sound like a cop in a movie, Brody. Very cool."

"Just don't expect this to blow over, Kirk. I don't think it's going to. Make the call."

"Don't tell Eve about this, okay? She'll go nuts."

"Eve's the least of your troubles. Tell the police everything. And stay safe, would you?"

"I will. No problem. So how's the shoot going? JJ working out? Eve's kind of quiet about it."

"JJ's doing great," he said with a sigh, struggling to shift topics. "She's smart, has a good eye and a lot of energy. She fit in right away."

Kirk hesitated. "So you don't miss me, then." His voice went soft and sad. "That's good, I guess."

"She's no wingman, Kirk. Of course we miss you. Eve especially. She's cranky as hell, picking on JJ all the time."

"That's Eve." He chuckled, sounding relieved. "I should give JJ some tips for handling her. I'll be back as soon as I can. I'll have to have an assistant for a while. No carrying the camera, but I'll be cool for Europe. Amsterdam rocks."

Kirk's enthusiasm put an ache in Brody's gut. Unless they chose a new Doctor Nite, there would be no European shoot. Before he could bring up the HBO job again, the phone clicked.

"Hang on," Kirk said. He came back in a second. "It's Eve reminding me about my PT appointment. She is so...*relentless.*" But he sounded pleased about it.

"Call me back after you talk to the police."

Brody turned off his phone, pondering the situation. If somebody was willing to break into Kirk's home to get the DVD and chase down a copy using force, something serious was at stake. He decided to poke around a little himself, try

Madden again on the cell phone. And he worked for a political guy…Jed Bascom? Who just might still be at the convention…

The front desk informed him Bascom had checked out, since the conference had ended the night before. Brody asked for Lars Madden and learned the man had not been registered at the hotel. Interesting. Of course it had been a hospitality suite, so the convention staff might have booked the room.

Next, he ran Jed Bascom through a Google search, which netted a dozen hits. The man was a California state senator, a conservative and former CEO of a family-values lobbying group. He showed up in a ton of recent news stories, where he was known for his antidrug, anti-immigration, antipornography positions. His name had been floated as a possible Congressional candidate.

To a guy like that, a video of him snorting coke from a stripper's navel could be a career killer. No wonder his staffer had offered Kirk big bucks for the footage. But a *copy?* As a souvenir? Bascom would want to wipe the memory of every person in the room if that were possible.

Maybe they didn't know for sure what Kirk, in his innocent idiocy, had actually shot and wanted to verify how much trouble they were in. Or maybe two groups were after the footage for different reasons. Whatever it was, Brody knew this wasn't over.

From the state legislature's Web site, he found Bascom's office number. The secretary said Bascom was due on the floor soon, but promised to convey Brody's message about an urgent matter related to the recent conference.

She resisted his banter, denied his request for Bascom's cell number, repeating robotically that the senator considered all constituent calls urgent and would return Brody's as soon as possible. In the end, he threw out a casual question. "Lars Madden around?"

"I haven't seen him, no."

"Could you ring him for me?"

"Mr. Madden does not have an office in the building," she said primly.

"Okay. Sure. I hate to trouble you, but I've been dialing his cell with no luck. Has he lost it again?"

"I don't believe so. Mr. Madden called earlier this morning to speak with Senator Bascom." So his friendly ploy had worked.

He thanked her for her time. Now he knew Lars Madden was alive and holding his cell phone, at least, and as soon as he hung up, he left another message for the guy: "Brody Donegan here. Wanting to make sure the DVD worked out all right for you." He left his cell number. It didn't seem wise to mention what he'd seen. Yet, anyway.

All he could do now was wait for Bascom or Madden to return his calls and for Kirk to talk to the police.

Now what? He was up early and starving. What about JJ? He could order room service and surprise her with breakfast in her room. And sex? Would that be part of the surprise?

The idea set him on fire. He'd love to fall into her warm bed and lose himself in the physical moment. But that would be wrong. He'd be hiding from himself and his doubts.

Besides, JJ had probably meant that about forgetting what had happened. She was a serious girl.

God, he hoped not.

Forget that. Get busy, you ass. So he ordered food to his room and sat down to work on *Night Crimes.* The best advice he'd seen was to make writing a daily habit. So he would do that. Just one page and he'd see where he went from there.

He opened the file. The P.I. scene was too sexy to continue with JJ only a few floors below him, rolling around naked in her bed, sheets twisted between her incredible legs…

Okkkaaaay. He made his way to that blasted pier where Trent was waiting for his next move. How would Trent feel? Nervous, wired and ready for action.

Exactly how Brody had felt last night trying to protect JJ. He pictured Meathead and his beady eyes and rode the adrenaline rush to the end of the scene. *Thank you, Kirk.* At least his mess had gotten Brody moving on his book. His mess and JJ, of course.

8

RIGHT ON TIME for the van to the airport, Jillian stepped out of the elevator into the lobby, her camera case over her shoulder, her heart banging her ribs at the prospect of seeing Brody again. So ridiculous. She was relieved to see he hadn't yet arrived. She had more time to settle her nerves.

She was still angry she'd allowed those lust-loaded dominoes to click out of control. As a result, she'd hardly slept, which was no way to face a film day. Her body ached with exhaustion.

She smiled at Brian and Bob, who headed out front. Through the glass doors she saw the rest of the crew beside the second van. Eve stood near the concierge desk, multitasking as usual, jabbing at her BlackBerry, talking via her wireless phone earpiece, an energy drink at her elbow.

Jillian headed her way, determined to be completely cool and confident with Brody, to set up all those dominoes as if they'd never fallen.

Brody was Brody, so his behavior was no surprise. Jillian had no excuse for hers. She was no swoony girl. She was a serious filmmaker with work to do and a mission to fulfill.

She would do just what she'd said—forget what had happened. Well, except for the mysterious gunman incident. She'd ask Brody about that when she could.

As she reached Eve, the producer frowned, but her absent stare told Jillian it was the caller who'd upset her. "I'm counting on you," she said. "Verify for me.... Call me back.... Okay.... A-S-A-P. Really." She touched her ear, evidently ending the call, then swiveled her miss-nothing gaze to Jillian. "Late night, I see."

"It shows?" She flushed and put her hand to her hair, which she'd pulled into her usual ponytail. Glancing beyond Eve, she noticed that Brody was headed toward them from the elevator.

"Of course. Puffy cheeks...pale skin...bloodshot eyes with big, black bags..." In typical Eve style, she listed the features like a checklist.

"You look fine," Brody said to her from behind Eve, who spun toward him.

"You look even worse, Brody, and you'll be in front of the camera. Your skin looks like school glue and your eyes are positively satanic. I thought you were turning in early."

He shrugged. "Doctor Nite is supposed to look beat-up."

"Thank God for eyedrops," Eve said, grabbing a small bottle from her bag and thrusting it at him with a sigh. "Let's go. She headed off at a snappy march, her behind twitching officiously.

Brody held out the drops to Jillian. "Want some?"

"I'm fine," she said, watching him apply the liquid to his eyes, liking the way the muscles of his throat moved. God, she was turned on by his *throat?* Hopeless.

He blinked at her, moisture sliding down his cheek.

"What if Eve figures out why we both look like roadkill?"

He leaned close to her ear. "Stop blushing and she won't."

She touched her cheeks.

"You look very pretty. I don't know what Eve's talking about." They looked at each other for a long, breathless moment, then Brody said, "We'd better go or she will figure it out." He put a hand to her back and led her toward the door.

Outside, the winter light had a bright cast and the brisk breeze cooled Jillian's embarrassment, at least. She could only hope Eve mistook her blush for a response to the cold.

"We don't have a minute to waste in San Fran," Eve said to them. "The sex store shoot has to be before the erotic bakery because the store owner wants to be interviewed. We won't use it, JJ, so mostly get B-roll."

"Sure," Jillian said.

"I'm serious. No fancy shots. Just coverage." She seemed to realize how harsh she'd sounded and softened her voice. "The clock's ticking, that's all I'm saying." She bustled off to talk to the crew.

Jillian let the bellman stow her camera, then slid under Brody's arms to sit beside him, alive to him, aware of his strength, his smell, the way his eyes followed her as she moved.

"Why is Eve so pissed at me?" she asked. She wanted to ask him if he'd slept with Eve, but that seemed too nosy.

"Not sure. She's pretty protective of Kirk. Maybe she's afraid I'll like you better."

"And do you?"

"You're not nearly as hairy."

She laughed softly, knowing they were treading on dangerous ground, but loving it anyway. "You don't think she suspects us?"

"Of what? I went to bed early. How about you? Wasn't that the idea? To forget last night?" His eyes glowed golden brown. "Did you forget?"

"Not really. You?"

"Not in a million years."

A shiver flew through her. Brody didn't sound one bit like a player. Last night seemed to have meant something to him, too.

"Of course, Eve could pick up the vibe anyway," he said. "Women have built-in antennae for that kind of thing."

"You've been in trouble before?"

"Enough to know better."

"There's a price for living the dream, I guess."

"Worth it, though." He grinned wickedly.

She couldn't believe she was joking with Brody about the very thing she despised—men toying with women's hearts, then escaping as if it meant nothing. She felt like an undercover cop who had to pretend to be one of the creeps she intended to bust.

Except she no longer thought of Brody as a heartless user. He was warm and aware and kind. Unless she'd misread him completely. Maybe her instincts were off. Libido could color your views as much as past experiences, she guessed, though it had never happened to her before. She'd never been in a situation like this, never reacted so intensely to a man.

"I talked to Kirk about the DVD, by the way," Brody said.

"What did he say?" She was relieved to have something else to think about.

Brody explained a burglary at Kirk's place had caused his injury and told her of Brody's calls to Lars Madden and his boss the legislator. She found it fascinating and liked that Brody was following up to help Kirk.

"Just don't say anything to Eve about this," Brody said, watching the woman out the window, where she seemed to be telling the drivers of both vans what route to take. "Kirk doesn't want her to harass him about it."

"So I'm not the only one she hassles?"

"Not by a long shot. It's her way, but she gets things done. I'm sure she'll calm down after a while."

"Should I tell her I'm not after Kirk's job?"

"She knows I'd never fire Kirk."

Jillian realized that was true. Brody was a loyal guy. He clearly cared about his crew.

"You're on the right track, JJ, praising her like you do. You're good, like I said."

Their eyes met and held. "Did you sleep much?" Brody

asked, as if the talk of the crime and Eve had been a mere sidebar to the real conversation that wasn't nearly finished.

"Not at all."

"Me, either." Had he thought of her? Longed for her? She shouldn't care, but his eyes searched her face, reading her, absorbing her, and she was doing the same to him. Could he tell that she'd wanted more? She'd half hoped he'd storm her room this morning to finish what they'd barely sampled.

Eve opened the front van door. "No fooling around today," Eve said to them.

Jillian whipped startled eyes to Brody, who looked equally alarmed. They burst out laughing.

"What?" Eve frowned. "We have to hit the ground running, that's all." But she glared at them like misbehaving children before she flounced around to tell the driver to hurry it up.

Jillian shrugged at Brody, and he chuckled and squeezed her knee in a friendly way that stayed with her all the way to the airport.

The flight to San Francisco was uneventful, except that Jillian drifted to sleep and awoke to find her head on Brody's chest. She jerked up, embarrassed. "Sorry I did that."

"It was a pleasure." He leaned close. "I got to smell you the whole way."

She smiled, then noticed a trail of saliva on his shirt. "I drooled on you." She reached to wipe it away, but he stopped her hand, holding it warmly in his, looking down at the wet streak on his shirt. "Very decorative. I like it."

"Stop," she said, pushing at his arm, then realized how intimate that would seem to anyone watching. Luckily, Eve, sitting across the aisle, seemed engrossed in the *Variety* she'd brought, iPod buds in her ears, drinking a Red Bull.

They landed at noon and within an hour they'd reached the first San Francisco location for Jillian's second day of shooting.

It would be a long one, with afternoon locations and a break to check in and rest before the night's action in the city's hottest clubs commenced.

With its sugary aroma, lacy white-metal furniture, red-striped upholstery and warmly romantic atmosphere, Eat Me Erotic Treats could have been any bakery, except that the brightly frosted cakes, pies and cupcakes that filled the display case were decorated like penises, breasts and vaginas.

Many customers recognized Brody and numerous women were happy to talk on camera about which sexy treats they would like for Valentine's Day.

Before long, she was taping a woman licking frosting from a penis sticking out of a cupcake while Brody looked on. "Oh, yummy," the woman said with an exaggerated tongue move.

"How's this for next?" Brody pretended to apply a finger's worth of frosting to his own zipper. So gross. Did he really enjoy all this vulgarity, or was this just the Doctor Nite act?

Relieved to leave Brody comparing notes on white chocolate versus dark chocolate penises on a stick, Jillian ducked into the kitchen to film the bakers squirting nipples onto breast-shaped layer cakes. When they left the shop, Brody was munching on a sugar cookie frosted with vulva. She sighed. This was all so strange.

They moved on to SenSations Emporium, a famous San Francisco sex toy shop, where the grandfatherly owner discussed the top sellers of various sexual accoutrements. "Now, for the ladies, your dildos are your biggest movers," he said in a monotone worthy of describing gardening tools. "Most go for the mid-range models, but you'll get your handful who want the deluxe with all the bells and whistles."

A group of women after bachelorette party favors were giggling in the vibrator aisle. The owner smiled indulgently in their direction. Jillian kept her camera on him. "What's funny?" she asked.

"Oh, they titter at first, the girls," he said, "but once they see what the new vibrators can do, they get real quiet."

Standing behind the man, Brody shot her an OK to indicate Jillian had nabbed a gem. She turned off the camera and smiled, pleased once more at what a good team they made.

Eve hurried over. "I'll get the cue cards for the Top Ten Tips on Sex Toys. Go ahead and set up for the segment."

Jillian chose the vibrator aisle and Brian and Bob got set, then departed, along with the owner, who was handling a sale, leaving Brody and her alone surrounded by sex toys.

"So, what do you think of this place?" Brody asked. "Lots of fun stuff, huh?"

She looked around. "I think sex is pretty good all on its own." The optional equipment and toy choices were dizzying.

"Come on. You don't have a vibrator?"

"Of course I do."

"Uh, would that be your basic dildo, the mid-range EZone 2000 or the Pleasure Master X, the deluxe model of self-pleasure devices?" He was imitating the owner's monotone litany as he picked up each in turn.

"That's a pretty personal question," she said.

"I think we've been pretty personal, don't you?"

She remembered instantly his mouth on her and felt a wave of desire that almost made her gasp. "I have the basic dildo. Simple to use. Batteries last forever. Dishwasher safe." She couldn't believe she was having this conversation. Somehow, Brody made it seem not only normal, but fun.

"How about an upgrade?" he said, holding up the mid-range model. "We'll buy it for you. How's that?"

"You wouldn't."

"Sure I would. You could evaluate it for us. It would be

research." He picked up the deluxe model, studied it, then set it back. The thought of trying it out with Brody had her trembling, and he noticed. "You okay?"

"How do you think I am?"

"Pretty damn shaky if you're thinking anything close to what I am." He grinned. "What do you say? I'll put it on our tab."

"Put what on our tab?" Eve asked. She held out the stack of cue cards, a Red Bull in her other hand.

"Energy drinks," Jillian blurted, needing to keep Eve off the trail. "I'm curious about brands. You like Red Bull best?"

"It's good. Sure." She gave her a strange look, but Jillian turned away to get on with the taping.

Soon they'd packed up to go and were waiting for Brody, who was supposedly thanking the owner. He returned to the van with a sack. A vibrator, no doubt. "Samples," he said to Eve, but he grinned at Jillian, clearly enjoying making her squirm.

They were headed to a bachelorette party, where Brody was to interview the women about Valentine's Day, when Eve got a call that canceled the event. "Shit. What do we do now?" Eve said.

Out the window, Jillian noticed a bridal shop. "How about there?" she said. "There will be bridesmaids getting fittings in there and they'll have plenty of opinions."

"Not bad," Eve said, signaling for the driver to turn around. She gave Jillian another look. *Maybe I underestimated you.*

An urgent phone call had Eve waving them on without her, so Brody schmoozed the shop owners and Jillian not only convinced several bridesmaids to sign releases and be interviewed, but she talked them into meeting the crew at one of the nightclubs for the planned segment on Valentine's Day pickup lines.

The crew loaded up the equipment van and she and Brody joined Eve in the other vehicle. "We okay?" Eve asked.

"Perfect," Brody said. "JJ talked the bridesmaids into

coming to the bar for the V-Day lines bit. Isn't that great? You love when a shoot does double duty."

"Yeah," Eve said thoughtfully. "It is great."

At five o'clock, on the way to the hotel, they stopped for food at a jam-packed deli and when Eve came to the table, she had three different cans of energy drinks, which she set in front of Jillian. "Thought you'd maybe do a taste test," she said.

"Thanks," she said, aware this was Eve's way of making peace. The three of them tried each flavor, taking turns guessing at brands, using a necktie from Eve's bag—why was it even there?—as a blindfold. After the relaxed moment, Eve declared it time to check in to the hotel.

Jillian sank into the van seat, sweaty and weary, though pleased with her work and the progress she'd made with Eve. The lack of sleep had taken its toll, and they'd done a lot of shooting.

She leaned forward to rub her neck, then felt Brody's warm fingers dig in. Mmm. He was as good with her neck as he'd been—well, elsewhere.

In the seat ahead of them, Eve flipped through her folders frantically, talking on the phone again. Abruptly she stopped dead. "What do you mean you didn't get permission? I asked specifically for the head gigolo. We have to have a one-on-one with Brody. No. Okay…I'll come out. I have to talk to them."

Meanwhile, Brody was dissolving Jillian from the shoulders down, hitting all her trigger points, turning her muscles to ribbons, so light and loose they would fly in the lightest breeze. "That is so good," she murmured.

"You're easy."

"You're ruining my reputation."

"It's a compliment, believe me," he said, which was exactly the right way to put it. The man had a gift for making people feel special. It was just the Brody Treatment, she reminded herself, but a girl could do far worse.

"Dammit!" Eve said from the front seat, then turned toward them. Brody dropped his hands just in time.

"I've got to go early to San Diego," Eve said. "The scout screwed up. I've got to meet with people and fix it. I knew I should have done it myself."

"You can't be everywhere every time, Eve," Brody said.

"We'll drop you off at the hotel, then I'll head to the airport," Eve said. "I guess you're on your own tonight and tomorrow." She huffed a breath, frowning. "Tonight's all arranged. Tomorrow's the florist, then the bachelor auction. They should be cool, but..." She bit her lip, worried.

"We'll be good," Brody said. "JJ's been a producer, too, remember. She can handle the details."

"You set everything up so well that I'm sure it will be effortless," Jillian added. She'd just made some headway with the bristly producer. No way did she want it to seem she could do the woman's job for her.

"Stay in contact," Eve said on a sigh. "Any questions, call. I'll track you." She said it like a mother threatening to spot-check teens being left alone for a weekend.

"You worry too much," Brody said.

"Let me see what else you'll need." She flipped through her folder, scribbling things down.

"She can't help herself," Brody whispered to Jillian.

They would be alone for most of tonight and all of tomorrow. The thought made her stomach jump and her heart flutter in her chest. She felt exactly like those teens planning a kegger while their parents were out of town.

Which was wrong. They'd agreed to forget what happened, not do it again. But when Brody squeezed her knee, warm and firm, she knew he felt a similar thrill.

When the driver pulled up to the Phoenix Hotel, Eve handed her folder to Jillian. "All the details are there. Call me if anything comes up. The envelope has your tickets and itinerary with confirmation numbers for the hotel. The flight's at two tomorrow. I'll meet you in the lobby at the hotel."

"We'll be fine. You don't need to meet us. Just take it easy," Brody said. "You'll need to after torturing San Diego."

Eve leveled a look at him.

"Thanks for everything," Jillian added. She climbed out the door the driver held, crossing Brody's body. He brushed her butt, as if to help her, but with an extra caress, as if he couldn't resist, and she felt so weak she had to grab the side of the van for support.

They stood together in front of the hotel and watched the van take Eve away, then turned to each other, intimacy rising between them like hot smoke. They took a ragged breath in sync, then laughed like guilty children.

"So, we have a few hours of free time," she said.

"Yeah. We do. Just us." He paused. "Want to see what we got?"

He shook the paper sack that held the vibrator he'd bought, and her knees turned to water.

"What do you mean?"

"The footage, of course," he said with fake innocence. "What did you think I meant?"

She rolled her eyes. "Leave that in your room and we'll be fine." She nodded at the sack.

Brody sighed. "It's possible to be too sensible for your own good, you know."

"I don't believe that," she said, but a tiny voice inside said, *Prove it, Brody. Pretty please?*

9

THE PHOENIX was a Fifties motor hotel that had been refurbished as retro hip and was known for its art gallery, sculpture garden and rock star guests—definitely a *Doctor Nite* kind of place. Best of all, Jillian thought, because so many celebrities stayed here, even the fans who'd come to see Brody greeted him without grabbing at him or shrieking, and no one asked for an autograph.

Jillian's room overlooked the fantasy pool that had a tile mural by a famous artist. From the open window, laughter punctuated the jungle sounds piped into the courtyard from the terrace cabana. Beyond that she could pick up the sounds of San Francisco. Somehow the rush of traffic, the sirens, the clack of tires over bumps, those normal city sounds, seemed more romantic here. San Francisco made her feel as if something exciting was about to happen any minute.

Her room was colorful—burnt orange and avocado with tiki influences and big tropical flowers—but she barely had time to soak up the ambience before Brody was at her door. He seemed uncannily able to appear out of thin air, just like her sexual thoughts about the man.

She figured they'd sit at the bamboo table, but Brody stretched out on one of the beds, lying on his side. "Table's too small," he said, patting a space for her, wearing a predator's grin she'd swear meant, *I double dog dare you.*

Now that she'd carved out her role as the sensible one, he

seemed to feel free to tempt her. She couldn't let on how difficult this was for her, so she joined him, head braced in her palm, mirroring his position, the laptop between them.

It was difficult to focus, being so close to him. She was aware of his cologne, the smell of his skin, his long body, bare toes, his big smile and sensual lips. She'd tasted those lips and they'd tasted her body, a memory that thrilled through her like electricity.

"So, let's see what we got," she said, starting the footage. She forced herself to watch the video and found she was startled by how different Brody seemed on the monitor than he'd acted when she was shooting. The crude talk, the frosted penises, the sex-toy banter, the leers and hints no longer seemed gross and crass. Instead, they were fun. Endearing. And Brody was clearly trying to amuse her behind the camera.

She did like his attitude toward the show. For all his casual style, he worked hard, demanded quality and knew exactly what he wanted: edgy and sexy and crude—but only so crude and no more. He knew what his viewers wanted and delivered it. She couldn't help but admire him for that.

She'd obviously begun to accept the ambience of the show, to become part of it. That was her gift in her documentary work—she was empathetic with everyone she interviewed, no matter how unsavory their actions or opinions. She managed, for those minutes, to see the world through their eyes. It made for powerful interviews, but it made her uncomfortable, too.

She preferred things to be clear-cut, simple to interpret, not sliding around, shifting in meaning and value. She liked to know where she stood at all times.

With Brody, things were murky now. It didn't help that their bodies brushed, forearms touching every few seconds. Fingers, too, and, now and then, legs and feet, and Brody was looking at her as if he wanted to eat her up. His gaze roved her body, her breasts, her hips, her face, her mouth.

They were in a hotel room lying on a bed together, for God's sake, jungle music drifting in the window, the drumbeat urging them to succumb to the desire pulsing between them.

She was nuts to allow this. Except after what they'd already done, any room could seem romantic, any moment intimate, any surface sexual. At least she didn't have any condoms.

Stop. Right. Now.

"Let's talk about the shoot tonight," she said, just to do something besides notice that their feet had overlapped and neither was moving away.

They went over some interview questions, their voices soft and low, intimate as lovers, laughter bubbling up over and over, the ideas bubbling out, too, clever and fun.

"Do you want to write some of this down?" she asked him.

"It's all up here." He tapped his skull. "This is how I work best."

"You do this with Kirk?" she asked, raising an eyebrow. "Lie on a bed and talk it all over?"

"You're forgetting the hair problem again." He winked. "Actually, Kirk's not so much on planning."

"How about you? What's your preference?"

"I like to plan, but I'm flexible. Kirk and I have a system that works for us. He's not all that…ambitious."

"You mean he's lazy?"

"Laid-back is how I'd put it. He's got good instincts. He thinks on his feet. And he's always there for me. I'm not the easiest guy to work with, as you already know."

"You want the job done right. I have no problem with that. A retake is a chance to improve. How did you come to hire Kirk anyway?"

"We were drinking buddies. He needed a job."

"Did you know he was good?"

"I asked around."

"But after you'd hired him, right?"

He shot her a look, as if surprised that she'd guessed correctly. "I guess, yeah."

"And you cut him slack because he's your friend?"

"Don't you give your friends a break?"

"Not if they're working for me. I expect the best."

"You're one tough cookie, Ms. James."

"So are you, Brody. You'd never have gotten this far if you weren't. You pretend not to care, but you don't miss a thing and you push yourself, too." From the moment they started shooting, she'd felt his urgency, his restless need for the best. "You owe it to yourself, to the show and to Kirk to ask more of him."

"It's not that simple. There are trade-offs. If I push Kirk too hard, he'll shut down and follow orders instead of coming up with his own ideas. When you're in a crew, you learn to work around quirks and idiosyncrasies."

"So Eve's being a bulldozer and Kirk's laziness are just quirks?"

"They're not that bad. I rein them in when they go too far. You know how it is. You hire crew, right?"

"When I can afford to, sure. But that's not often."

"Yeah. The money's shit in documentaries. Why did you choose that, anyway? With your eye and need for a plan, I'd think you'd want more control. Real life is pretty messy."

"I'm into pain?" she joked. "It's tough, no question."

"Not to mention the fact that every Joe with a digicam thinks he's a filmmaker these days."

"Very true. The festivals are clogged with lame stuff."

"So why you? Why this?" He watched her, waiting, as impossible to resist as she tried to be when she did interviews.

"I guess it's that documentaries are these incredible living puzzles, you know? A mix of reality and story and always with secrets to uncover."

"You started out in broadcast news, right?"

"I thought I wanted to work for a newspaper at first. But in college we had a class in electronic media and the minute I had that camera to my eye, I knew this was where I belonged. I worked news in Fresno, then San Diego, but I loved the investigative pieces, so I started on my own stories on the side. I sold a couple of ideas to my station—one on beauty pageant scams, another on smugglers ripping off undocumented workers' families. I saved my money and three years ago, I quit the station to do documentaries full-time."

"No regrets?"

"None. This is what I love. Things get clear behind the lens. Distractions disappear and I really see."

"I get that about you," he said.

"Of course I want to change the world, too."

"Don't we all?"

"You want to change the world?" She hesitated, realizing she might have hurt his feelings, but Brody chuckled.

"Sure. 'Sponsor a wet T-shirt contest, save the world.' Doesn't sound like me, I know. Don't laugh, but I started out in journalism, too. Except that meant I had to attend class, actually study, which seriously cut into party time."

Brody covered his true feelings with self-mockery, she could see. She wished, suddenly, that he felt safe enough with her to stop that. She was also glad she hadn't turned on her camera. This conversation was personal.

"How did you end up with your show, Brody?"

"You really want to know? I'll give you the PR version, then the real story, how's that?" He leaned back against the headboard, getting into story-telling mode. "My *Variety* bio has me as a rags-to-riches guy. I hitched to L.A. the day after I graduated high school, took every job I could get—delivering dry cleaning, landscaping, gofer to the stars.

"A gig as vacation fill-in on a hot radio talk show led to my own radio show. A thousand pitches to a thousand producers got me a shot at *Doctor Nite* and here I am."

"And the real story?"

"Pure luck and good friends. I told you I made friends with everyone in school, right? So a friend got me into a hot fraternity at UCLA and we made money putting together parties. After college, I would get calls from all over the country from frat brothers and their friends wanting to know the hot bars, where the women were, all that."

"So you were a human Fodor's guide?"

"You got it. I had friends in the industry, too, who introduced me around. A friend of a friend got me a pitch meeting. More friends worked the angles—especially the sister of a network exec I was dating—and, poof, I had *Doctor Nite*. The truth is..." He leaned over to tickle her ear with a whisper, "I slept my way to the top."

"Come on. You were smart, you had talent."

"I was lucky."

"Luck is the meeting of preparation and opportunity."

"It was right place, right time, right people."

"I guess you get to tell it the way you want, but you seem to go out of your way to belittle yourself, Brody."

"In this business, you have to keep your ego in check. Success turns on a dime. I can't forget for one minute that the only difference between me and the guy watching my show from a bar stool, machine oil under his nails, debts up the butt and tons of regrets, is a few lucky breaks."

"That's very humble of you."

"You start believing your own PR and you end up facedown in your custom pool, too drunk to lift your head and save yourself."

"Wow, Brody. That's quite...profound."

"I'm a deep guy. Don't sell me short. I could surprise you." He grinned at her.

"You already have," she said, aware that her opinion of Brody was shifting by the minute.

"Glad to hear it. So, that's me. What about you? What keeps you going when things go wrong, JJ? Besides your love of pain?"

"You mean when the big interview falls through at the last second, the rental equipment breaks when you're miles from a city, the grant money is too little or too late or includes a script rewrite?"

"Exactly."

"Sometimes I wonder." She smiled, then got serious. "I guess it's when flashes of truth burst out in a piece. Doing a documentary is like being a detective after clues or like the Inuit carvers who release the animal they believe is already in the wood."

"That's a cool image."

"See, you go in with a plan, of course, a theme and a framework, something you want the audience to get, but it always changes. You have to stay open. You can't be stubborn or you'll miss what's really there."

"You? Stubborn? I can't imagine."

"Yeah, well. It happens. My tendency is to draw quick conclusions. But I can be wrong. Like with *Lost Childhood,* I thought the issues were lack of funds and bureaucracy. Then I spent weeks in a foster home and shadowed some caseworkers. I saw the situation through the eyes of the kids, the foster parents and the social workers themselves."

"And that wasn't it?"

"Lack of money is the overarching problem, sure, but what's equally serious is burnout and overload—caseworkers and foster families trapped in an overextended system, doing their best, but stretched too thin. The cracks have to show."

"Sounds like an important message."

"It was heartbreaking. I went with a foster mom on a field trip taking her fosters to prison to visit parents serving time."

"They let you film at the prison?"

"I had to do some fast talking, let me tell you." She told him about introducing the officials to the kids, working her way into their confidence through mutual acquaintances and just never giving up. She talked so long her throat grew dry.

"I'm going on and on, Brody. I'm sorry. I get carried away talking about this."

"I like seeing you all fired up. Your eyes are glowing. I admire your passion." He paused. "I'd like to feel that way."

"You love your show, don't you?"

"Sure," he said, but he wouldn't meet her gaze. There was something more here, something he wasn't ready to say. "So did your foster care movie change the world?"

"Hardly. Other than a few screenings, no one's seen it."

"But you won festival awards."

"Awards don't guarantee airtime. I couldn't get a distributor. Everyone liked the piece, but it was either too local or too grim to buy."

"Bummer. What about this new project? The one you're interviewing me for? It's on…*dating?*" He looked at her questioningly.

She couldn't tell him her real angle. Not yet, anyway. The better she knew him, the more complicated that angle became, which made her stomach twist.

"It's got a commercial hook, that's the point. A movie that no one sees is like one hand clapping. There's substance to this one, too, though. I promise you that."

"Look, I'm the last person to criticize you for being commercial." He leaned in, touched her cheek, trying to cheer her. The warmth was so nice. "Which reminds me, I promised you an interview, didn't I? Why don't we do it now? We have time."

"Now?"

"Sure. It would give us something to do besides what I can't stop thinking about." He brushed her arm with his finger, making her shiver.

"Good point." She sighed. He was right and this was exactly what she needed. She just felt so dreamy and aroused…. She forced herself to focus. "Let's do it."

"You have a way with words," he murmured.

"You know what I mean." She slid off the bed, away from temptation, determined to make the most of this chance.

"Where do you want me?" Brody said, still lying down, teasing her still.

"Where do I want you? Please. Don't make this any harder."

"Oh, it couldn't be any harder," he said, low, meaning it exactly how she took it.

Her knees sagged. "Brody…" She fought to stay strong. "Sit up maybe. The painting behind you is nice." She turned the light on the nightstand to its brightest setting, fighting the way her fingers trembled.

He sat for her. "Look okay?"

"You look great." Almost edible. Her heart was hip-hopping in her chest and she was glad to have something to do besides fall on the man and claw his clothes off.

"So what do you want me to talk about?" he asked.

She turned on the camera before setting it on the tripod to catch any early gems. "Your show, your dating advice, what your fans tell you. Whatever comes up."

"I like how subtle you are," he said. "And how tricky. The way you slip in and out when you work, almost invisible. Like, for example, you're already recording me, aren't you?"

She jerked her head up, caught cold. "Does that bother you?"

"It shouldn't. It's how the game is played, right?"

"Good." His words relieved her deeply. He probably wouldn't even be surprised about the secret taping. "I appreciate your suggesting this. You could be doing a lot of other things."

"We both could," he said, and she felt the familiar heat burn through her. "The Pleasure Master X awaits us in my room." He wagged his eyebrows, clearly teasing her.

She laughed, grateful for his playfulness. "So, Brody, *Doctor Nite* is the top show on your network. What do you think accounts for its success?"

"That's easy. I talk about what's on men's minds."

"And that would be…?"

"Sex, of course. Sex is always on men's minds. Every seven seconds, isn't it, that a man thinks of sex? So we talk about clubs and sports and beer and cars, but the point is always sex."

"And your approach to sex is…?"

"Sex is a game. My job is to help guys be better players."

"To score?"

"To score, sure. That's the point, after all, isn't it?"

He was giving her perfect lines. "And that makes dating…?"

"Dating is the pregame show."

"It sounds more like a war. Women are the enemy, trying to trap men into marriage. Men must avoid capture at all costs."

He laughed. "All I know is what my guys tell me and, believe me, they're not asking me how to, quote, take it to the next level, unquote." He winked.

"Talk about that a bit, would you? You encourage men to stay single?" As an aside, she added, "If you could repeat the question for me, so we don't need my voice in the final cut."

Brody nodded. "Do I encourage men to stay single? I encourage them to get what they want from life. If they don't want to be dragged into a mortgage payment and a minivan, they should stay clear of the *R* word."

"You're something of a role model, aren't you? For younger men? Say teenagers?"

"Hold on." He honed in on her, warning in his tone. "My show is clearly labeled adults-only. If a kid sees me as a role model, something is wrong at home. As for teens watching my show, that's what the V-chip is for, people."

"Certainly. That makes sense. And certainly the bulk of your audience is over twenty-one. There's a bar game, isn't there, that guys play? Would you describe it?"

"Yeah. Supposedly whenever I say the line, 'The Doctor is *in*,' people drink a shot. Any excuse to get smashed, I guess."

"You're being modest, Brody. Men revere you. You're an icon. Do you feel you're shaping a trend? Or at least contributing to it? The idea that men should shun commitment?"

"Am I shaping a trend? Am I an icon? Hardly. I'm just doing my job, entertaining my audience. They seem to like it so far."

"And you? Do you like what you do?"

"What's not to like?" Tension sparked in his eyes and made his cheek muscle flicker.

"Doesn't it get to be too much?"

He grinned at her. "Come on, you're talking to Doctor Nite here. Too much is never enough."

Okay, he was fully into his role. "So, what's next for Doctor Nite?" she said, letting him plug his show.

"Who knows?" he said, then paused for a breath. "We're working on Europe. London, Paris, Amsterdam. Lots of possibilities there." He suddenly looked utterly done in. She was startled by the change. He looked as if he'd rather be anywhere but here. Or certainly Europe.

"You look tired, Brody."

"I am," he said, trying to smile.

"Shall we pick this up another time?"

"If you don't mind."

"No. Thanks. That was a great start."

Brody got up from the bed, looking preoccupied, his eyes far away. What had bothered him? Going to Europe? Whether he loved his show? She was dying to find out.

"I should head to my room, catch a nap before tonight." He shoved his hands into his pockets and fidgeted. Something crackled. A candy wrapper probably. He moved to the door.

When she met him there, standing close, he smiled, studying her face, the weary distance erased again. He touched the side of her head, then tapped the scrunchie that held her hair. "You mind?"

"Go ahead."

He tugged away the band and fluffed her hair around her shoulders. "When I'm close to you like this I want to have my hands all over you." He traced her arms with his fingers, lingering on her skin, watching her reaction in her eyes.

"I know," she said, wanting to lean into him, her body so eager she had to fight to keep from shaking. If he kissed her, she wouldn't want to stop him. "You should go," she said, opening her door with a trembling hand.

"You learned a lot about discipline in Bondage School." He reached into his pocket, she assumed for his key, but something else fell to the floor.

She bent down to get it and so did he. She saw it was a strip of brightly colored condoms. She picked them up, caught a sweet smell and sniffed. "Fruit flavors? Banana. Strawberry. Orange. Hmm. Where did these come from?"

"They were in the gift basket in my room," Brody said, grasping one end of the strip and standing with her.

"You got condoms in your gift basket?"

"You think Doctor Nite gets cheese and crackers? There were also body paints, flavored lubricant, a thong and an erotic video. The savvier hotels give me theme baskets hoping for a mention on the show."

"But you brought these to my room." The strip crackled between them. Or maybe it was the air. Her heart thudded in her ears. They stared at each other across the protection they'd needed the night before.

"Be prepared, right?" He tugged on the strip, coming away with the banana one, which he rolled over his knuckles like a magician's quarter.

"You don't strike me as the Boy Scout type," she said, the reality of what was happening sinking in, the strawberry and orange condom dangling from her fingers.

"If we'd had these last night…" he said.

"You'd have been inside me," she finished and their eyes connected along a line of invisible fire.

"Damn," he breathed, his eyes dark except for a hot white spark in the center. A muscle in his jaw ticked. He was trembling, holding back, she could tell. "I want you so much. You're making me crazy."

That made her feel so powerful, so sexual. It was all too much. She'd never felt this way before, never wanted a man so much. Lust pounded through her like a giant, irresistible tidal wave. "Maybe we should finish what we started," she said, knowing how dangerous those words were. "We only had the appetizers, right?"

"Appetizers?" He looked utterly confused.

She grabbed his shirt with both hands, the condoms crinkling as she tightened her grip. "And we owe ourselves the whole meal." She yanked him close and kissed him, turning him so his body slammed the door shut, acting wilder than she'd ever behaved with a man.

"So we know what we missed, right?" Brody managed, kissing her back, his tongue sweeping her mouth. Totally getting it.

"Just this once," she mumbled, then went back to kissing. They kissed for long moments, stoking the fire to a roar. Jillian knew that if she paused for one second, let one sensible thought enter her head, she'd lose her nerve.

Brody sensed this, too, judging by the way he gripped her

bottom, lifted her and walked her backward to the bed. When she hit the mattress, she let herself fall, bouncing on the tropical flowers that covered the quilted spread.

Brody went at her clothes, then his, stripping her so smoothly she hardly knew how she ended up naked. She didn't want to think about all the practice he'd had. She was just grateful there'd been no fumbling with clasps or buttons or hooks or belts. Here he was, warm, erect and bare to her touch.

His chest felt so good against her breasts, and he moved one thigh between her legs to nudge her sex. She locked her knees around that thigh and slid up and down, getting a rush of sparks and stinging fire.

They shifted slightly to the side and Jillian ran her hands down Brody's back, around the curve of his backside, loving his smooth skin and firm muscles. Her heart was going a mile a minute.

He stroked her bottom, his mouth on her throat, his erection an insistent pressure against her belly. He kissed down her neck to her breasts, sliding his tongue around each nipple in turn, sucking, pressing, sending charges of electricity everywhere, zipping and zapping and making her jump.

This was going to be so much better than the appetizers.

Don't stop. Don't stop. Don't ever *stop.* The words thumped through her mind like a heartbeat. Brody's fingers kept moving, varying their pressure and stroke—soft and teasing on her stomach, firm on her bottom, delicate on the underside of her arm and down her sides. His tongue pressed the flesh beneath the swell of her breasts and she felt alive and hot and desperate.

Ohohohoh...mmmmmyyyy.

He was turning every inch of her into an erogenous zone. Her hips pivoted and her sex tightened, ready to explode. She was about to come and the man hadn't even gotten inside her yet.

She threw out an arm, feeling for the condoms she'd dropped. There. She clutched at the two still connected.

Brody pulled back the covers, opening the bed, and helped her between the cool sheets.

"Strawberry or orange?" she gasped.

"Lady's choice."

"Strawberry," she said, tearing it open with her teeth, thinking they might need the orange and the banana, too, which had fallen to the floor somewhere. No. They'd made a deal.

"Just once, right?" she said, reminding herself, too. Maybe it wouldn't even be that good, the sex.

Yeah, right.

Brody didn't speak. He didn't seem able to. He was flushed, his eyes shiny with the same hunger she felt. This seemed the only thing they could do.

He sheathed himself before she could even attempt one of the approaches the women in the segment had demonstrated—putting the condom on with their lips, rolling it down superfast or superslow, with tongue or without. She was just glad the thing was on.

Hovering over her, holding himself up by his strong arms, Brody stilled. "You sure about this?" he said huskily. He wanted her to be certain. He wasn't allowing this to be a mindless coupling, a frantic act. How annoyingly mature of him.

"I'm sure," she said.

"Thank God." She knew Brody had been with dozens of women, but he looked at her as if he'd never wanted a woman this much.

She lifted her hips and opened her thighs to him.

He eased into her body with slow care and when he looked at her, the strangest sensation shot through her. *I know you. There you are.* As if he were someone dear she'd once had and wanted again.

"JJ," Brody breathed, his voice full of wonder, too.

"Jillian," she said. "Call me Jillian." Jillian for her family, her friends, the people she loved.

"Jillian," he said and pushed deeply into her. "You feel so damn good," he groaned, pulling back, then digging in again.

She grabbed his backside, loving the way the muscles tightened and released as he drove into her again and again. His strokes coaxed her upward, higher. Tight, then tighter.

She loved the rush and burn, the sweet ache of their bodies combining, separating, finding each other again and again in this most ancient, most intimate act. She was so glad they'd gone all the way, not settled for less.

She lifted her hips to meet each thrust, wanting more and more. Brody would not let her look away or close her eyes.

She felt so...*naked.* So open to him. The way she expected to feel with the man she eventually loved and made a life with. If she ever found him, if what she wanted was even possible.

That was too much, way too much, so she was glad when Brody's moves intensified and she lost herself in the physicality of the moment. She wanted to relish every second, make it last, but she couldn't hold back, couldn't stop her climax, which struck as violent and bright, as lightning-quick as a hot summer storm.

Brody met her with his own release, saying her name like a prayer. She closed her eyes, and let her climax roar through her, wave after wave, gradually slowing to low rumbles and zings and gentle shudders that got fainter and fainter, fading to soft laps of pleasure.

Brody's arms were tight around her and she felt his heart pounding as hard and his breath coming as raggedly as her own.

They settled down slowly, breathing and pulse returning to normal. Brody lifted his head and looked down at her. "It'll be okay," he said. "Whatever you do, do not panic. We had to finish it—the meal, like you said."

"I'm fine," she said. She felt great. Of course, she had every reason to panic. She'd had sex with the man who stood for everything she hated about the player mentality, the man who was her boss, the subject of her documentary. She'd sworn not to do this, knew it was wrong, but she'd done it anyway.

And she was grinning like an idiot, proud of herself for throwing caution to the wind and going for what she wanted so badly. She would come to sensible earth soon enough.

Right this minute, she'd revel in pure glory.

10

UH-OH, Brody thought, watching the dreamy expression fill JJ's face like a pink cloud in a kiddie cartoon. He knew that look—he'd gotten it a couple of times in college when he'd let a serious girl slip under his radar. She thought they'd *connected,* that this was *big,* that they'd started a *relationship.*

He was in trouble now. This was exactly why he only slept with party girls or groupies. Women who didn't make sex a big deal, even when it was this good.

Okay, great.

Jillian would make too much of what had been a pleasant—all right, phenomenal—physical moment between two willing—okay, desperate—people.

He should have known better. He knew *himself* better. From the minute he plucked that strip of condoms out of the basket on the way to her room, he knew he was up to no good.

He was as weak as he was stupid. He'd just had sex with a woman who took *everything* seriously. She'd asked him to call her Jillian in that warm, forever way that made his skin crawl.

Maybe not *crawl.* More like a hot shiver, like stepping into a steamy bath. Which felt pretty damn good. And he'd gotten this warm stab in his chest. He'd felt…homesick.

And sure, he wanted to settle down, make a home, but not until he had his new life figured out, and it wouldn't be with someone who knew him as Doctor Nite.

And, for God's sake, what was JJ thinking? He wasn't her type at all. It was some bad boy thing. Doctor Nite had charmed her. That was what he did. That was his deal.

Of course, she'd charmed him, too. Right now he was running his fingers through her hair and kissing the impossibly soft skin of her neck, breathing in her smell, holding it in, as if it were some kind of healing vapor.

The sex had been effortless and *real.* He hadn't been performing or watching himself from a distance—a sensation he so hated he'd avoided sex for weeks.

It wasn't that he wanted some small-town girl like his friend Cal's wife, who baked bread and made baby quilts for every family in town. And maybe the girl he found would be *like* JJ—smart and funny and no bullshit, dedicated to her career and dynamite in the sack. But it was too soon. Like hooking up right after a divorce. On the rebound, you arrived with all the baggage from your past love—or, in his case, your past life.

At the moment, he wanted to talk to her about quitting the show, writing his book, changing his life. He hardly knew her, of course, and they'd spent most of their time with her looking at him from behind a camera.

In a few days her see-all, digging-at-him, green eyes would be replaced by Kirk's go-along, let-it-be brown ones, so he should forget it, not get carried away.

His job now was to wipe that dreamy look off JJ's face without hurting her. Doctor Nite had gotten him into this mess, that lady-killing SOB, so Doctor Nite would have to get him out of it, too.

"You were great," he said, shifting away from her delicious skin, stuffing an arm behind his head, going for a casual tone.

"Don't exaggerate," she said. "I doubt I'm in the top third, performance-wise, of the *countless* women you've had."

Countless? That sounded pretty empty. And she'd meant it that way, he could tell. "Not countless. There's a number."

"You kept track? You have a black book with stars? *Gives great head. Goes all night?*" She was teasing, but it didn't seem so funny right now. At least she'd stopped looking dreamy.

"No, I don't have a black book."

"You don't need one, right? It's all up here." She tapped his forehead. He didn't appreciate her mocking him.

"Do you ever sleep with the same one twice?" She rested her cheek on one palm and traced his nipple with her other fingers. Was she laughing at him?

"Sometimes, sure. If I'm in town long enough. If it works out. The timing. The mood. The woman."

"I'm sure they're all happy to go again with Doctor Nite. You're very good, after all."

How did she manage to make a compliment sound like an insult? And she had this wicked glint in her eye. She rolled on top of him and kissed him deeply, so that he went hard as stone, despite his irritation with her.

"Mmm," she said, looking at him like she was ready to take a bite. "I'm game, if you're up for it." She reached for his obliging erection. "Oh, yes. You're *very* up for it."

But he wasn't in the mood. Or at least he didn't want to be. Besides, it was better to clear these things up quickly, he knew. "We said once, didn't we?"

"Technically, sure." She squinted past him at the clock. "We've got ninety minutes before we have to be anywhere."

"And we have a long night ahead of us," he said sternly, regretfully shifting away from her incredible fingers.

She stilled, blinked, and her face colored. "Oh. I get it." She sat up, her hands on her naked hips. God, she looked good. "You think I'm too into you."

"We agreed, that's all."

"We agreed? You're holding me to a contract?" She was clearly hurt, but anger crackled in her eyes.

"I just want us to be clear."

"Oh, we're clear. Hang on and I'll grab a Sharpie so you can autograph my boobs. I'll never wash them off."

"That's not what I mean—"

"You were into this as much as I was. I saw your face."

"I know. I was. Don't get all wound up."

"Wound up? What? You think because I want more sex that I'm choosing bridesmaids and picking out china patterns? You are the most arrogant man I think I've ever—"

He kissed her. What else could he do? She was getting him all wrong and he had to smooth it out.

Except it was like mashing his lips against a door. So he'd have to explain. "Sure I'm into it, JJ. I'm just mixed up lately. So it's better to put the brakes on. For me, not you. You might think that's bullshit…."

"Oh, I do." Her eyes snapped at him. "Whatever you say, Brody. Have it your way." She bent down, grabbed his clothes and tossed them to him, smiling a cool smile that had no effect on the heat in her eyes. "I'm taking a shower. I'll meet you in the lobby at eight. For work."

He sat there holding his balled-up clothes while she waltzed her gorgeous ass into the bathroom. Even the shower sounded pissed off when she started it.

Unfair. He'd done the honorable thing, passed up great sex, told her the truth, but he'd ended up in trouble anyway. What the hell was he supposed to do?

Back in his room, he was grateful for the distraction of a call from Kirk. Brody hadn't heard from either Madden or Bascom.

"The cops said they couldn't do much unless I was threatened," Kirk told him. "I'm staying at Eve's right now, but picking up my messages. And today there was one from a guy who said I had something he wanted and he'd be back for it. He didn't give his name and at the end he says in this, like, menacing voice, 'I hope you'll be more careful on the stairs.'"

"Sounds like a threat to me."

"Yeah. So I called the police about it and, meanwhile, they've been in contact with some investigator who's after Bascom, I guess? So, long story short, you'll get a call from a guy named Brian—no, Ryan—Jeffers. He's from the Attorney General's office, he said when he called me."

"What's it all about? The investigation?"

"Not sure exactly. He's coming to talk to me, too. I'm sorry I got you into all this, Brode."

"No big deal. We just have to get you out of it. For good."

"Yeah. I'm staying clear of strippers with Web sites, for sure. I'm done with freelance, I think. Eve says I waste money. Too many surfboards. Too many cars. I could cook more for myself. Eve thinks my quesadillas are ab-fab."

"She does, huh? I didn't realize you two had such deep discussions." It sounded like Eve not only produced his show, but was working out the details of Kirk's life for him, too.

"You gotta give her time. She comes on all tough and bossy, but she's a marshmallow. She can't stand movies where any animal gets hurt. Not even a horse in an old Western. So, don't tell her about the cop thing, okay?"

"I won't. How are you feeling?"

"Not bad. Sore in the morning. Mostly I'm bored as hell. I can't play Grand Theft Auto worth shit. I can't wait to get back on the road with you guys. Don't have too much fun without me."

"No problem there." Now that JJ was mad at him, the fun was definitely over. He doubted she'd crack a smile the rest of the trip. *No sex with crew.* Some rules weren't made to be broken. Especially his own.

IN THE SHOWER, Jillian ran the water boiling hot and scrubbed herself raw, totally disgusted with her behavior. She'd acted like some heartsick groupie. It was just that Brody had been so damn smug, as if he thought she wouldn't be able to resist falling for him. *Pul-eeze.* At least she'd managed to act angry. She could only hope Brody hadn't seen through to her hurt.

Maybe she'd misread his reaction, that naked desire, the surprise of sudden intimacy she could have sworn he felt, too. Maybe he'd been faking. That would be so Doctor Nite.

This was an important lesson. She was glad to learn it now. The best part was that she had no interest whatsoever in having sex with the man ever again.

No interest. Whatsoever. Ever again.

She dressed, checked her spare media cards, made sure her batteries were charged and grabbed her camera, determined to be the consummate professional during tonight's shoot. Brody would completely forget the woman who'd moaned and quivered in his arms.

As it turned out, Brody made it very easy to forget the tender, attentive lover he'd been, being Doctor Nite to the tenth power—obnoxious and sexist at every turn.

At the flower shop, Brody mimicked the sex act with flowers, mashing an amaryllis, the red flower with the penis-like stamen, into the labia-like petals of an orchid. It was so childish, she thought, making nature seem tawdry.

During the bachelor auction segment, he advised the bachelors to stuff their boxers for higher bids, then, after one man earned a particular high price, Brody advised him to "check for shackles and a shotgun in the basement, pal. That lady's going to want her money's worth."

By the time they headed to the club where the bridesmaids were meeting them to talk over Valentine's Day pickup lines,

Jillian had bitten her tongue so much she needed ice for the sore spots.

Set to shoot the four women at a high round table while Brody asked questions, Jillian braced herself for more offensive remarks.

"So what does a guy say that makes you want to rip his clothes off?" Brody asked the women, eyes moving from face to face.

Jillian rolled her eyes without moving her camera.

"Just the basic compliments," said the first girl. "If he tells me I'm pretty or I have nice eyes or he likes my dress."

"Got that, boys?" Brody winked at the camera. "Slather on the flattery like cream cheese on a bagel and you'll score."

"It's more if he's thoughtful," the second girl said. "If he notices my drink is empty and orders me another of the same."

"Ah. I get it." Brody lifted her martini glass, half full of pink liquid. "Barkeep, another 'tini-weenie, please?" He turned to the girl. "Does that mean the Doctor is *in?*"

"Oh, yeah," she said, planting a big kiss on him. Brody's hand went to her back, probably to keep the woman from falling off her stool—she was pretty loaded—but it reminded Jillian that he'd done the same thing to her. It was just the Brody Treatment. Nothing special.

The next girl said, "What gets me hot is if we never run out of things to say. We just talk. I can't explain it…."

"Give me the words, doll. Be specific. What do I have to say to get *in?*"

He was just doing a bit, but it hit Jillian wrong. She signaled for a break—she had to change cards—and took the camera from her shoulder. "It's not a *line* that gets you in, Brody. Ask real questions and care about the answers. Get to know the woman as a person. Give something of yourself. Be freaking sincere! Maybe then you'll get into her pants!"

It was abruptly quiet and Jillian realized she'd yelled that last bit. People stared at her and the four bridesmaids' eyes were wide. "Sorry," she said, her cheeks hot. "Gotta get another…" She held up the media card.

"No problem," Brody said, clearly trying not to bust out laughing, which annoyed her even more.

She returned and managed to keep her opinions to herself while they finished those interviews, then went on to ask men about their "score lines," and finally Brody called it quits.

Thank God.

"Can I buy you a beer?" he asked softly, clearly wanting to make peace, his dark eyes digging in. "I promise. No lines." He crossed his heart. Even when he was a jerk, he couldn't help being cute. Before she could answer, a couple of guys at the end of the bar hollered at Brody to "Get *in,*" one of them holding out an overflowing beer stein.

"They're singing your song," she said.

"They can wait," he said, holding her gaze.

"It's fine. I'd like to interview some women for my documentary anyway. Go drink."

"Later, then." He squeezed her arm in farewell and the warmth stayed with her, along with her annoyance.

The four women she'd selected were real estate agents from the same office, all in their thirties, and they were happy to tell Jillian what they thought about the Peter Pan syndrome.

"There's a bunch of 'em," said the first, a brunette with spiked hair and hoops the size of saucers, waving at a clump of late-twenties guys bellowing at each other like apes. "I bet at least two still live at home."

"Or in a guesthouse on their parents' property," said a blonde with big bangs that got caught in her false eyelashes whenever she blinked. "They've had an equity setback or they're artists or they're chasing a dream. Whatever. They love their Xboxes and their sports cars and their mom's cooking. They get laid now and then and they're perfectly happy."

"It's so depressing," said a third woman with black hair and tired eyes, an empty martini glass before her. "Why did I come out tonight? I have more fun watching a movie with my cat on my lap." She shook her head. "Sex is just not that important to me and all these guys want from us *is* sex."

"I know," said the fourth woman, a redhead with long, wavy curls and flawless makeup. "I'd like to buy a house, but that's impossible without a second income. A guy makes you feel like you're after his freedom, when all you want is to share a life. He doesn't even have to mow the lawn. I mean, I *like* yard work."

Jillian's heart went out to these women, disillusioned, but still hoping. They'd come to this singles bar, after all. "What do you think causes these guys to want to stay single?"

"It's their mothers," said the redhead. "All those Eighties stay-at-home moms spoiled the little princes. Now they expect to be pampered and praised and have everything handed to them on a titanium platter. They certainly don't want to share or compromise or change diapers."

Brody drew close, eavesdropping, a beer mug in one hand.

"Plus, we never look good enough," added the flawless redhead sitting in front of Brody. "They want runway models, mannequins. Real women get cellulite and their boobs droop, guys. Get used to it!"

"I wish I could have sex like guys do," said the glum blonde. "Just get laid, then be my own person, happy on my own."

The women all nodded agreement.

"Here's Doctor Nite," Jillian said, motioning toward him. "What do you think of his message to men to stay single?"

The women turned and booed him.

"Hey, don't shoot the messenger." He raised his hands in mock surrender. "You don't want a guy who's not interested, right? In the meantime, ladies, I'm here to dry your tears."

Brody tapped his beer against the blonde's wineglass and she couldn't help but smile. Before long, the women were joking with Brody, taken in like everyone else.

In a bit, Brody signaled to Jillian that he was ready to leave and they headed out of the bar toward their van.

"You still pissed at me?" he asked as they stepped into the cool night air. "For a while I thought your posse was going to break beer bottles over my head."

"No way. They melted. Doctor Nite charmed them as usual."

"Yeah. I get sick of that guy." He sounded disgusted.

"Really?"

"Nah. I'm just messin' with you." He tried to laugh, then grabbed her camera bag to carry it to the back of the van. But he'd meant what he said. She stood and stared at him.

He caught her looking. "Let's go. Forget it. It's been a long night and too many people bought me beers."

But she had to know more. Brody had all but confessed what she hoped was true—that Doctor Nite's life made him miserable.

They made small talk on the way to the hotel and in the elevator Brody caught a call from Eve, who wanted to be sure the evening's shoot had gone okay without her. When the elevator opened on their floor, he was ready to barrel down the hall away from her. She had to catch his arm to stop him. "How about a nightcap?" she said, flustered, but anxious to get deeper with him. "We can unwind, look over the footage or just…talk."

"You want to *talk?*" he said, arching an eyebrow. *After what happened last night?* was the unspoken question.

"I'm too wound up to sleep. How about you?"

He smiled, intrigued despite his reluctance.

"Come on, then." She waved him toward her room, then let him in, nervous as she fetched a scotch for him and a Grand Marnier for herself from the minibar.

"I'll get ice," he said, picking up the ice bucket.

As soon as he was gone, she set up her camera in case she could use something Brody said to her. She shifted the night-stand lamp closer to the one on the table and set both on their highest setting to maximize the light. Then she placed a chair where she wanted Brody, setting a glass and the whiskey bottle there to cue him where to sit.

Brody returned, smiling when he saw her standing at the table. "So you're serious about this talk, huh? The table instead of the bed?"

"This seems better," she said, scooping ice into their glasses. The sound seemed loud in the night-quiet of the room. She twisted off the lid on the scotch.

"Just a hair," Brody said, holding his hand partway over his glass. She'd noticed he actually limited his alcohol intake, only pretending to keep pace with his fans at the bars.

She poured half the scotch and all of the Grand Marnier into the glasses, the silky liquids slipping silently over the ice.

They sat down facing each other.

"Cheers." Brody held her gaze for a moment before taking a sip, then putting down the glass. She was aware of his cologne, the clink of the ice, the privacy of the room.

"Cheers," she said back.

They watched each other in a silence that was suddenly awkward. She didn't know where to start and Brody seemed to have something on his mind he didn't really want to talk about.

"So, Kirk called me…" he said, clearly avoiding what was on his mind. He explained about Kirk's threatening phone call and the investigator who would be contacting Brody.

"So this is a big deal, then?"

"Seems to be, yeah." Silence settled between them again.

Abruptly, Brody leaned closer. "Are you okay with us? I know I offended you six ways from Sunday, but I didn't mean to."

"I'm fine. Really."

"I would love more time with you, Jillian." She loved the way he said her name, low and slow, using all three syllables.

"No. I got testy. It's because I don't do this kind of thing very often."

"Neither do I."

"Please. You have women sneaking into your room every night, you told me yourself."

"Not in a while." He evidently read the doubt in her face. "You think you've got me figured out, but you don't."

"Correct me, then," she said softly, caught off guard, realizing her camera had been a mistake. This conversation would be too personal. She would delete this afterward, along with the foot massage clip, which she hadn't taken care of yet.

"You were right. It gets to be overkill and you end up going through the motions." He sighed. "I mean, face it, these women aren't sleeping with me. They're after Doctor Nite. And Doctor Nite gets old, believe me." He steadied his gaze on her. "You are way too easy to talk to, you know that?"

She held her breath, not saying a word, letting him talk.

His smile was so sad. "After a while, it's just too many parties, too many bars, too much booze, too many strangers who want to be my best friend."

His words were *perfect* for her movie. *Perfect.* But she couldn't use them. He was speaking from the heart to her alone. "I've noticed you seem weary," she said. "Kind of lost."

"I am, I guess." He swallowed, as if there were more he wanted to say. "The thing is…" His eyes traced her features. He smoothed her hair, one side, then the other. "I feel good with you. You're different from the women I know. I like being with you, but I might be hiding out, you know? I'm not in shape to be with anyone right now. And that's not bullshit, okay?"

"I understand," she said, startled by the pain in Brody's eyes. He was so different now, so real and open and human.

Except, he suddenly seemed to regret what he'd said and gather himself. He slapped his palms on the table as if at the end of a meeting. "So it's late and you're too good a listener." He smiled softly. "Thank you, Jillian."

"You're very welcome, Brody."

"I should go." Then he stopped. "Unless…how about if I give you another interview. I think I can ad-lib something—say, Doctor Nite's Top Dating Tips? You could contrast it with all that bitching the bar girls were doing about men."

"You want me to interview you? Now?" Watching him become Doctor Nite again before her eyes was like being dragged awake from a great dream, but this was what she was after. "Okay. Sure." In a haze, she moved her camera to its tripod, checked the card memory, brought out a fill spot, and in a few seconds she was set to shoot.

"Okay," Brody said, "Doctor Nite's Top Ten Tips for Dating. This is guys-only, ladies, so go powder your noses for a tick."

He pretended to lean forward. "Listen up. Write these down. Tip Number Ten…don't call it a *date*. You make it official and she'll drag out The Rules—three dates before you screw, must call the next a.m., all that BS. Ask her to catch a flick, grab a beer, get a meal. Never take her on a *date*."

He held up nine fingers. "Nine…keep her guessing. Get predictable and you're dead. Change up the nights you go out and when you call. Resist habit. In her heart, she doesn't want a routine, either." He shifted, working the angle perfectly.

"Next, Number Eight…give her a plausible story for why you have to stay single. Workaholism, a bad breakup, elderly parents who need you, your therapist says you're a hazard to women, whatever. Give her an it's-not-you-it's-me rationale for when her girlfriends start nagging her to pin you down."

As he retreated deeper into his Doctor Nite role, Jillian

realized she felt relief. The tender, troubled man who'd looked at her across the table was entirely too appealing.

"Seven…" Brody continued, getting into it now, "if you're stupid enough to say you'll call, for God's sake, call. Women treat those words like an oath of office. If you don't want to see her again, be so dull she'll beg to hang up. Talk about your athlete's foot, all the pets you had from birth or your fave video game. And never, never dangle another get-together unless you mean it. That way lies madness, my friend." He winked.

"Six…spend money. Even women who make more than you want that. It proves you're an adult, not some girlie man who cries at Julia Roberts movies. Besides, with women, we always pay, don't we?"

Ouch. But this was just what she needed. He'd volunteered the Ten Commandments for Peter Pan Boys, which hit her theme head-on. She should be thrilled, but she felt strangely disappointed in him.

"Five…appearances count. Don't let women tell you they don't care what you look like. Check her out—she's bleached her teeth, shaved herself in special ways, done her nails, bought a dress. How you look counts with her, believe me." He raised a hand as if swearing to the truth.

"And if you've ever worn a pair of sweats into a restaurant, boyo, get female help with your wardrobe. Accessories are key. Save dough on Kmart pants, if you must, but break the bank on shoes, belts and a watch. Women *know.*

"Subset of that is the car. It's like whipping it out, men. Rent or borrow if you have to, but do not show up in a Focus, unless it's nitro'd out and has a sound system that makes you bleed from the ears. It's all about your genitals, man. The boys make the man and the car makes the boys."

He laughed, and something flickered in his face for a second.

That weary look again. He seemed to catch himself and continued in his smart-ass voice.

"Four...listen more than you talk. This will blow her mind. *Cosmo* and her mom have taught her it's all about the guy's ego. When you don't blab on about yourself, she'll be awed. Good Listener Geek gets laid ten times more then Garden Variety Geek.

"Three...use what you learn. When she tells you she loves spring flowers or Barenaked Ladies, she's giving you ammo, man. Swing by the drugstore on your way over and snag some daisies or a CD. Be casual. No big deal. You're just a thoughtful guy. She'll be so weak in the knees you'll have to carry her to the door...and help her out of her clothes, while you're at it."

Again he paused, looked away, then seemed to struggle onward. "Two...she calls the shots on Go Time. Seriously, man. Walk her to the door, tell her you had a nice time, act like you're leaving, but keep condoms in your wallet and a Tic Tac in your mouth, bro. Because if she thinks you can take it or leave it, you'll get it, I guarantee."

"And the number one tip...?" He paused, took a breath. "Number one..." He looked straight at Jillian and his expression changed completely. His eyes blazed with heat and when he spoke, the showman's tone was gone. "Don't listen to another word from Doctor Nite. Turn off the TV right now and find yourself a woman you want to spend time with. One who keeps you guessing."

He was looking at her, not letting go, talking to her behind the camera. "Someone smart, who makes you laugh, whose smile lights your world. Find someone who believes in you, someone you want to be proud of you. Then make her proud."

"Brody?" she said, moving away from the camera to stare.

"I'm quitting the show," he said softly. "I'm done with Doctor Nite, Jillian."

"You are?" she said. "You're...done?"

"Turn off the camera." He pushed to his feet and walked toward her, holding her gaze as he strode closer, his hunger for her taking over his expression, making her melt.

She turned off the camera, her heart pounding.

"I don't know why I told you that," he said. "I don't know why I'm here, either. I'm just glad I am." He cupped her face, his dark eyes huge, his face raw with emotion. "I don't want to figure out what it means. I just don't want to fight it anymore. What about you? Are you in?"

Her heart turned over in her chest. "Yes," she whispered, not hesitating. "I'm in."

11

THEY STUMBLED TO THE BED, pulling at each other's clothes, desperate like before. Except this was different, Jillian knew. This would change everything. She could tell by the way Brody looked at her, how he touched her and how her whole body seemed electrified by the brush of his skin, his lips, his gaze.

This wasn't *finishing what they started* or *getting it out of their system* or even that ludicrous thing she'd said before, *releasing tension*. This was not Brody's intimate handshake, either. This was different for him, too.

She refused to consider the consequences. She'd had enough of consequences. Instead, she grabbed the remaining fruit-flavored condoms from where she'd placed them in her nightstand, as if she'd known all along she would need them.

This time when Brody kissed her body, he seemed to take possession of each part—her mouth, her throat, her breasts. He held her with his eyes, fully hers, while his body moved over hers, lowered and entered her. Diving deep, scooping into her, he seemed to take her and give himself at the same time.

She lifted her hips, welcoming every inch, taking and giving, too. She'd never felt this way before, been so consumed by desire, so sure this was where she belonged.

She closed her eyes, focused on the wonder of the way their bodies fit, the smoothness of Brody's skin, his deep groan of pleasure, his power and grace, the way her own body tightened, reaching for the climax she knew would arrive as effortlessly as the first one had. And the second. And third.

There. She was off, riding through space and time, holding on to Brody, feeling connected to him somewhere deep, their differences gone completely.

"Jillian," he breathed and surged inside her body, holding her, too. His heart pounded so hard against her own she got their beats confused. He kissed her hair, breathing hard and fast. She buried her face in his neck, feeling so close to him, feeling like part of him.

Gradually, gradually, they settled down, calmed. Brody looked down at her, smiling softly.

Somewhere she was still holding her breath. Could this be real? She knew not to hope too much. Maybe it was just good sex between two people in the right mood at the right moment.

No, her heart cried, *this is more.* She didn't buy that nonsense about finding a soul mate. You counted on yourself and maybe worked something out with a compatible person. But her heart remained stubborn. *This is big.*

Or maybe she was as much a fool as her mother had been.

"I knew you were trouble the minute I met you," Brody said with a soft smile. "I just didn't know how much."

"Sorry," she said, managing a quiet laugh.

"You're the only person I've told about leaving the show."

"Brody…" She was so touched she didn't know how to put it in words. "I'm honored that you would trust me." Now she knew what the weary, empty-eyed look had been about.

"I think I told you because I'm starting to have doubts. I mean, my life is good. Why quit? Maybe I should ride this train to the end of the line."

"You have to trust your instincts," she said.

"Maybe I just need a break. Maybe it's just burnout. The

devil you know, right? The network will go nuts. I'd be throwing away tons of money. My friends won't get it at all."

"You need to feel passion again, Brody." She held his troubled gaze, willing him to truly hear her. "You pretend you took the easy road, that you slept your way to the top, but you push. I see you. You're ambitious and determined and smart and you have good instincts. That's what got you here. Use those traits to take the next step."

"You don't really know me, Jillian." He stroked her hair.

"You forget I've studied you through my camera for days now."

"And you see more clearly through the lens. Yeah."

She liked that he remembered everything she said. She'd never been with a man who paid so much *attention*. On the other hand, she'd never allowed anyone to get that close. Or wanted to.

"I don't have to tell you to keep this to yourself, do I? If it gets out, it's trouble. I hinted to Eve I was bored and she flipped right out. That's why she's always watching me, keeping me busy, overdoing everything."

"I wondered what was going on."

"Before I tell the network, I'm going to try to hook Eve and Kirk and the crew with new projects."

"That's nice of you to look out for them."

"They shouldn't suffer because I can't do this anymore." Brody was a loyal person with a big heart. She'd clearly underestimated him. She was used to being surprised by the true story when she worked on a movie, but this shook her up in ways she wasn't ready to examine.

"You inspired me, you know," he said. "When you talked about your work. You're so sure. No shortcuts, no compromises. I want to feel that way, too."

"I'm no saint, Brody," she said, her heart sinking at how much credit he'd given her. "I make compromises. I have doubts." She had some right now. She'd secretly taped the man, after all.

But she wouldn't use any of the private conversation. Should she explain her original intent? Was that important now? Would it ruin what was between them? And what, exactly, *was* between them?

Things were getting scarier by the second. She was in over her head, and whichever direction she flailed her arms seemed to take her farther from shore.

YOU'VE DONE IT NOW, Brody realized, running his hands across the smooth skin of Jillian's warm stomach, looking down into her beautiful face, so glad he was here, holding her, despite the fact he'd just blurted his biggest secret to her.

Why had he done it? Was he crazy, losing it for good?

No. It had been Jillian's steady eyes, her integrity, the way she made him want more, made him think he could be more. Smack in the middle of his bullshit dating tips, he'd wanted her to know the truth about him.

When they'd made love, he'd felt a shift inside his soul, like puzzle pieces snapping into place, making a new shape, a better one that felt…right. Even now, post-sex and nearly back in his right mind, he wasn't sorry he'd told her.

"So what's next? After the show?" she asked, innocently enough, confident he must have a plan.

"I want to write, I think," he said. "Maybe a novel." He wasn't ready to talk about his thriller. She'd offer to read it, then be too honest not to tell him it was shit if it was. He wasn't ready to hear that. Not yet, anyway.

"I'm sure you'd be great as a writer," she said. "If that's what you want to do."

"You sound like my mother—you can be anything you want to be, son." He laughed, warmed by her automatic confidence in him.

"First I smell like your mom's cooking, now I sound like

her? I'm not sure that's good, unless she's brilliant and gorgeous and way young for her age."

He chuckled. "Ma's a great person. I see her differently than I used to. Same with my pop. Figuring that out is sort of why I decided to change my life."

"How so?"

"Pop had a heart attack last summer, so I went home."

"How bad was it? The attack?"

"Not too bad, as it turned out. They put in some stents. Now he has to exercise, watch his diet and take some meds. It was a wake-up call, really. For me, too, as it turned out. I hadn't been home in a while."

"Where's home?"

"Los Baños—a little farming town in central California that I couldn't get away from fast enough after high school. I visited as little as I could."

"Why is that?"

"It's a long story. See, we're really from Chicago. My dad owned this great bar there. Loud and crowded, listed in the travel guides as a must-see neighborhood tavern."

"Sounds like something you would do," she said.

"True. Except Pop got caught up in the fame and the fun. He held too many tabs, comped too many rounds, drank too much himself and threw us into bankruptcy. Ma had a sister in Los Baños, so we were basically banished to the boondocks."

"That must have been hard."

"For them, yeah. I didn't really notice, since I was only four at the time. Pop became a mechanic—he always loved cars—and Ma spent her time picking on Pop for losing their money and shaming them back home. All this bitter Irish guilt every single day. I just hated hearing it. Ma bitching and Pop hunched over like he thought he deserved the abuse."

"As a child, that would be difficult to grasp."

"Don't get me wrong. They loved me and I never lacked for anything. But it seemed like all they did was make each other miserable. I just wanted out."

"Until you went back this time, right?" He liked how eager she sounded, how interested in his story.

"Yep. I hardly recognized them. They were in the hospital, of course, and they'd had a scare, so they'd be a little different, but this was more. They seemed so close, reading each other like books, behaving like halves of a whole. Maybe I'd remembered them wrong, maybe they'd changed, but they were clearly deeply in love, not at all like I remembered."

"You saw them as people, not parents? Could that be it?"

"Partly, no doubt." He liked how she reached for the deeper meaning and offered a fresh take. It was exactly how she worked. "It was like you and your camera lens. They came clear for the first time. I got the real story."

"Wow. That's wonderful."

He kissed her, brushed her hair from her face, more relaxed, more himself than he ever remembered being with a woman. "So, while I was there, I started thinking about what I really want in my life. I knew I was bored, but I finally admitted to myself that I was done with Doctor Nite. And that I wanted a more stable life. Hell, I was ready to grow up."

"That was some visit home."

"No kidding. The whole trip hit me that way. I saw my old high school buddy, Cal Taylor, too. He designs the most amazing furniture. Sitting on one of his chairs is a religious experience, I'm not kidding."

"I'd like to try that."

"The guy belonged in New York, right? He was doing great there, too, until his high school girlfriend called him back to Los Baños. And, being totally *whipped,* he went. I tried to talk him out of it, but no. He got married and, boom, she trapped him with two kids. Such a waste."

"She *trapped* him? You know it takes two, don't you?"

"I've heard rumors, yeah."

"Did he keep making furniture, even trapped as he was?" She used that smart-ass tone he liked. He liked that she made him defend his attitudes.

"He has a shop in a barn. Does mail order, has some decent accounts, but nothing like he'd be doing in New York."

"So he sacrificed for his family."

"Except you'd never know it by how he acts. I figured he was making the best of a bad deal, putting a smile on his disappointment. But this trip I realized he was truly, honestly happy."

He paused, remembering the visit, the homemade lasagna, the happy confusion and baby-soap smell of bedtime at the Taylor house. "He adores his kids, and when he looks at his wife, it's obvious he can't wait to get her in bed again."

"That's nice," she said with a little sigh.

"I mean, he's not rolling in it and he has to drive to Fresno for mediocre sushi, but he's got what he needs—good work, a wife who loves him, great kids. The man's content."

"And you want that, too? To be content?"

He looked into her green eyes, so deep he could drown. And not be sorry to go. "I'm not moving back to Los Baños for an old girlfriend, of course. But I want a place that feels like home. And a woman to match. Someone who's a friend, you know? And smart."

"Someone who makes you laugh, whose smile lights your world?" She was repeating his speech, but with reverence, not ridicule. He loved that about her. How she really listened.

"Exactly," he said.

"And you'll put a ring on her finger and an SUV in her garage?" She sounded just a tad skeptical.

No wonder. He laughed. "Not very Doctor Nite of me, huh? But people can change, can't they?"

"It would be pretty hopeless if they couldn't." But she hesitated, as though she didn't believe that, only wished that were true. Maybe he didn't, either, deep down.

"And what about you?" he asked. "You after the ring and the SUV?"

"I want to make a life with someone, sure. Down the road. Right now my work is the most important thing to me."

"Have you ever been serious with a guy?"

"I've had boyfriends. The longest was for a year. When he headed to Australia to work on a film, we ended it."

"You didn't want to wait for him?"

"It didn't make sense."

"Obviously, you weren't in love with the guy."

"Sure I was. I missed him, but I got over it."

He shook his head. "No way. If you didn't feel like your insides had been shredded, if all the color hadn't drained from the sky, if a piped-in love song in the grocery store didn't bend you over with sobs, you weren't in love."

"And what makes you such an expert, Mr. Marriage is Death?" she asked, joking, but he could see she was troubled by what he'd said. "You've been in love? Felt all that?"

"Not yet, but I want to. Not the crying over sappy love songs or the shredded insides, but I want to be in love. I guess I want what my parents have—without the years of bitching at each other."

"Maybe years of bitching is part of the package. Maybe that's how it works. It can't be all picnics in the park."

"What about your parents? What are they like?"

"My parents should never have married." She sighed. "My dad cheated on my mom. I mean a *lot*. She just put up with it. What could she do? She loved him. That was her excuse."

"You knew about it as a kid?"

"Oh, yeah. I used to tell her to kick him out, but she never did. They finally divorced a couple years ago. I'm not sure whether she told him to go or he just left. I didn't ask. I doubt my mother would want to admit I was right."

"Are you two close?"

"Not really. Holiday visits, calls on birthdays. Too much stuff hangs in the air between us. Same with my dad, except I don't visit him."

He could tell this caused her some pain. "Is that how you want it to be?"

"Not really, no. But I don't know what to do about it."

"Maybe start thinking of them as people, not parents? Like you said happened with me?"

She gave him a thoughtful look. "I guess I push the pain away, try not to think about it." She smiled at him. "Maybe I ought to try to see things through their eyes a little. Good tip, Doctor." She paused. "You know, it's funny. If your show had been on when my dad was young, maybe it would have given him permission to stay single, saved all that heartbreak...."

"What are you saying?"

"Listen closely—I've found one good thing about your show. If you keep players in the field instead of faking it as faithful husbands, that's positive."

"You mean *Doctor Nite* is a public service?"

"It's *some*thing anyway." She sounded as if she had to scrape the barrel of decency to find a way to make his show acceptable. He felt a spike of irritation, but pushed it away. He was too happy, too content to argue at the moment.

All he wanted was to keep smelling her hair, holding her body, making love to her all night long. The rest of it, the fallout? Well, it could just wait.

WHEN SHE OPENED HER EYES, Jillian found herself facing Brody across the pillow. As if he'd heard her lids flip up, his eyes opened, too, and a slow smile filled his face, lifting his pillow-creased cheeks. He leaned in to kiss her, morning breath be damned, and she melted into the bliss for a few precious seconds before she had to face reality.

"Now what do we do, Brody?" she asked quietly.

"We make love. The flight's not until two. Back in my room, there's a brand-new, whizbang vibrator to play with...."

"I mean about us."

As if on cue, both their cell phones went off—Barry White growled from the floor, muffled by Brody's pants, and Jillian's no-nonsense chime sounded from across the room in her purse. Brody leaned off the bed and fumbled in his pocket. He sat up to speak. "Yes?" he said, sounding suddenly alert and serious. It must be an important call.

Jillian fished her phone from her purse and was startled to see We Women Network in the readout. Here she stood, stark naked near an equally bare Brody, with a crucial career call waiting to be taken.

She ducked into the bathroom for privacy, pulled a towel around her body to feel more normal and answered the phone, her heart pounding. "This is Jillian James," she said as calmly as she could, pulling her towel tight, hoping her lack of attire wouldn't show in her voice.

"Jillian, May Lee, We Women Network. How are you?"

Jillian opened her mouth to respond, but May Lee kept talking, "We are *so* excited about your project. Marketing went *wild* about the Doctor Nite exclusive. That will really give us a sales hook."

"That's so good to hear!" Jillian's heart soared. She did have two exclusive interviews at least. The newest had his dating tips—well, not the last one about finding a special woman, of course, but—

"You've got the dirt, right? The skinny? How Doctor Nite is really a lonely guy with an empty life? It'll be 'The Misery Behind the Magic.' See, I'm writing promo copy already."

Jillian's excitement faded. She had the dirt, all right, and the skinny. But she couldn't use a word of it. "I have two interviews and hope to get more."

"Overnight us a screener," May Lee said, then rattled off the courier number.

"I haven't placed the interview footage yet, though, so—"

"Slam it in, girl. Get it *here.* Marketing locks promo on the series ASAP. You're in or you're out. By Monday, 'kay?"

"Sure. I can do that. By Monday." She could slide Brody's interviews in with a narrative voice-over easily enough. She had time before their flight and in San Diego before they started the night's shoot. She'd planned to visit her friend Callie, who was still at the San Diego news station where they'd worked together, but she had time.

She just didn't have what they wanted. Not unless Brody would go on camera with the truth? Would he? Now that he was quitting? It seemed too soon. He'd barely admitted it to himself and she was the only person he'd confessed the whole story to.

It was too soon. May Lee made enthusiastic small talk while Jillian's heart sank and sank. Her dream was within her grasp and she had to let it float away.

She emerged from the bathroom just as Brody was finishing his call. "That was Ryan Jeffers from the Attorney General's office," he said. "He needs me to look at photos to ID Madden and ask me about what happened, so we're meeting in San Diego."

"Sounds pretty serious if they're coming to meet you."

"Evidently." Then he really looked at her "You okay? You look sick." He moved closer.

"No. I'm fine. Just…tired."

"Who was on the phone?"

"Follow-up on my movie." She wasn't ready to tell him about We Women. She had to think about the right approach. Maybe this wasn't as hopeless as it felt.

Brody's phone rang again. He looked at the readout, then rolled his eyes before he answered. "Yeah?… What am I up to?" He glanced at Jillian, then winked. "No good, as usual. And you?… Sounds good. We'll see you there. Sure… We're fine. We won't forget." He rolled his eyes, then hung up.

She tried to smile. "So that was Eve? Wonder what she'll think about all this," she said to make conversation.

"Yeah. That." He cleared his throat. "I'm thinking we should keep it between us for now. Eve would just give us grief."

"That makes sense. And the last thing we need is grief." She wasn't even thinking about what she was saying.

"I believe we were discussing vibrators…" He moved in to take her in his arms, but she pulled back, still preoccupied by the phone call. She'd like to look at what she had, start embedding the interviews at least, see if she had something May Lee might like.

"Actually, I should put in some time on my movie," she said. "There's time before our flight."

"Okay, sure." Confusion flickered in his eyes.

"Not that I'm not interested, Brody. I just think—"

"You have work to do, sure. Makes sense. Yeah. I mean, we have plenty of time to be together." Was he hurt, relieved? She couldn't tell. He seemed troubled and tense.

What was that about hiding it from Eve? Was he backing out? Freaking out? She didn't know how to broach the topic.

They'd been so intimate the night before, discussing hopes and dreams, even their childhoods, and now they didn't know what to say to each other. She had new feelings for Brody, but her plans had been turned upside down and her documentary was in limbo. Everything had happened too fast. She had no idea what to do about any of it.

JILLIAN WAS WAY TOO QUIET on the plane, Brody thought. She'd used work as an excuse to avoid him before the flight, and now her smiles seemed forced, she barely spoke and she acted preoccupied and distant. Maybe she was hurt because he'd suggested not telling Eve about them. But how could he? It was too new and raw to have Eve picking at them like a bird after a juicy worm. He felt peculiar, too. He'd blurted his secrets and now he felt…buck naked in the cold.

Should he ask Jillian what was wrong? Did he want to know? He'd never been nervous with a woman before. But then he'd never felt this way about one, either.

This was probably the usual deal in a relationship. God, he was already thinking the *R* word. *It's not all picnics in the park,* she'd told him. Lord. He hoped it wasn't a walk across egg shells or hot coals, either.

He glanced over to where Jillian was reading. The sight of her made everything in him go tight. He wanted her so much. Just the way she moved her head or trailed a finger down the page made him want to nail her in the cramped plane lavatory.

He'd get used to this, he hoped. They both would.

The hotel where they were staying was close and a half hour after they'd landed, Brody guided Jillian into the spacious lobby of the refurbished nineteenth-century building, where they were instantly mobbed by fans. As often happened, somebody had figured out where they were staying and posted it on the blog.

He used to love these moments, but lately he just wanted peace and quiet. "Hang on, I'll move us through," he said to Jillian, who looked stunned by the crowd.

Soon he was being tugged at, shouted at and had papers and notepads shoved at him to sign. Cameras flashed again and again. He kept smiling and moving, being as gracious as he could, as he made his way to Eve, who held out room-key envelopes. "Everything go all right?" she asked him.

"You know it did. You called us three times."

"With all your advance work, it went like clockwork," Jillian said, her cheeks bright pink. A clue, if Eve were paying attention, but she didn't seem to be.

"We've got a couple changes to go over," she said. "The nude synchronized swimming is out. It's a logistical nightmare. Blurring the nipples and pubes will wreck the effect. Sorry. I know you were hot for that."

Jillian arched an eyebrow at him.

"It's art," he said. "An athletic challenge. Requires tremendous muscle control."

"It's naked women in water," Eve said. "Who are you kidding? But no matter, since I nabbed a twofer instead. The bar where we're holding the whipped-cream bikini contest will do your frou-frou drink-off, too."

"Frou-frou drink-off?" JJ asked.

"Yeah," Eve said. "To see which cocktail scores a tit flash the fastest. It's Brody's idea. Isn't it great?"

"Who wouldn't love knowing how much booze it takes to get women to give up their dignity and self-respect?" she said. "Do they at least get plastic beads out of the deal?"

"Yeah, right," Eve said with a laugh, but Brody could see Jillian was disgusted. Had she always been sarcastic or was it worse now?

"Maybe the drink-off is too much with the bikini contest," he said to Eve. "Maybe save it for another show?"

"What's wrong with you? You were pissed when I couldn't get it to happen on the last shoot."

"We do a lot of T and A. You said yourself we need variety." He glanced at Jillian, hoping she was pleased by his concession, but she was looking into the distance, not even paying attention. What the hell was wrong with her?

"You're acting all weird," Eve said, staring at him as if he might have chicken pox. "Too much alone time," she declared.

"Don't worry about me, Eve." He felt a spike of annoyance—at Eve for watching him like a hawk and Jillian for making him self-conscious about his show.

He loved *Doctor Nite,* even if he wanted to move on. Boob flashing might be trashy, but it was popular. It was his job to use trends, not judge them.

"Let's go with both for now," Eve said. "We can edit it out if we need to. We've already got a gap in the schedule. Tomorrow is more or less free. Maybe I'll bump our flights up a day."

"Leave it, Eve," Brody said. "We need a break."

Some alone time away from the shoot might help him and Jillian. At least he hoped it would. She was acting strange and he had no clue what to do about it.

"*You* want a break?" Eve demanded.

"JJ, too," he said. "This is your old stomping ground, right?" She'd mentioned a friend from her old job she wanted to see. "You'd probably like some free time to relax." *With me,* he meant and he could see the idea catch and hold in her eyes.

"Some time would be good." She looked at him with relief, as if she suddenly remembered who he was and what they'd meant to each other in bed.

She looked so good to him. Light made her eyes shine and streaked her hair with gold. She'd worn it down, the way he liked. He wanted to pull her into his arms and reassure them both this would all work out just fine.

"I'll try to come up with something to do," Eve said, ignoring them both. "Maybe the male escort segment will lead to a follow-up."

"So that's a go?" he asked. That had been one of the problems Eve had to come early to sort out.

"Yep. The top gigolo has agreed to tell you his secrets for

pleasing the ladies. Like you need that. You could give him lessons." She pretended to jab him with her elbow. *Come on, Brody, be your old self.*

"It's not sex, though, right? They just talk." He wanted Jillian to know it wasn't sleazy. She'd become an uptight voice in his head, ragging at him about stuff he never worried about before.

"Supposedly not," Eve said. "The clients are women too busy to date. The gigolos cozy up on the couch with champagne and roses and they dish about the boss, the kids, the ex, the latest shoe sale at Nordstrom's, whatever. These guys *have* to be gay. What straight man gives a hang about shoes?"

"Not me. I swear." Brody held up his hands.

"Personally, I don't get the women," Eve continued. "If you need to talk, pay a shrink or do two-for-one margs with a girlfriend. Use a man for what he's good for. Right, JJ?"

"Huh?" Jillian blinked, as if startled by the question.

"We use men just like they use us, right?"

"We do? I mean, I guess." Jillian swallowed, then shot Brody a quick glance. She looked...*guilty.* What? She thought she'd *used* him? That was weird. Nobody had *used* anybody in that bed last night. It had been totally real, totally personal and completely from the heart. At least for him.

What was going on in her head? He had to know. He needed to get her alone, away from the show, and ask her, tell her what he was feeling, and together they'd figure out what to do about it.

Like a punch in the gut, it hit him that he was about to say the words he taught men to run from: *We have to talk.*

At this rate, he wouldn't have to quit—he'd get fired as a traitor to the show, his fans and his entire sex.

12

"We appreciate your taking the time to meet with us, Mr. Donegan," Ryan Jeffers said. *We* and *us* made it sound as though there was a whole investigative team at work when it was just Jeffers and Brody in a back table at the lobby bar.

"Whatever I can do to help," Brody said, sipping his beer. Jeffers hadn't touched a drop of the coffee he'd ordered.

He'd asked for a rundown on the Xanadu incident, then took copious notes on a leather-bound legal pad. "And you say Madden wasn't registered at the hotel?"

Brody shook his head.

"And he hasn't contacted you since then?"

"No. Madden hasn't returned my call. Bascom, either, for that matter. Supposedly, he treats all constituent concerns as valuable, so I have to assume he's avoiding me."

"Okay. Thanks. Now we need you to verify the man's identity." He took a folded paper from the flap beside his notepad. It was a gray, blurry photocopy of a driver's license. "Was this the man you gave the DVD to?"

Brody was startled to see that though the name on the license was Lars Madden, the photo was of Meathead. "That's the guy who stole the briefcase."

"Really?" Jeffers looked at the picture, as if that would answer his question, then up at Brody. "You're sure?"

"I'd recognize those beady eyes anywhere," he said. "So, Meathead is Madden and my guy was pretending to be him?"

"That appears to be the case. This changes things. Describe the gentleman you met again."

He went through the details: *tall, thin, sweaty, rumpled, ill-fitting suit, scribbled name tag.* "I thought it was odd his tag was handwritten, since I'd seen preprinted tags on other people at the convention. He rushed me out, too, acting nervous. Maybe he wanted to get out before the real Madden showed up."

"Interesting..." Jeffers said. Brody could tell his mind was racing and Brody wanted in on his thoughts.

"So, who ordered the DVD from Kirk?" Brody asked. "The real Lars Madden or my imposter? I don't think Kirk ever saw the guy. They talked over the phone. And who robbed Kirk, by the way? My guy or Madden or Bascom? Or someone else entirely?"

"Hold on," Jeffers said, lifting his hand in a stop gesture. He gave a tight laugh. "How about you allow us to handle the investigation, Mr. Donegan?"

"I'd like to help if I can," he said. "I'm already involved, remember? And I've got calls out to two of these clowns."

"We appreciate the information you've provided us. Thanks to you, we know that someone besides Mr. Madden is involved."

"Exactly. And he wanted just a copy, not the original footage. Why? And who is he, anyway?"

"We don't know. We'll have to discover that." He tapped his pen on the pad, his eyes narrowed in thought. He looked upset.

"You know I told Kirk to make another copy. Maybe I should call my guy and offer to sell it to him."

Jeffers stopped tapping. "Interesting."

"I'd be happy to do that. It would be easy. I've got the number. He knows my voice."

"We hesitate to involve civilians in our investigations," Jeffers said, but he was clearly interested. The guy wasn't a cop. He worked for a state agency.

"So I make a phone call, big deal. Maybe I meet with the guy, sell him the DVD. He knows me, after all."

"A meeting's out of the question. You could be in danger."

"My guy wasn't armed."

"The situation may have escalated."

Brody left that idea alone. "Is Kirk in any danger?"

"We don't believe so, no. He's away from his place, staying at a friend's. As a precaution, there are local police officers at his apartment…." He hesitated. He clearly had more to say. "Let me make a call," he said, grabbing a cell phone from an inside jacket pocket. "Will you excuse me?"

Brody nodded, then drank his beer, watching Jeffers walk away, talking rapidly on the phone. No way was Brody leaving without knowing exactly what these guys were up to. He had to look out for Kirk's interests, didn't he? Besides, his crime writer instincts were fully engaged. He was loving this.

When Jeffers returned to the booth, he looked relieved. "As it turns out, Mr. Donegan, we would like you to call your contact. Flushing out the imposter may aid our investigation."

"And what exactly are you investigating? Jed Bascom, I assume, but surely a lap dance and a couple lines of coke don't concern the AG's office."

"That's very astute of you, Mr. Donegan." He played with his mug, shifting it back and forth on the table with his fingers. Then he lifted his gaze, trying to decide what to tell Brody.

"I'm part of the case, Ryan. I need to know what I'm getting into."

"This case involves more than one jurisdiction, which makes the chain of command complex, but I don't imagine there's any harm in briefing you."

"Good. Go." Brody made a rolling gesture with his hands.

Jeffers leaned forward, looking eager to talk, like a guy at a party with a hot stock tip. "We believe that Mr. Bascom has been engaged in bid-rigging with some disreputable construction companies."

"So he's getting kickbacks?"

"That's the least of it. You may recall the fire in a low-cost housing complex last year? Three hundred units burned to the ground. Ten people killed?"

"I remember that."

"It was poor construction by firms in the back pockets of Bascom and others—legislators, judges and commissioners. We've had Mr. Bascom under surveillance for months. In fact, we believe he received a payoff at the party where Mr. Canter filmed him. We tried to witness this exchange, but your producer was quite militant about the guest list." He spared a smile.

"Eve's tough, that's for sure."

"Yes. So. We've been gathering evidence, but slowly. When Mr. Canter called about his burglary and mentioned your encounter with Lars Madden—who works security for Bascom, by the way—we were automatically contacted by the police. Of course we were eager to see the footage of the party."

"Looking for the bribe handoff, right?"

"Yes, except it wasn't there. If it took place that night, it happened away from the camera, we were sorry to discover."

"So you can't use the clip to prosecute him?"

"Unfortunately, no."

"Does Bascom know you're after him?"

"We don't believe so, no. We think he wants Mr. Canter's film because of the perceived damage to his reputation over his illicit activities at the party."

"The stripper and the coke?"

"Exactly. So, assuming the bungled burglary will be repeated, we have set up a sting at Mr. Canter's house, using a dummy hard drive, and we've gotten word to Bascom's office through our contact there."

"Okay, so why did Madden offer to buy a copy of the DVD in the first place?"

"You're assuming it was Madden and not your imposter who placed that order."

"True. Madden may have learned of the purchase and wanted to keep my guy from getting it. And why would my guy want a copy?"

"Good question. He could be with a competing candidate wanting to embarrass Bascom."

"Or it could be blackmail."

"Always possible."

"Fake Madden must have been affiliated with the convention somehow, since he had a key to the hospitality suite. He wasn't registered at the hotel. He had to know someone. Hmm."

Jeffers cocked his head. "You're thinking like a detective."

"That's the idea, I guess." Maybe he wasn't wrong to attempt a crime novel, after all. "Shall I call him now? Fake Madden? I have his number on my cell phone."

"Yes. If he's interested, tell him you'll have the DVD delivered to him in L.A. and we'll take it from there."

"I can make the delivery. I'll be in L.A. tomorrow."

"Let's take it one step at a time."

"If you involve someone else, he'll get suspicious."

Jeffers studied him. "Let's see how the man responds." They talked over what he would say and Brody called the number—and got voice mail. Damn. He left a message saying he had another copy of the DVD if Madden wanted it and left his cell number.

"Good," Jeffers said when he hung up. "The minute he calls back, call me. You may have to ad lib, depending on his reaction. Use your judgment. Lead him on, if you can. Meanwhile, we'll get the word about a second copy to Bascom's people. Thanks for your help, Mr. Donegan."

"Call me Brody. We're working together now. If there's a

handoff, I'll do it." He found the idea exhilarating and his writer's mind was ticking away.

"Hopefully that won't be necessary, Mr.—okay, Brody." He shot him a quick grin. "I used to love your show, by the way." He gulped his now-cold coffee.

"Used to?"

"Until I moved in with my girl. She hates it. She thinks my watching it means I secretly want to break up with her."

"That's a shame." Poor guy. How could he let a woman control his cable habits? Talk about *whipped.* And the girl's attitudes…so judgmental.

Kind of like Jillian, now that he thought about it. Hadn't she more or less called him a sexist ass from the moment they met? But she'd been joking, right?

Still, he felt uneasy. Would he end up like this sad guy, watching every word for fear it might offend her feminine sensibilities? Jillian didn't strike him as the bitch type, but women changed once they had you in their grip.

He'd ask her about this when they were together for the day.

Oh, and how would that go, Brody?

So, Jillian, you're not going to turn into a raving bitch once we get together, right? Oh, yeah. That would work just great.

WITH A FEW HOURS of free time before the San Diego shoot was to start, Jillian went straight to her room to work on her rough cut for We Women. Before the flight here, she'd slugged in the women interviews. She still had to slip in the Brody segments. She wasn't sure it was worth the trouble, but she might as well see what she had.

She stripped out of her clothes, donned her robe and got busy. Opening the clip files, she noticed the secret footage she'd forgotten to delete—their first kiss, the foot massage, the oral lovemaking.

She was glad she still had it. Maybe watching it would help her see more clearly. Her heart jumping in her chest, she cued the footage and began to watch. The light was dim, but she could see their expressions as Brody murmured that she wasn't really crew and they kissed. She turned out to be the one who'd eaten up the last inch between them and pressed her lips to Brody.

Watching their mouths press together aroused her so much she began to squirm in her chair. She skimmed forward to the beginning of the foot rub, where they'd bantered about marriage and Brody had claimed he would have been all over her in high school. His hands slid up her shins, she pointed out he was no longer rubbing her feet. *Do you want me to stop?* he asked and she answered him by opening her knees to him.

Wow. She sat there and watched herself climax, stunned and aroused, and so embarrassed her ears burned. Her hands were trembling, her breathing was ragged and she felt woozy.

No way could she watch Brody go down on her, so she stopped the clip and put her head down until she quit feeling faint. Wow. At least it was clear how they'd ended up in bed together.

She moved on to the first official interview with Brody. It was fine, but nothing We Women would squeal over. The most controversial element was the bit about him being a role model for teens, but he'd handled that smoothly.

She clicked onto the dating tips interview. He was completely Doctor Nite, of course, his tone cocky and bold and offhand. Tonight she would shoot him getting women drunk enough to bare their breasts to him, then licking whipped-cream bikinis off their bodies, accompanied by male hoots and wolf calls.

The contrast between the warm, open man who wanted a loving relationship like his parents and the guy who cooked up lascivious stunts to amuse drunken fans troubled her.

Which was the real Brody?

Then she reached the part where Brody gave his number one dating tip, his tone soft, his expression hot with desire for her. He told his fans to turn off *Doctor Nite* and find a woman who made them laugh and think, who lit them up inside.

Could she be that woman for Brody? He was quitting the show, after all. He wanted to change. He was better than Doctor Nite.

Her heart swelled with hope and emotion. Love? It couldn't be love. Not in so short a time, no matter how intense.

She had to reassure herself that she hadn't imagined what was between them, that there was more going on than the head-on collision of her lust and his turning point. She had to see him. Right now. He was surely back from meeting with the investigator.

She tightened the belt on her robe, grabbed her ice bucket as a joking reminder of that first night together, and padded barefoot down the hall, anticipating Brody's happy surprise when he saw her.

Except when she rounded the corner on his hall, she was startled to see twin blondes in spike heels and minidresses knocking at his door.

Maybe it was a mistake.

Except the door opened, the first girl said something and Brody let them in.

Jillian felt suddenly ill. Were they fans or friends? Distant cousins? College pals? Please. Those women hadn't trotted over here in spike heels and tiny dresses to chat about old times. She put two and two together and came up with a three-way.

Why not? This was normal behavior for Doctor Nite when he had a free hour on his hands. Brody had warned her he didn't know what he was doing, that he had no business sleeping with Jillian. Now he was proving it.

She was standing there, mortified and bereft, when she noticed someone hustling toward her. Someone familiar. Eve, holding a folder against her chest, papers sticking out all over.

Damn. The woman was about to catch Jillian flat-footed and empty-bucketed, yards beyond the ice room, almost at Brody's door wearing only a robe.

Jillian tapped her forehead, as if she'd just realized she'd overshot her goal, spun on her heels and went back for ice, mashing the button so the grind and rattle made it impossible to hear Eve calling her name.

Eve burst into the small space. "Hello?! Didn't you hear me calling you?"

"Sorry." Jillian fought for a calm smile. "What's up?"

"I can't find the releases I gave you for the San Francisco shoots. Did you take them out of my folder?"

"You didn't give me any releases, Eve. And if you had, why would I take them from you? That's ridiculous." Jillian was in no mood for false accusations from Eve. As it happened, Jillian had used her own forms, since Eve hadn't provided any.

"I *always* get releases," Eve said, looking panicked.

"Not this time, you didn't." She thought about leaving Eve hanging by her nails a bit longer, but the woman's eyelids began to twitch. "It's okay, Eve. I used mine."

"You got releases? You're sure? On everyone?"

She nodded. "I keep a pad with me."

"Oh, thank God!" Eve sagged against the ice machine, clutching the folder to her chest. "I thought we were sunk."

"You knew you didn't give me releases, Eve. Admit it."

She grimaced. "Okay. Sorry. You're right. I was consolidating checklists and I must have left off the releases." She gave a humble smile. "I don't know what's wrong with me this trip. I'm usually so organized."

"Don't beat yourself up. You have a lot to juggle."

"Do you suppose I can get the releases from you? For my files?"

"Certainly. Come on." She motioned toward her room,

pausing to glance toward Brody's, where the twins were no doubt naked by now. Heat and hurt burned down her spine.

This was an important reminder. Brody might want to be different, but that didn't mean he could be. In her heart of hearts, she wasn't sure people ever changed. Her father sure hadn't, despite the promises, despite her mother's tears and foolish optimism.

But Brody had said she was different than the women he knew. Of course. He liked variety. He was clearing his palate. She'd let herself feel too much, expect too much. She'd acted like some naive girl who believed every line a guy delivered. If she wasn't more hip than that, she had no business dipping a toe in this particular hot tub.

Inside her room, she headed straight for her pad of photo releases and tore off the used ones for Eve.

"You saved me, you know," Eve said, accepting them. "We would have had to blur so many faces the segments would have to be trashed."

"We're a team, Eve, even if I'm only a fill-in. I'm not Kirk, but I won't let you down."

"I know that." Eve looked at her for a long moment. "I've been kind of a bitch to you, haven't I?"

"Kind of. But forget that now. How about a drink? I could sure use one." Especially after seeing the call girls toddle into Brody's room.

"I'd love a P.I.N.K.," Eve said, sinking into a chair with a loud exhale. "I've been so stressed lately."

Jillian rummaged in the minibar for the drink, which was vodka mixed with an energy drink—the perfect cocktail for Eve—grabbed herself a Grand Marnier and poured both drinks, admiring the way the orange and pink concoctions matched the funky room.

"This trip has been so confusing," Eve said, leaning back

in her chair, kicking out her legs. "It's mostly Kirk. Since he had his accident, he's been so jumpy and he won't tell me what's wrong. Kirk is not a man who's easy with a secret, let me tell you."

Jillian knew Kirk was tense about the robbery and the stolen DVD. She'd promised Brody not to say anything to Eve though. "I'm sure he'll be back to himself soon."

"I hope so. I miss the guy." She stirred her drink with a finger, looking thoughtful. "Brody's been weird, too, lately."

"Really?" Eve knew he was discontented. Jillian wondered how she would describe the problem.

"Yeah. Sometimes people try to be something they're not, you know? Take me. I started out wanting to direct, but it was so *hard.* I puked up my guts before every shoot."

"New experiences cause anxiety. That's normal."

"This was terror, not anxiety. Plus, I sucked. Now, the producing part was different. I was so serene. The stress and frustration that had everyone else freaking felt natural to me."

"You seem pretty in touch with who you are."

She shrugged. "In this business, you have to be to survive. Brody used to be solid. Since his dad's heart attack he's been moping. He'll be better once we hit Europe. New people to charm, right? He can flirt in seven languages." She brightened. "We just have to get him past this rocky spot."

"You think that's all it is?"

She sipped her drink. "Actually, since you've been here he's been better. I guess he wants to impress you." She gave her a puzzled glance, then went on. "We have a system—Brody, Kirk and I—and I guess I was nervous about how you'd fit in."

"I can imagine. You've worked together a long time." Jillian could see that Eve was as loyal and devoted to Brody as he was to her and the rest of the crew.

"Yeah. I almost didn't get the job, you know." She sipped

her drink, leaning back, musing. "I blew the interview. Nerves. So I was leaving the building, tail between my legs, practically whimpering, when Brody caught up with me and took me out for a beer with Kirk. The two of them made me laugh and relax and by the second round I had the job."

"That was nice of him."

"He saw my potential. Brody's great that way."

"He seems to be." Jillian hesitated, then decided to ask the question she'd wondered about since Eve first bristled at her. "Did you two ever…? I mean…it's none of my business, but—"

"Did Brody and I hook up? God, no." But Eve turned the color of her drink. "I had a crush on him, of course. Everyone falls for Brody. Brody loves women. That's his trick."

"It's a trick?"

"No. It's his *way,* I guess. He's sincere. He's so attentive and intense that you think it means more than it does. Women are, like, I don't know, his hobby. He tries out every model. It's not personal. He can't help himself."

Jillian listened hard, taking in the truth in Eve's words. "So, how did you…stop? Your crush, I mean."

"It wasn't easy. First, I picked out things about him I didn't like—the way he belches when he drinks beer, that strip of beard he always misses when he shaves, how he calls women *doll.* I hate that. Plus, all the winking. So hokey."

"And it worked?"

Eve rolled her eyes. "So, next I tried this negative stimulus thing I read about. I put a big rubber band on my wrist and every time I had a hot thought about Brody I snapped myself."

"Did that do it?"

"Not completely, no. What worked was focusing on making *Doctor Nite* the best show it could be. I realized if I was all hot over Brody, I couldn't do my job. Now *that* worked."

"How did you get so smart about men?"

"Self-defense, of course!" Her eyes widened. "I got dumped a few times before I figured it out. See, I used to think I could guard myself against the pain. See the signs, you know, and dump the guy before he dumped me. It never works like you expect. That's the deal with love. It's always a surprise. Falling in and falling out, it's like ba-bam, you never see it coming. It's a game of gotcha."

Jillian laughed. "Wow. That was great." It almost made her feel better about Brody. "You know, what you're saying would be perfect for my documentary."

"On dating, right? Brody said you were interviewing him."

"Yeah. I'm talking to single women, too. Would you mind? You can promo the show, too, while you're at it."

"I guess I could do that." She sucked down more of her drink. "Let me put on some makeup." She rose.

"You're welcome to use mine in the bathroom."

"You're forgetting who you're dealing with." Eve patted her gigantic messenger bag. "So many shiny foreheads, so little pancake."

Jillian laughed.

Eve returned in a few minutes, looking gorgeous, and gave a terrific interview, retelling her dating wisdom so that it sounded fresh.

"What do you think about settling down yourself?" Jillian asked, moving to new questions.

"Down the line, sure. L.A.'s no place to fall in love. Too much ambition. Thinking you'll survive love in L.A. is like standing in the Five at rush hour expecting not to end up roadkill. My horoscope says I'll know when the time is right."

"You believe in astrology?"

"It's better than thinking too hard about it. That's just depressing, and who needs it?"

"In your opinion, does the attitude Doctor Nite promotes, that marriage is death, hurt women?"

"Women can take care of themselves. We're tough. It's simple. If you're looking for a husband, you don't go to a bar with *Doctor Nite* on the plasma." She shrugged.

"Do you think Doctor Nite will ever eat his words and settle down?" Jillian's heart banged her ribs as she waited for Eve's opinion. Which was ridiculous, since Brody was the only one who could answer the question and right now he was frolicking with twin blondes. Wasn't that answer enough?

"Not a chance," Eve said, utterly certain. "His whole career is built on being single. His fans would be devastated."

"Thanks," Jillian said. "You gave me some great stuff, Eve." And reminded her of a truth she'd been stupidly ignoring since she and Brody made love.

She turned off the camera, then slid the release to Eve.

"So, you're into women's rights?" Eve asked, signing her name. "You think The Man keeps us down?" She looked up.

"I believe women don't get a fair shake, yes. Women make up half the U.S. workforce, yet they make only seventy cents for every dollar a man makes. Of the Fortune 500 companies, only eight have female CEOs."

"Maybe women don't want to be CEOs."

She just looked at Eve.

"Okay, so that's a problem. But when it comes to sex and dating and marriage, it's a two-way street. Men and women screw it up together in their separate ways." She paused. "So what's your deal? Who pissed you off so much? A boyfriend? Ex-husband?"

"My ex-boyfriends and I are on good terms, and I've never been married."

"Then your dad, right? Mine left my mom when I was five. He was a divorce attorney and he ran off with a client, if you can believe that. We kind of got screwed on the child support/alimony deal, too. But I still love him. Kind of."

"That's mature of you. My dad was a player and my mom put up with it for years."

"Sounds like you're mad at your mother."

She had a point. "I'm not really mad at either of them. Disappointed, I guess. I know no one's perfect. I mean, Prince Charming had great PR."

"Yeah, but with a dad like you had, you probably figure deep inside that all men are rats. Who knows, maybe they are. I try to take them on a case-by-case basis and trust my instincts."

"And your horoscope?"

"That, too." She laughed. "I've got time, anyway. I'm only twenty-seven." She paused. "You're...what? Brody's age? Thirty-seven or so?"

"Just thirty, thanks."

"Sorry. You just seem...mature. Brody doesn't like to talk about his age."

"Really?"

"Yeah. He's sensitive about it. Want to know another secret?" She leaned in. "He's writing a book. He hides it, but I sneaked a peek. It's a detective story, from what I can tell."

"Really?" Funny he hadn't mentioned it to her. But then he hadn't mentioned the twin call girls he'd ordered, either.

"Do not say a word."

"Oh, I won't," Jillian said.

"Guys get touchy about the funniest things. Like Kirk can't stand any movie where an animal dies. He actually cries. He pretends it's allergies. I think it's kind of sweet. I pretend I can't stand it, either...for his sake."

"You sound really close, you and Kirk."

"What?" Eve blinked. "That's work stuff, not...well, it's not..." Now she turned bright red. "You can't get sucked in by working together. It's, well, it's just stupid." She leveled her gaze at Jillian. "You know, with Brody, when he wants to impress someone, he pulls out all the stops. Keep that in mind."

"Thanks. I will. I appreciate the tip." Jillian rattled the ice in her drink and sipped at the remaining drops, realizing she'd done exactly what Eve had warned her about on the first day. She'd fallen for the Brody Treatment.

"Too late, huh?" Eve said.

She looked up to find Eve holding out a thick purple rubber band. "Sorry," she said with a shrug.

Jillian laughed and put the band on her wrist.

"It's easy to do. The man is delicious. I had such fantasies. That grin and those eyes."

"They do pull you in."

"Yeah. His best feature." Eve took another swallow of her drink. "The six-pack's good, too, though." She made a sizzling sound.

"Not to mention his butt," Jillian contributed. "You can bounce a dime off it."

"No lie. When he walks around in his boxers...Jesus, Mary, Joseph, and the little burro, too."

Jillian laughed and snapped the rubber band. "Ow!"

They tinked their glasses together, swallowed and sighed in synch, both envisioning a nearly naked Brody, she'd bet.

There was a knock at the door. Eve went to the peephole. "It's him," she hissed. "Brody!"

"What could he want?" Jillian tried to act cool, jumping up to tug her robe tight as she approached the door Eve had opened.

"Well, speak of the devil," Eve said to him.

"You were talking about me?" He held an empty ice bucket and looked at Jillian with an expression of longing that burned through her like flame through dry grass.

Finished with the twins? Sarcasm was her friend at the moment. She didn't dare forget what she'd figured out.

"You're having a party, Jillian, and didn't invite me?" He gave a look of mock hurt.

Eve turned to stare at her. "He's calling you Jillian now?"

"Friends do. You can, too, Eve. If you want." She didn't have time to be embarrassed. She had to let Brody know she knew what he'd been up to. "When I went for ice, I noticed you had *company.*" She folded her arms.

"Company? You mean the two blondes? You saw…? They had the wrong room. Didn't they, Eve?" He gave her a stern look. "Since when do I have to pay to play?"

"Just keeping you busy."

"You sent them to him?" Jillian said, trying to keep the relief out of her voice, but Eve was busy giving Brody her attention. "What are you doing here, anyway, Brode?"

"I thought Jillian and I could go over the shot list for tonight like we did in San Francisco."

In San Francisco, they'd made wild love. Jillian's heart thudded in her chest so hard she couldn't concentrate or even breathe. Brody had sent the twin vixens away and come to see her. She was way too happy and far too relieved.

"I guess I'll leave you two alone," he said, backing away, "Unless you'd consider a pillow fight in your undies?"

"We'll let you know," Eve said, closing the door on him.

The last Jillian saw was Brody looking at her as if she were a Christmas present under the tree. She could hardly breathe.

Eve turned on her, hands on her hips.

"What?" Jillian said.

Eve reached out to snap the rubber band.

"Ouch. Cut it out."

"It would be a mistake," Eve said. "We talked about this."

But Jillian knew it was too late and as soon as Eve left, she set off for Brody's room running.

BACK IN HIS ROOM, Brody got blasted by the pricey perfume the call girls had left in their wake. Seeing their empty eyes in their doll faces had made him crave Jillian. Warm, natural Jillian. Smart and funny and honest. He just felt good when he was with her. She made him feel he could be who he wanted to be in his heart.

It was too soon to get freaked about her attitudes and moods and his own defensiveness and doubts. They had a day to spend together tomorrow. He'd just show up and see how it went.

Right now, he had to see Jillian. He didn't care if Eve knew. He was about to call her room, ask her to get down here, when there was a knock at the door.

He didn't even look through the peephole, simply yanked open the door, delighted when Jillian, in that goofy robe, threw herself at him, leaping up to wrap her legs around his waist, making him stumble and almost fall.

"Thank God," he said, kissing her, burying his nose in her hair, lifting her up and swinging her around. "How could you even think I'd have sex with those girls? The only woman I want right now is you." It hurt that she'd think that.

"I don't know. This is so new between us," she said, putting her hands on his cheeks, studying his face, looking for some answer she was desperate to find.

He noticed a rubber band on her wrist. "What's this?" He touched it.

"Eve gave it to me." She laughed. "It's a long story. She tried to warn me about you. She says women are your hobby, that you can't help charming us all."

"Is that what she said?" he said. "Interesting." And not very flattering, he realized.

"And I know you're at a crossroads. You don't really know what you want, what you'll do, who you'll be."

"How about we take one thing at a time? Right now I want

you in bed." Desire welled up in him, blocking his doubts. This he trusted—this heat, this hunger to have her.

He waited for her eyes to catch fire, then he kissed her. It was the only thing to do.

They were naked in seconds and made quick use of one of the condoms he'd bought from the gift shop.

She met him with her body and they fought their doubts with every stroke of his cock, every lift of her hips. He tried to tell her how he felt with every touch, every shift of weight, every kiss. Once he got inside her, he never wanted to leave.

Afterward, he collapsed onto the thick pillow and pulled her against him, reveling in her sweat-slick body, the way she melted into him, boneless and fragrant.

Outside a fire engine blared.

Brody laughed. "That was a four-alarm fire, boys," he called toward the window. "We got it out for now, so you can go back to the station. We may need you later if we get out of control." He ran his hand down her body. "We could break out that vibrator, go for a five alarm. What do you say?"

Jillian groaned happily. "We've got work soon."

"So we rest a bit," he said, stroking her breast until the nipple tightened happily. The female body was such a miracle of delights. And Jillian was…ah…so much more. He buried his nose in her neck, reveling in her softness, the warm pulse, her delicious smell.

"You're smelling fruitcake again?" she said. "I have to say that's not very sexy."

"Ah, but sure and it is," he said in an exaggerated brogue. "You don't know the whole story of *barmbrack*. At Halloween it tells your fortune. The tradition is to bake in symbols for luck. A ring meant you'd marry that year, a pea meant you wouldn't. A stick predicted an unhappy marriage, a piece of cloth meant you'd be in rags. A coin meant wealth."

"How fun."

"Ma adapted it a bit, took out the marriage stuff and made all the fortunes good ones. A bit of peppermint meant you'd make a mint. Orange rind meant to keep your eyes peeled for good luck."

"She sounds sweet, your mother."

"She is. And Pop, too. I still don't know if they mellowed or I just finally saw them as people, like you said."

"Does it matter?"

"Maybe not. And it's probably both. Few things are cut-and-dried, one or the other. They worked out their differences."

"Unlike my parents, who are probably happier apart."

"Have you asked them? Maybe if you talked about it you'd feel better about what happened when you were younger."

"You analyzing me again, Doctor Nite?"

"I just want you to be happy."

"I am," she said with a soft smile, then yawned.

"You want to catch up on sleep? We've got all day tomorrow. What do you want to do?"

He cupped her pubic area and she sighed. "More of that."

"Yeah," he said as renewed lust surged through him. "We might never leave this bed."

"I did promise my friend Callie we'd get together."

"I need to meet with my agent, who's here for some sailing event or other. But after that, I'm all yours."

"I'd like us to have a normal day. We could do couple things. Go to a park, hang out, have dinner together."

"Sounds great," he said, burying his nose in her hair, happy to escape Doctor Night for a while, be the new Brody, see what kind of a couple he and Jillian might make.

13

THANKS TO her friend Callie, Jillian had the perfect day planned for Brody. Since Callie was headed out on assignment, she'd offered them her condo, and Jillian planned to fix Brody the perfect Irish meal, just like his mother used to make.

They would relax, spend the night together, away from the hotel, the crowds, the pressure cooker of the show. They would be an ordinary couple, falling in love in the ordinary way.

She'd put her documentary on hold, too. When they returned to L.A. on Monday, she would figure out what to do about We Women and the rough cut they wanted.

She had this tiny hope that Brody might let her use his tip about forgetting *Doctor Nite* and looking for the right woman. Maybe he'd even tell her on camera about how he'd changed.

She could be dreaming—caught up in the magic of the moment, missing reality completely—but hope swelled inside, all the same.

For all their differences, she and Brody were similar, too. They both wanted to change the world, to feel passion for their work. They were both curious. They'd been self-sufficient, but lonely. They both had issues with their parents. And Brody claimed they'd felt the same isolation as kids—she because of her weight and he over his weird humor. They both wanted one special someone and weren't quite sure it was possible.

They'd found each other, hadn't they? Or maybe she was

making up a story to excuse all the rules she'd broken. She hoped to know for sure by the time they left San Diego.

The dinner was to be a surprise. After Brody finished with his agent, he was to join her at Callie's—supposedly to meet her old friend for a quick beer. Instead, he'd find them alone for a romantic home-cooked meal and the luxury of time alone together.

Before heading to Callie's to get the key and at least get a hug before Callie took off, Jillian had nabbed recipes from the Internet and gone to a store for ingredients, even scoring novelty gummy candies for their *barmbrack* fortunes.

By noon, she'd made a salad, put the stew on the stovetop, had the pasties and the *barmbrack* in the oven, and set the table. The finishing touch—a bouquet of pink star lilies and deep purple irises—gave a dreamy beauty to the scene. Pleased with the homey nest she'd created, she went to take a shower.

A few minutes later, dressed and happy, she was humming to herself as she rounded the corner to the kitchen, expecting that great smell, imagining Brody's face when he walked in and smelled his childhood kitchen at full strength, real time.

Except there was no smell of warm beef and baked pastry in the air. The stove and oven were dead cold, the food still raw. Damn, damn, damn. Had she blown a fuse? Callie hadn't mentioned electrical problems.

She had mentioned her neighbor Skip, though, as a good resource if she needed anything. So Jillian dashed over to ask about the fuse box.

With a name like Skip, Jillian expected a yuppie lawyer, not the bleary-eyed biker in a doo-rag, tattoos of twisty reptiles on his forearms, who came to the door. "Yeah?" he said, pot smoke and heavy metal music billowing out behind him.

"Skip? Hi. I'm Jillian. Sorry to bother you, but I'm using Callie's kitchen and I think I blew a fuse. Do you know where the breakers are?"

"You're cooking in Callie's place? She's a total takeout chick. Let me take a look."

Precious minutes flew by while Skip mused over the breakers, which were fine, then opened the back of the stove and concluded there'd been some kind of short. Duh.

He sat up, brushed dust from his hands on his jeans and looked up at her. "Tell you what. How about you use my stove?"

"I wouldn't want to inconvenience you." But it was a reasonable solution. "It should take just an hour."

"It's cool. I got time. And maybe I get a taste?"

"Sure," she said. "Of course."

They carried the uncooked items to Skip's house, walking through a surprisingly orderly living room that held a gleaming motorcycle, into an equally neat kitchen. Jillian thanked him and promised to return when the food was ready.

When she knocked at his door an hour later, however, no one answered. The door was locked and she saw through the window the bike was gone. Damn.

Twenty minutes too late, Skip roared back. She jumped from the step where she'd been waiting and met him at his door.

He held out a twelve-pack of beer. "Something to wet our whistles with," he said, beaming at her.

The stew had cooked down to a thick gravy, the *barmbrack* smelled burnt and the pasties were very dark. So much for a perfect home-cooked meal. She hoped it was edible. She grabbed two of the dishes with hot pads, planning to come back for the *barmbrack*, but when she got to Callie's door, she found she'd forgotten about the knob lock and locked herself out.

"Damn!" She sank to the steps in dismay. She'd have to call a locksmith just to get her purse out of there. She balled her fists in frustration. So much for a normal day with Brody.

Skip appeared, carrying the *barmbrack* pan, chewing a piece he'd pried off. "A little tough, but not bad," he said, trying to cheer her up, it seemed, oblivious to the fact he'd caused the problem. He sat beside her and reached for a pastie. "You mind?"

"Help yourself," she said gloomily. "I locked myself out."

"Not bad if you eat around the crust," he said. "The onions give it a nice flavor. You can cook, all right."

"You know a good locksmith?" she asked miserably.

"Why?" He leaned around her to shift the geranium pot far enough to reveal a key, which he handed to her. "Happens to Callie all the time. That little knob lock is a bitch."

"Why didn't you tell me…? Never mind. Thanks." She threw her arms around him and hugged him hard. He laughed, still munching on the pastie.

She'd been rescued, the day redeemed, even if the food was less than perfect. Back in the house, her cell phone beeped, telling her she'd missed a call and had a message. It was Brody, calling from someplace noisy. His words broke up, but she was able to catch that he wouldn't make it to meet Callie. Something had come up and he'd see her back at the hotel later.

Damn, damn. Double damn. If she'd told him about the dinner, instead of trying to surprise him, he might not have canceled so readily. She looked at the table she'd lovingly set, the flowers gracing the scene, thought about the food she'd wrangled into shape, despite a dead stove and a tardy biker. Disappointment roiled through her.

Then her stubborn streak kicked in. She would not be defeated. If the man wouldn't come to the *barmbrack,* she'd bring the *barmbrack* to the man. She'd take the meal to the hotel. Why not? She'd make this a perfect day one way or another. She didn't give up on her documentaries, why would she give up now?

Barely thirty minutes later, she set two big shopping bags holding the food, wine and flowers on the floor beside Brody's room door and knocked. He didn't answer, so she assumed he hadn't returned. Good. She'd set up and surprise him. She used the key card he'd given her, but she got the surprise.

"Jillian!" Brody jumped to his feet from the bed where he'd been sitting. "What are you doing here?"

Why hadn't he answered? And what was the electricity in the air about? It felt like fear. Then she saw that Brody had company—a grim-looking man with a swollen face and glittering eyes sat in the shadows of the room, at the desk, hiding something in his lap with a folded newspaper. Meathead. Had to be. The real Lars Madden.

"I wanted to surprise you with a home-cooked meal," she said, thinking fast. Tension crackled in the air. Brody had left a message for Fake Madden, but hadn't heard back. Why was this guy here?

"We're in a meeting," Brody said. "If you could come back?" She could tell he wanted to shove her out the door for safety, but no way would she leave him in danger.

"No problem," she said, acting bubbly and oblivious for Meathead's benefit. "I've got plenty. Too much. We don't want it to go to waste, do we?" She moved closer to the gunman, between him and Brody, thinking that he wouldn't harm a bystander. She hoped not, anyway, and maybe he would leave because of the interruption.

"It got a little overcooked, but it will still be good, I hope." She gestured as if to let the guy look in the sacks, acting like a ditz, but needing to break the tension somehow.

The man shifted his weight at her approach, as if to warn her away, and the newspaper slid to the floor. She saw that he'd been hiding a handgun. Lifting her gaze, she met his and saw that he was going to take action, point the gun, shoot maybe?

Without thinking, she swung the heavier sack—it had the cast-iron pot of stew—at the gun and it flew out of his hand and hit the wall. It fell to the carpet and Brody and Meathead lunged for it.

Jillian swung at the guy's head this time, connecting with a dull thud, and Brody got the gun.

Madden staggered forward, looked at Brody, now armed, then at her, looking stunned, before he stumbled to the door and out into the hall.

Brody set the gun on the table and rushed to her, grabbing her by the arms. "Are you okay?"

She nodded, trembling. "That was that guy—Meathead—right?"

"Yeah. The real Lars Madden. I've got to call Jeffers." He led her to the bed and sat her down. "Will you be all right for a sec?"

She nodded, feeling numb, dazed by what had happened. In a fog, she listened as Brody apologized to Jeffers because the guy ran off. It sounded as if Jeffers had been on his way over. Her attention faded in and out and she noticed her teeth were chattering. She felt ice-cold, but she was sweating, too, and her fingers still vibrated from smacking the guy's head with the pot, which had leaked stew onto the sack at her feet.

Brody was insisting he was glad to help…wasn't about to back out now…something about going back to Plan A and not needing a bodyguard.

Her mind raced and stalled and sputtered, clutching at wild thoughts. Was there any stew left in the pot? Was dinner ruined? The flowers had fallen out and Meathead had trampled them. So sad. Such a waste. Tears sprang to her eyes.

Brody clicked off the phone and reached for her. "Hey, you're trembling." He pulled her into his arms and squeezed her close.

She tucked her face against his chest, grateful for the comfort and warmth of his arms. "Did I mess things up for you?" she said against his shirt, then pulled back to look at him. Her teeth still rattled, her chin vibrated uncontrollably.

"You could have been killed." He rubbed her arms, as if to get her blood circulating. "You were way too brave."

"He saw me see the gun. I was afraid he'd shoot. I just acted on reflex." Her voice wobbled. "What was he doing here?"

"After you left, Fake Madden called and I promised to get him a copy of the DVD when we return to L.A. Meathead got wind of the deal somehow. I was heading out to meet my agent—he'd delayed our meeting, which was why I couldn't come to your friend's place—but Madden caught me at the elevator and demanded the DVD."

"But you don't have it."

"No. I pretended to be calling Kirk, but I called Jeffers, who was on his way with the DVD when you arrived."

"So I wrecked it? Would they have arrested him?"

"No, as it turns out, this is better. They want Bascom to take the bait at Kirk's place. We've still got the Fake Madden deal going in L.A. Jeffers thinks this near miss will make them more anxious."

"So I did good?" She felt so weak, and her words were faint.

"You did great. It's okay, Jillian. We're both okay." He brushed her hair from her cheeks. "What did you hit him with anyway?" He seemed to be trying to distract her from her panic.

"A pot of Irish stew."

"You hit him with a pot? It was quite a clunk. He probably has a concussion."

"I certainly hope so. He wrecked my perfect Irish meal." She was joking to get her head above the waves of fear washing over her. She'd never seen a gun that close before. She *could* have been killed. Brody, too. To her chagrin, she began to cry.

"Just let it out," Brody said. "It's okay. And your meal's fine. We'll eat every bite. Shh…shh." He rubbed her back, comforting her, and she just hung on to him and cried it out.

Brody held on to Jillian with all his might, his heart aching over what she'd done, the risk she'd taken. "It'll be okay…don't worry…we're good…." He kept mumbling soothing words, but his chest was a knot of emotion.

He wanted to protect this woman, make everything right in her world. She had beaned a gunman with a pot of Irish stew to save his sorry ass. What a gift she was. She smelled like buttery pastry and onions and flowers, and he never wanted to let her go.

After a little while, she seemed calmer and lifted her tear-streaked face from his chest. "I'm better," she said, trying to smile.

He wiped her cheeks with his fingers. "Are you hungry?" Food would help her, he thought. "Because I'm starving. Let's see what you brought me."

He went to the tipped-over sacks and picked up the crumpled flowers in a cracked vase. One sack held a bottle of wine that hadn't broken, a seriously tossed salad and the pot, which still held a couple inches of stew. The other had a plastic baggie of something crumbly, and a plastic-wrapped loaf of… "You made me *barmbrack?*" He was so touched he didn't know what to say.

She nodded. "Burned it, though. Callie's stove had a short, so I had to use the biker's kitchen next door. And he went for beers and came back late. Then I got locked out of Callie's. It's a long story…" She took a shuddering breath.

"While we eat, you can tell me all about it." He cupped her face, so dear to him. "We'll share each other's day like a normal couple, huh?" He'd do anything to cheer her up.

He arranged the small table on the terrace, put the bedraggled flowers in place, poured the wine and served them the salad, the pasties from the baggie and the dregs of the stew in the bowls she'd brought.

"This looks nice, Brody. Thank you," she said faintly, trying to smile.

He took a spoonful of stew. "Yum," he said, though it was more like gravy and a bit salty. "Better than Ma's."

"Don't exaggerate." She gave a sad smile.

"It's good, Jillian. Especially considering the battle conditions in which you were working." He took a bite of the pastie. "Now, this, this is delicious. I like a well-cooked crust."

"I wanted this to be perfect." Tears welled in her eyes.

He squeezed her hands. "It is perfect. I love it. You did a very thoughtful thing. I'm happy, aren't you?"

"Yes, I am." She held his gaze, her eyes shiny with tears and relief. Her color had returned, so he thought she was out of shock and almost back to normal.

"I don't know about you, but I'm ready for dessert." He unwrapped the *barmbrack,* which was black on the bottom.

"We can eat the top part," she said, taking the loaf from him. "At least enough to find our fortunes."

"You put in fortunes?"

"Of course." She handed him a piece.

Inside, he found a green gummy candy shaped like sunglasses. "Ah." He licked it clean and held it out.

"That means your future's so bright you've got to wear shades." He saw that she held a yellow candy shaped like a sun.

"And yours means...?"

"Good fortune will shine on me."

"Sun and shades. Our fortunes match," he said.

"That's because they're the only shapes I used."

"It was fixed? You're a girl after Ma's heart." His own heart felt so big he thought he might crack a rib. He leaned across the table to kiss her. "I'm so lucky I met you."

"Lucky? I begged you to hire me."

"Then I'm lucky I said yes."

She smiled. "I feel lucky, too, Brody. Very lucky."

"Ma will love you." The words just burst out of him.

"You want me to meet your mother?"

"That's what people who care about each other do, right? Meet the parents?" Too soon maybe, but, hell, he didn't know how this all worked. He'd blunder through as best he could.

"But we hardly know each other, Brody," she said, her eyes full of hope all the same.

"I know all I need to know about you," he said, hoping it was true. "What I don't know I'll figure out. Isn't that how it works? You uncover the story after you get the footage."

"That's what I always say," she said, but there was a hesitation in her voice, a flicker in her eyes, as if something bothered her about that.

"There is one thing I want to tell you," he said. "Remember I said I might want to write a novel? The truth is I've already started one. It's a thriller called *Night Crimes.*"

"Really? That's wonderful, Brody."

"Except I'm stuck at the moment. So I'm thinking that if you read it you'll give me some ideas. Would you do that? I know you'll be honest. You're the most clear-eyed person I know."

His words seemed to trouble her. "I'd be honored to read your book, but don't give me so much credit. I'm not clear-eyed all the time. I get confused, I change my mind, I don't always know what I'm doing. There are things you need to know, too."

"We'll get there. Don't worry." He was hoping out loud, behaving as if he were as clear-eyed and sure as Jillian always was. Maybe he was getting there.

14

Two days later, Jillian was back at the Xanadu, the shoot finished and the wrap party that night. Her work with *Doctor Nite* was over. But her relationship with Brody was just beginning. They were falling in love, which excited and scared her all at once. What would happen when they returned to their ordinary lives? Would they grow closer or fall apart?

Brody's words haunted her: *What I don't know about you I'll learn. Isn't that how it works? You uncover the story after you get the footage?*

What he didn't know about her was the full scope of her documentary. She needed to share that. Instead of telling him, she'd decided to show him her rough cut.

With a hopeful sigh, she slipped the DVD she'd just made into its plain brown case and set it on the table beside her laptop to wait for the right moment.

First, Brody had to do the DVD handoff with Fake Madden—a prospect that scared her, though Brody seemed excited about it.

After that, in a calm moment, she would show him her movie and ask him if he would tell the truth about *Doctor Nite* on camera, turning her documentary into one We Women would buy.

The timing would be tricky, depending on when he planned to leave the show, but it could work. Love made all things possible, didn't it? Or was she dreaming?

Brody was due any minute. The meeting with Fake Madden was in a couple of hours. She was worried, even though police would supervise. Brody had insisted on making the handoff and Fake Madden had acted skittish enough the investigators had reluctantly agreed to let him.

She didn't like to think of Brody in danger. The idea hollowed her out inside. Fake Madden had never been armed, but still… She hoped the police stayed close.

There was a knock that sounded like Brody's, so she yanked open the door. There he stood, so handsome in his bomber jacket she could hardly stand it, could hardly believe he was hers. He gave her a quick kiss, then patted both pockets. "DVD here… Tape recorder here."

"Are you scared?" she asked.

"Not really. My guy is a sweat-stained wimp, Jillian."

"Be careful, okay?" She bit her lip, nervous for him.

"Come on. I'm a hard-bitten thriller writer, remember?"

"When are you going?"

"He should call to confirm in an hour." He took off his jacket and set it on the table beside her computer. "You working?" He nodded at her laptop, which she'd left on.

"A little. Yeah."

"I sent you *Night Crimes* as an attachment. Check your e-mail while I'm gone."

"I can't wait to read it," she said.

"I think you'll like the P.I. She's this wisecracking woman with hair like red licorice sticks, a smile that lights her eyes and a no-bullshit soul." He pulled her into his arms and murmured into her hair, "She's also very good in bed."

"Brody," she breathed, feeling the familiar rush of heat and need.

He lifted her onto the table, leaned her back, kissing her, shifting her body, knocking things from the table, making her laptop wobble. She didn't care. She loved when Brody behaved as if he had to have her, as if she were absolutely irresistible.

He swooped her up into his arms and carried her to the bed, chasing away all her doubts. Maybe it would work out. Brody was leaving Doctor Nite in his dust. Maybe he would help her with her movie and she'd have everything she wanted and then some. It seemed too much to hope, but she hoped it all the same.

THEY'D FINISHED making love and Jillian was in the bathroom when Barry White sang from the floor where Brody had tossed his pants. *Good timing, Fake Lars,* he thought with a smile, going after the phone.

His readout said, *Private Call.* Probably the guy. "Hello?" he said, his body tensing, his breathing shallow.

"Donegan?" It was him. "We're on. One hour. Aviation Services." Fake Lars had already declared that the handoff spot at LAX. Jeffers had gone over the directions with Brody ad nauseum. An LAPD team was probably already on-site, prepared to make the arrest.

"I'll be there," Brody said, then hung up, startled to see Jillian wrapped in a towel, looking on, her forehead creased with worry. "It'll be over in a couple hours. Relax. Go take your shower."

She didn't move.

He dialed Jeffers, dressing as he listened to another lecture about recording all he could, asking questions, but none that would make Fake Lars suspicious, backing out if things got hinky, and on and on.

When Brody hung up he went to kiss Jillian, who'd stayed in place, listening, eyes wide. "You worry too much."

"I can't help it, Brody. If anything happens to you..."

"If there were real danger, they wouldn't let me near. Go take your shower. No, make it a hot bath. A long one. With wine. I'll think of you getting all pink and soft and warm. Maybe I'll be back before the water cools." Not likely, but he had to calm her somehow. She looked so sweet and small and scared.

"I wish I could come with you," she said, gnawing her lip.

"What, and bring a pot of Irish stew, just in case?"

"I'm thinking the *barmbrack*. It was hard enough to take out fillings." She tried to smile.

"I'll be fine. There's a SWAT team out there already."

She threw her arms around him and held him tight, trembling. "Just be careful, Brody. I love you." She put her fingers to her lips, as if she'd surprised herself by saying that.

He stilled, realizing this was the first time either of them had said the *L* word, though they were both feeling it. "I love you, too." He kissed her again, his heart filling with emotion. This was scary, but good. Very good.

He liked having a woman care so much about him. "Now, go." He turned her toward the bathroom. "Make it long and hot."

She gave him a quick smile, then did as he'd said. He waited to hear her start the water. Loud. Full force from the faucet. She was doing a bath, like he'd suggested. She must really be scared if she was taking his advice.

He bent for his jacket, which had fallen with everything else when he attacked Jillian at the table. When he lifted it, his mini tape player tumbled from the pocket. Bending to grab it, he noticed the DVD had slid under the table.

That would have been a disaster, showing up without that. He shoved both items into his pocket, then headed for the door.

His pocket felt bulky, so he reached in to move the recorder to the opposite side—no way did he want that falling out in front of Fake Lars. He felt two DVD cases. Two? Huh?

His DVD must not have fallen. He'd picked up one that had slid from the table. Something of Jillian's.

The two cases were identical. Which was Kirk's? Damn.

He decided to check on Jillian's laptop. He slid in one and

clicked the Play button. Instead of strippers and men in suits, he saw a woman he recognized from one of the bars where they'd shot the show. She complained about men who only wanted sex, not marriage. There was a quick cut to another who claimed the Peter Pan boys were spoiled by their stay-at-home moms. This had to be Jillian's movie. A title zipped onto the screen. *Peter Pan Prison: How Men Who Play Pay.*

But her documentary was on dating, wasn't it? Weird. He was about to stop watching, get going, when he caught a visual from his show and Jillian's voice began to narrate:

In a woman-hating milieu of beer-guzzling bachelors, Doctor Nite exhorts men to seduce, score and escape. The show is a runaway hit and Doctor Nite has become an icon, the heroic ideal for the unattached male. Just as women today can't be too thin, it seems a man can't be too single.

Wait a minute. Next came a head shot of a woman with bookshelves behind her, a Ph.D. after her name. *Of course, this man and his television show are symptomatic of a culture of self-worship, of narcissistic self-involvement. This man is the express embodiment of the Peter Pan syndrome.*

The Peter Pan syndrome? Huh? He had to get going, but he was frozen in place, like someone watching a car wreck, unable to take his eyes off the disaster. He could hear Jillian's bath still pouring. He could get to LAX in forty minutes easy.

On screen, a male psychiatrist described Doctor Nite's personality: *misogynistic...egoistical...self-hating fear...dysfunctional role models in childhood.* The guy was insulting his parents now?

Next, Brody's face filled the screen. He recognized the dating interview he'd given Jillian. In the context of the preceding insults, the Brody on screen sounded arrogant, crude and bombastic. He'd been showing off, dammit, laying the Doctor Nite act on thick to help Jillian with a film that was supposedly about *dating.*

But that wasn't it at all. Her movie was a hit piece on him. She'd described him as a selfish, woman-hating scumbag, then set him up to prove it with his own words. Very clever.

The water was still pouring in the bathroom and he thought he could hear her humming. He wanted to demand an explanation, but he had to *go.* This instant, if he didn't want to be late.

Numb with shock, he hit Stop, made sure he had the right DVD in his pocket and headed out, this new pain in his chest taking out any tension he felt about the handoff.

TRAFFIC WAS GOOD and he'd lost little time, so Brody parked on the outskirts of Aviation Services right on schedule, fighting to focus on the task ahead, feeling the weight of what he'd learned like a lead suit dragging him down, making him sluggish.

The reception area seemed ordinary enough—cheap paneling, plastic chairs, chipped laminate table with faded magazines, and the sour smell of day-old coffee from an ancient coffeemaker on a card table in the corner. No one sat at the reception desk, but a guy in a golf shirt and khakis seemed to be expecting him and led him down a short hall, not saying a word. Brody turned on his recorder, set on voice activation.

At the first open door, the guy waved Brody inside a small office, then retreated. Brody was surprised to find Fake Madden had company. He slumped in a chair beside a cheap desk, where a man sat with an open laptop. Behind him stood Meathead, the real Lars Madden, and he sneered at Brody in recognition. Was that a lump on the side of the guy's oversize skull?

Good going, Jillian.

"What's going on?" Brody asked Fake Lars, realizing this must be a repeat of his first encounter. "What's with all the company?" He didn't see any guns, but he felt menace in the air.

Fake Madden shrugged, head down, as if he'd gotten caught. "Just give him the DVD," he mumbled to Brody.

The guy at the desk held out his hand.

"Who are you?" Brody asked, wanting the guy's name for the recording. Did the police outside know Fake Lars had company? Had he been ambushed? Or was this all part of the plan?

"Explain to the man," Computer Guy said sharply.

"The DVD belongs to them," Fake Lars said. "Hand it over."

"I don't know…" Brody said, trying to read the situation, his neck tight, hairs prickling.

Meathead moved closer to him, looming, his body language and beady eyes saying, *Give me an excuse, smart guy.*

Brody got the message and handed the case to Computer Guy. "What is this all about?" he asked, hoping for more for the police.

"Pay the man," Computer Guy said to Fake Lars, not looking up, busy putting the DVD into his computer.

Fake Madden pulled an envelope from his ill-fitting jacket—brown instead of navy this time—and held it out to Brody. "It's okay," he murmured. "Just go."

"Wait!" Computer Guy snapped.

Meathead moved to block the door.

Uh-oh. Brody was considering a side kick to the guy's kneecap, when Computer Guy said, "I'm verifying. Hold on."

In a few seconds, Brody heard from the computer's speakers the muffled sounds of laughter, chatter, ice rattling, along with the heavy beat of stripper music—definitely party noises. Computer Guy clicked around for a bit, then nodded at Brody. "You can leave."

Brody left, wishing he'd done more, racing for his car, dialing Jeffers as he went. Sitting inside the car, he told Jeffers about the surprise.

"Sounds like you handled it well," he said. "We've had a

change of plans. There's been a break at Canter's. Contact has been made, possibly as a result of your exchange. We want to follow that before we tip off anyone where you are."

"We still don't know my guy's name or how he fits in."

"We'll put someone on him."

At that moment, Brody saw Fake Madden step out of the building, blinking in the sudden sun, slumped with defeat. "He just came out," he said into the phone.

The guy started across the lot and seemed to be heading across the street. "I'm going to talk to him," Brody said.

"Don't. We'll follow him. We're a block away."

"The guy's not armed. If I talk to him, he doesn't have to know the authorities are involved yet." He clicked off before Jeffers could object, watching as Fake Lars reached the far side of the street and the lot crowded with cars. Brody sprinted to catch up, approaching from the passenger side. He watched as Fake Lars hit his electronic key and when he heard the clunk of the locks releasing, Brody opened the door and slid into the passenger seat.

"What are you doing?" Fake Madden slammed himself against the driver's-side door as if he feared an attack.

"I'm not here to hurt you. I want the story, Lars."

"My name's not Lars, okay?" He relaxed and shook his jacket into place.

"What is your name?"

The guy looked at him for a few seconds, then shrugged. "I'll tell you while I drive." He started the car and pulled out of the lot.

Brody clicked on his tape recorder, noticing a car waiting on the street. No doubt police who would follow.

"My name is really James Toomis, okay?" he said.

"Why did you pretend to be someone else?"

"Because Jed Bascom is a lying, cheating sack of shit and I had to prove it to my sister with that friggin' DVD."

"Your sister?"

"So she would divorce the bastard. She's married to him, okay? What a joke. Have you seen him on TV, that self-righteous ass, all moral about drugs and pornography? Meanwhile, he's shooting heroin at sex parties with you and your crowd."

"Hang on. That wasn't a sex party. And there was no heroin. Or needles."

"Whatever," Toomis said gloomily.

"So you hate Bascom? Is this a blackmail deal?"

"Blackmail? Are you kidding? I was trying to save my sister."

"How did you get into the convention? And how did you know about the DVD in the first place?"

"I work for Bascom, right? I was between jobs and Lydia—that's my sister—got him to give me this gofer job. Getting coffee, making reservations, fetching dry cleaning. I'm this flunky, like some college intern. So, I'm about invisible to them—like maids and janitors, you know? And I happened to overhear them meeting after the robbery got flubbed. Bascom was all hot about what might be on the film, and Madden insisted they check out a copy and see how bad it really was before they harassed the guy with the camera again."

"And you wanted the DVD first."

"To show Lydia, yeah. To prove how blind she's been. Except Madden arrived too soon and caught me. They made me call you the second time. But it's all for nothing, anyway. I told my sister what it was about. She doesn't believe it. She thinks I want to ruin her marriage. She's mad at *me*. *Me*. I think if I showed her the DVD this minute, she'd still find a way to deny it."

"Sometimes people don't want to see the truth."

He should know. He probably should have seen that Jillian was lying to him. She'd given him enough clues about her attitude. He'd been as blind as Toomis's sister.

"I just want the guy to get what's coming to him," Toomis said, pounding the steering wheel. "He's a lying, cheating hypocrite."

Brody glanced in the rearview mirror and saw the driver behind flash his headlights. He noticed Ryan Jeffers was in the passenger seat. Brody smiled. "I think I can help you out here, James," he said. "See the car that's following us?"

"Huh?" He swiveled his head to look at the car.

"Careful there. Eyes on the road. How about you pull into that parking lot?" He pointed.

"What's going on?" Toomis turned into the lot and stopped the car.

"If you tell these guys what you told me—" he pointed at Jeffers and his driver, who wore a badge around his neck, heading their way "—I believe Mr. Bascom will get everything he deserves."

"What are you talking about?"

"The authorities are interested in Mr. Bascom's activities, too. Answer all their questions. Someday your sister will thank you." Brody got out of the car and handed Jeffers the tape recorder. He told him what had happened, accepted his thanks and, after extracting the promise of an update, got a ride from a detective back to his car.

It was ironic that Bascom had committed assault with a deadly weapon and burglary to cover up his stripper encounter, having no idea he was in trouble over his dirty deals. The man would get nailed for going after a video that couldn't even be used against him. Even Toomis didn't intend to use the video except to help his sister. The case was about perception and reputation and truth and intent and what you missed until you knew the whole story.

Now Brody had more truth to learn. He headed back to Jillian, his heart heavy. Just as she'd predicted, he had seen everything more clearly on screen.

JILLIAN PULLED OPEN the door to her hotel room and for one instant Brody wanted to forget what he'd learned about her. "I was so worried," she said. "Are you okay?" She started to hug him, but hesitated, sensing his stiffness, no doubt, and backed up, letting him enter. "What's wrong? Did something bad happen?"

"Yeah. It's bad. But nothing to do with the case." He closed the door and walked to her laptop. "I saw part of your movie before I left." He hit a key and the screensaver disappeared. The picture was right where he'd left it, on his face while he gave his dating tips.

"You did? Why did you—"

"I thought mine fell out of my pocket and picked yours up by mistake. I had to check to be sure I had the right one."

"Oh," she said. "It's fine, really. I made the copy for you. I wanted to show it to you after you got back. How much did you see?"

"Enough. Plenty. I saw all I needed to see."

"You're angry?" She seemed surprised.

"Of course I am. This isn't a movie about dating. It's a hit piece on me."

"No, it's not." She looked startled. "It criticizes Doctor Nite, that's true, as a symbol of a negative cultural phenomenon, not you. Not Brody Donegan."

"I told you before. I *am* Doctor Nite."

"You're more than him. And you're done with the show anyway. You told me yourself." She seemed shaken by his anger. "In fact…I was hoping you'd give me an interview about your plans, about how you've changed your mind. We'd have to work out the timing, of course. After you tell everyone."

"You thought I'd go on camera and tell people Doctor Nite is full of shit? Are you nuts? And let me say for the record, contrary to what your experts said, I am no misogynist. I love women. I'm not Peter Pan, either. And my parents are good people who raised me right."

"I know that, Brody. That's academic theory."

Brody felt fury rise in him. She was flat-out denying what he'd seen with his own eyes, what was clearly, plainly there. "There's nothing wrong with my show," he said tightly.

"But you're sick of it. You said your life was empty."

"That was personal. Between you and me. And you want to put it out for the world to know? What's wrong with you?" It suddenly occurred to him how bad this really was. "This is why you begged for this job? To expose me to ridicule and insult me? From the beginning you meant to attack me?"

"I had some harsh ideas at first, I admit, but I learned about the tender, generous, warm man you truly are, the real Brody, not the crude TV personality. That's the man I fell in love with." Her voice went soft and shaky and he abruptly wanted to hold her, forget what he'd seen, believe what she said.

But he couldn't. It was all right there and he wouldn't deny it like she was trying to do. "For a woman who claims to want the truth, you spend a lot of time lying to yourself."

"Brody!" She looked stung.

"You weren't uncovering a story, JJ. You were proving a point. You're pissed at me. No, at men in general."

"That's not true."

"You think men are all players, who'll use you and cheat on you, right? Like your father? This film is payback, right?"

"That's not fair," she said, anger flaring in her gaze. "You didn't even see the whole movie. At least do that."

He was relieved she was fighting back, instead of looking puzzled and hurt, as if he were the one who'd misled her.

"If you're so proud of your show," she continued, "you should laugh at my experts, shrug off the criticism. But you know I'm right and that upsets you. Don't hide behind Doctor Nite. You know you want more."

"I want *different,* not *more.* And not better. There's nothing wrong with me, with my life or with Doctor Nite."

"You can't mean that." She stared at him. "Are you joking?"

Anger spiked in him. "You were right before, JJ. We hardly know each other. And I thought you were better than this."

She gasped and her cheeks went red, as if she'd been slapped. "I never meant to hurt you," she said levelly.

"What are you talking about? Your intent from the beginning was to make me look like a Class A prick. You took this job for the *purpose* of hurting me."

"That's not true."

"I trusted you. I opened my arms to you. I offered you interviews, told you to tape anything. What a schmuck I was."

"I'm sorry, Brody." She sank into herself for a moment, looking lost and small, then pulled herself up, as if wrapping her confidence around herself like a coat against the cold.

"I'm sorry you feel that way. I won't use anything you said. And for the record, I would never expose you in a negative way. I thought you'd agree with me. I wish I could make you understand."

"Oh, I do," he snapped.

She swallowed hard and tears sprang to her eyes. Fool that he was, his heart lurched in sympathy. He'd made her cry. She searched his face. "We can't get past this, can we?"

He fought the urge to touch her cheek, to hold her, tell her never mind, but it just hurt too damn much. "No," he said, "we can't."

She nodded slowly, accepting defeat. "I know you won't believe this, but I want the best for you, Brody. I know once you quit, you'll see more clearly."

"Quit? Who says I'm quitting?" And, like that, he decided. "Doctor Nite is just fine. In fact, he's heading to Europe." He lunged for the door, throwing it open. "Goodbye, Jillian. Have a nice life. I know I will."

He slammed the door and marched away. No one was going to tell him what to do or who to be. He'd move on when he was damn good and ready. He was having too good a time to walk away now.

"SO HOW WAS WORKING for Doctor Nite?" Nate asked Jillian, when she sat in front of his editing bay a week later.

Wonderful and awful. Thrilling and devastating. She wouldn't have missed it for the world, and she wished she'd taken no for an answer outside Score that night. She couldn't say any of that to Nate. She was too raw. "It was...interesting."

Her cousin kept staring at her, so she nodded at the monitor. "Let's roll, okay?" She hoped to salvage something she could work with once she'd removed all references to *Doctor Nite.* After the fight, she'd called May Lee and explained the documentary wasn't what the network wanted. May Lee was disappointed, but left her with a polite invitation to send in future projects Jillian thought might be right for them.

Nate readied his equipment to play back her rough cut. She hadn't told him what she had in mind. She'd see what she had, then decide what to do. She'd been floundering lately, indecisive and lost. Not herself at all.

A week had passed, but she still missed Brody desperately. She'd snapped that purple rubber band until she gave herself welts, then removed it so people wouldn't think she'd been abused.

She'd replayed their last conversation over and over in her mind. She'd assumed Brody would understand. Instead, he'd felt betrayed. Maybe if she'd been able to give him the context before he saw the snippets. He'd seemed so ready to assume the worst about her intent.

She suppose she didn't blame him. From his perspective, she'd lied to him, used him, tried to humiliate him.

She'd been wrong about him. They'd been wrong about each other. Even without the movie between them, they saw the world and each other too differently.

Brody was Doctor Nite and would always be, at some level. People didn't change. Not really. She could never love a man who treated women like toys to be played with, then set aside. That wasn't quite fair, she knew. Brody was a good person in his heart. He just wasn't right for her.

She wanted so much to erase the hurt from his face, to somehow make it better. He'd claimed she'd been proving a point, not seeking the truth. That bothered her and was a big reason she was here in Nate's studio to watch her documentary start to finish. Sometimes you got too close to your work.

Before they could start, Nate's bell rang. At the door were two young women—tall, blond and leggy, wearing silk robes and holding gym bags. Models from the condo next door, no doubt. "We have go-sees and Jessica's hogging the shower," whined the first, batting her eyes at Nate. "Can we use yours, pretty please?"

"Sure. Come on in," Nate said, blushing and beaming.

The girls walked through the living room, headed for the hall. Jillian watched them and Nate came to sit down. "What a generous neighbor you are," she said.

"We help each other out," he said, watching the girls' behinds disappear into the bathroom.

"They use your shower and you…what…borrow sugar?"

"It works out." Nate shrugged and they settled in to watch.

The movie scrolled forward and Jillian began to feel dismay at how repetitive the scenes were. First single women, then expert after expert condemned Doctor Nite and bachelors for being juvenile and self-involved. The same point over and over.

Nate gave a low whistle. "And I thought you had a thing for the guy."

"It's kind of monotonous, huh?" She'd done the newbie thing of venting her spleen, not trusting her audience to understand, hitting them over the head again and again with the same idea.

"So, did he piss you off or something?"

"No. I..." This wasn't her style at all. She kept an open mind, uncovered the story gradually. This felt like a hit piece. Brody had been right. How had she been so blind?

The *Doctor Nite* promo rolled across the screen and her mortification was replaced by the familiar ache of missing Brody. Every single day she hurt for him, scalp to toes.

"Whatcha watchin'?" The models, towels around their bodies and hair, leaned in to look. "Oooh, Doctor Nite," the first one said. "I love Doctor Nite."

The second nodded. "He is *sooo* cute."

"Jillian was his cameraperson last week," Nathan explained to the models, who gasped in wonder and delight.

"You are so lucky," one said.

"What do you think about Doctor Nite's attitude toward women?" Jillian asked, truly curious this time.

"His attitude? He loves women. What's not to like about that?" They all watched the screen where Brody was joking with a table of chunky women in low-cut spandex, who beamed at him. He treated them the way he treated everyone he interviewed, men and women, fat, thin, gorgeous, ordinary. Brody loved people.

Some of his bits were obnoxious, but men were as much the butt of his humor as women were. And he poked fun at himself more than anyone else.

Jillian remembered the advice a wise film instructor had given: *The angle of your brain is more crucial than the angle of your camera.* She'd gone into her movie with a closed mind. Why had she been so happy to believe the worst of Brody?

Her own history, no doubt. Was she pissed at men? Brody was right that the past colored her views. She had resented her father, been hurt by years of rejection because of her weight. She mistrusted men in general, she supposed. She hoped for decent men, but she didn't quite believe they were out there.

Before Nate's neighbors left, they waltzed off with his supply of beer and chips for a party they were having that night. They clearly had him wrapped around their little French-tipped fingers. Women had their tricks and maneuvers, too. What had Eve said? When it came to sex and dating, men and women screwed it up in their separate ways.

She looked at Brody on screen, at his smile, at those eyes. How she loved him. She'd hurt him, taken advantage of his generosity, convinced herself that exposing his show had been for the greater good. Believing she'd been open and fair, she'd actually stacked the deck against him.

She wanted him to be different than he was, but you had to love someone for who he was, not for his potential. Could she love Brody that way? Could she truly open her heart?

She would never like Brody's show, but she could respect him, honor his intent, see his side, couldn't she?

And, if she could, would Brody want her? Maybe she'd been his transition lover. Maybe she'd hurt him too deeply.

He'd not responded to her critique of his book, which had included a heartfelt note about how good it was. Maybe he was too angry. Maybe it was too late. Her heart squeezed tight in pain and hope. She intended to find out.

15

IT WAS 2 A.M., and Kirk and Eve were the last guests at Brody's blowout party at Score, Doctor Nite's favorite hangout. It was a week after the Bascom sting and Brody's breakup with Jillian and the place had been packed with crew, publicity staff, assistants, equipment guys, hell, even a couple of strays from the mail room they'd gathered up.

The party had rocked. Brody had kept the booze flowing and made sure everyone knew how important they were to him. It had been tons better than that subdued mutter of a celebration the last night at the Xanadu.

Jillian had had a soda, thanked everyone, then took off, claiming to need sleep. He'd been relieved, since he'd kept his eyes on her the entire time she was there, fighting the urge to pull her into his arms and just smell her hair.

Now he and Kirk and Eve were tossing back one last drink. "The Doctor is *back!*" Brody said, dropping his shot glass of whiskey into his beer. Kirk and Eve did the same, then all three banged their overflowing steins together and guzzled the workingman's highball, slamming down the mugs with resounding clunks.

"You had us worried," Eve said. "Didn't he, Kirk?"

"Nah. I knew he'd be cool." Kirk grinned, adjusting the sling strap around his neck.

Brody didn't feel cool. He felt awful. Miserable. Lonely.

Heartsick. *Dammit, Jillian.* He was still in love with the woman. Either that or he was having some kind of slow, agonizing heart attack—his chest ached constantly.

He'd stopped being angry, at least. He'd felt so betrayed, so set up. He'd thought she had integrity and, hell, standards. But she was human, too. Nobody was perfect.

This was still L.A.

He didn't really blame her—professionally, anyway. If her aim was to make a commercial project that would score airtime, *Doctor Nite* was an attractive target. Personally, though, it hurt like hell.

Of course, something else gnawed at him. After it was over, he'd felt *relieved.* As if a weight had been lifted off his shoulders, as if he'd dodged a bullet.

Knowing she believed in him, he'd gotten a knot in his belly, a pressure in his head. She expected him to be a new man. She was in love with her image of who he could be,.not who he actually was.

And who was that? Good question. His relief about resuming his old life hadn't lasted a day. He felt like a shadow now. When he talked about the show, he heard an echo, as if he stood in an empty room. There was nothing wrong with being Doctor Nite awhile longer, he told himself. He'd move on when he was good and ready. He was only thirty-seven. He had plenty of time to write a novel, find a woman and settle down. Right?

"I almost forgot the latest on Europe," Eve said. "We're this close to getting BBC to do a documentary on you. The working title is *An American Sex God Crosses the Pond.*"

"Sex God? No way," he said, dread filling him at the prospect. *An American Sex Fraud* was more like it.

"So we negotiate a better title. It's a good thing," Eve said.

Brody owed her and Kirk the European trip, he figured, and it gave him something to focus on.

"I want us to do more arty shots, Kirk," he said. Jillian had made him realize that. Working with her had perked him up.

"Only if Kirk gets medical permission to do handheld," Eve said, looking Kirk over, her face softer than usual. Her voice, too, now that he thought about it, and she was looking at the man the way Brody remembered Jillian looking at him.

JJ, he corrected himself. Jillian was fake, the fantasy of the warm and wise woman he'd imagined for himself.

"Oh, and did you see the paper?" Eve said, pulling a folded newspaper from her messenger bag. "I can't believe you didn't let them use your name, Brody. This would have been faboo publicity. You got major crooks totally nailed."

"I'm not interested in more PR," he said, but he was proud of his role in the case. Getting the word that the DVD Brody had handed over held scandalous content, Bascom's people went after the phony drives at Kirk's place and were arrested.

Bascom was caught completely cold and immediately sold out his partners in crime. Subpoenas had been rolling out for involved legislators, state regulators, even a judge.

It turned out Brody had lots of fans in state government and law enforcement. He'd signed countless autographs and had his picture taken with tons of people.

"And you!" Eve leveled her gaze at Kirk. "You could have been killed. Don't keep secrets from me like that."

"I didn't want to scare you," he said softly, looking like a puppy who just had its belly rubbed. Kirk always bobbed his head while Eve gave him shit, grinning like a goon. Brody had always interpreted it as a sister-brother deal.

"So, how come JJ wasn't at the party?" Kirk asked. "I watched some of the editing. She did great work."

"She declined," Eve said. "She seemed…upset." She turned to Brody. "It's not your fault, Brode. I warned her you weren't the kind of guy who settles down."

"Oh, yeah?" He felt irked by her confident judgment of him.

"I mean you're a great friend—generous and lovable and fun. But you need variety and action, right?"

"Right," he said faintly.

"Yeah," Kirk said. "Trying to make guys like us settle down is like teaching pigs to fly. Who needs a bunch of bruised bacon?" He clicked his empty glass against Brody's, but when he caught Eve's eye he seemed to hold still, as if he hoped she would disagree.

"Did you ever consider the pig might *want* to fly?" Brody said, sounding crankier than he'd intended. "Did you ever think about *that?*"

Kirk and Eve gave startled laughs.

"Good one," Kirk said hesitantly.

"Wait," Eve said. "You mean it, don't you, Brody? Oh. Hey. Is it JJ? God, I had no idea. I'm so sorry. Was it too much free time, because I'll be sure that—"

"Forget it. Just, for the love of God, Kirk, get some balls. No, make that wings. Be a damned flying pig. You want her, go after her."

"Go after her?"

"You mean…?" Eve let her words trail off as they both figured it out. They stared at each other, faces pink with embarrassment, eyes shiny with hope. Lots of hope. Brody felt an answering pang in his chest.

He left them still staring at each other. At least he'd learned one thing from being with Jillian. He'd learned what love looked like.

People could change, dammit. And he wanted to. He wanted out of *Doctor Nite*. Now. He'd gone back partly to spite Jillian. And also because it wasn't easy to make that big a jump, to flap those tiny, unused pig wings.

Back at his place, he went straight to the trash can under his desk where he'd tossed Jillian's feedback on *Night Crimes*—

he'd felt too angry and shaky to read it. Of course, the do-not-disturb sign on his office door meant the housekeeper hadn't emptied the trash, which he'd known when he pretended to dispose of the fat envelope.

Now he flipped through the printout, reading Jillian's remarks in the margins. They were helpful, insightful and steady, the same way she'd been behind the camera. After the last page, she'd written him a note:

> This is good, Brody. Finish it. I've made suggestions here and there. Remember, first drafts are never perfect. It won't be easy. Nothing good ever is. But I feel your heart in this. No matter what you believe about me, believe in my faith in you.
>
> Love, Jillian.

He blinked. *First drafts are never perfect.* Not even the first draft of a new life.

He couldn't go back in time, pretend he hadn't decided to quit the show. He would help his crew as much as he could, but it would be soul-killing to deny who he wanted to be now.

He'd need help to stick with it, though. He'd need Jillian. *Believe in my faith in you.* These words from her buoyed him, made him feel stronger.

He needed her for support and inspiration, for his own happiness. He needed her to help him see past his own bullshit, dig for the truth of whatever he needed to know and do and become.

And she needed him, too, dammit. To soften her edges, to show her that human weakness could become strength, to show her more than one way to see the world.

He had to talk to her.

But first, he had to say goodbye to Doctor Night. All hell would break loose, he knew, but he was ready for it now.

TWO DAYS AFTER she'd seen the truth about her documentary, Jillian burned a DVD to leave with Brody at his network office. Once he saw it and called her, they would talk. The idea made her heart jump so high into her throat she could hardly breathe past it.

The DVD was a rough narration with a few clips of her new project, which had the working title, *Taming the Beast and the Shrew: How False Expectations Keep Us from Happy Relationships.*

It was about the games both sexes played, whether out of selfishness, fear, insecurity or past pain.

At the end, she'd tacked on a speech just for Brody, telling him she'd been wrong and that he'd taught her about herself and her fears and unfair assumptions.

It was an apology and it was an offer to try again. Because she loved him still. Her voice shook at the end, but she didn't care. Her whole heart was in that speech.

She printed out a label, placed it on the DVD case and headed for her car to drive to his network's offices. Maybe he'd be there and maybe just seeing him would tell her everything she needed to know.

An hour later she was stunned to learn that Brody Donegan no longer had an office at his network. "But he's the star of *Doctor Nite,*" she said to the receptionist, whose desk she'd finally reached.

"Not anymore," she said with a smile. "I can take your package, but it might not get to him."

Had Brody quit? She left the office building and dialed his cell phone, only to get voice mail. Okay, no biggie. If he didn't call back, she'd track him through Eve. No way was she giving up without a fight.

She drove home, her head throbbing, her body tight with frustration. When she got blocked by the garbage truck working its way down her street, she almost bellowed out the window in rage. Instead, she whipped around the truck and drove too fast to her house, squealing up the driveway and jamming on her brakes. She calmed herself before getting out of the car.

She noticed her neighbor and several women huddled on the porch talking. When the group shifted, she was startled to see Brody in the middle of the women. Brody? At her house? He'd come to see her! Her heart seemed to break open with warm joy.

He said something and the women laughed. He was doing his thing, charming every female in sight. That was Brody's gift—to share his spark of fun and mischief and deep interest in people with everyone he met. This was the Brody Treatment. And a girl could do far worse than that.

She grabbed the DVD and took the sidewalk toward her neighbor's place. Brody caught sight of her and grinned so broadly she knew, head to toe, everything would be fine.

She was so lucky to know him. She loved him just as he was, Doctor Nite and all. If she was really, really lucky, she'd get to love him for the rest of her life.

He said goodbye to the group on the porch and skimmed the steps, heading straight for her. She wanted to run into his arms, but she stood on the sidewalk and let him come to her, glad when her neighbor waved and retreated into the house with her friends.

"I was asking your neighbor when you'd be back," he said when he reached her, standing close.

"I went to your network, but they said you were gone."

"I quit, Jillian," he said, his dark eyes so familiar, so warm. She'd missed his close attention. "It was time. Like you said in your note, nothing good is ever easy."

"Your book is so good. Are you still working on it?"

"I'm starting in again. Starting on my new life, too."

"When you quit, how did that go?"

"Like I expected. The network gave me hell, threatened to sue. My agent thinks I'm crazy. The crew flipped out."

"Eve?"

"The worst. Thank God Kirk calmed her down. They're together now, you know."

"I wondered about them. That's good to hear."

"They figured out there's life beyond *Doctor Nite*, too. They'll land on their feet. I guess I always knew that. Everybody's calming down. There's always a new show."

"I'm glad you're through the worst of it."

"You were right. I had to go with my gut. And my heart."

"And you were right about my documentary. I didn't mean for it to be a hit piece, but that's how it came out. Here…this explains it." She held out the DVD.

He groaned. "Haven't we had enough trouble with movies?"

"This is my new project. You'll like it." She had to stop talking while the garbage truck roared behind her. "There's a message from me to you at the end and—"

"You have the master?" he interrupted.

"Yes, but—"

He tossed the case into the garbage truck.

"Hey!" she said. "What are you doing?"

"Tell me what you said. I want it live." He scooped her hair behind her ears and looked at her in that way he had, taking her all in, showing her she was the most important person in the world.

"Okay…. I said I did have a closed mind about you. And about men. Maybe because my father was a rat, maybe because of my fat-girl past. I'll never love your show, but I love you. As you are. Without a single change."

"Without a single one? Come on. You wouldn't be a woman if you didn't want to fix your man."

"You know what I mean."

"I'm new at this relationship stuff, Jillian. I'll screw up and I'll make mistakes."

"Me, too. I can't even make *barmbrack* right."

He laughed, relieved it seemed. "We'll figure it out together, I guess." His face filled with emotion and he pulled her close. "God, I missed you," he said into her hair, and she felt as though she'd come home at last from a difficult journey.

He leaned back and grinned. "I mean, hell, a woman who can turn Irish stew into a weapon…now that's a rare woman. I'd be an idiot to let her go."

"Damn straight."

"I want to take my own advice," he said, serious again. "Remember Dating Tip Number One? I want to settle down with a woman who's smart, who makes me laugh, who lights me up inside. Someone who has faith in me. I want to make you proud, Jillian."

She felt tears in her eyes. "You already do."

"I need you to help me see my own BS for what it is, to get things straight, to know what I want and to go for it."

"Cross my heart," she said, as she'd said when she got the job. "I won't be able to help myself."

Brody laughed. "I love that about you. And I'll help you stay open, to see both sides, to cut us both some slack."

And then he kissed her, soft and strong, full of hope and heat. "Too bad I gave up my show. I've got a great Top Ten list for makeup sex forming in mind."

"I'd rather live it than film it, Brody."

"Don't you see better through the lens?"

"Not when it comes to you," she said. "I see you just fine. And when I don't, something tells me you'll set me straight."

"Mmm. My pleasure." He leaned in for a kiss.

"Let's go inside. You make me too weak in the knees."

He gestured for her to lead the way, but she tucked herself

against him so they walked together, half on the sidewalk, half in the grass, no one leading, no one following—partners on the journey of becoming a couple.

She'd given Brody the courage to be the man he wanted to be. And he'd helped her open her heart and mind, see more than she'd allowed herself to see. Two sets of eyes, after all, were better than one, especially when they belonged to two people in love.

* * * * *

Look for Dawn Atkins's next book,
coming in August 2008
from Harlequin Blaze.

Look for LAST WOLF WATCHING
by Rhyannon Byrd—the exciting conclusion
in the BLOODRUNNERS *miniseries*
from Silhouette Nocturne.

Follow Michaela and Brody on their fierce journey
to find the truth and face the demons from the past,
as they reach the heart of the battle between
the Runners and the rogues.

Here is a sneak preview of book three,
LAST WOLF WATCHING.

Michaela squinted, struggling to see through the impenetrable darkness. Everyone looked toward the Elders, but she knew Brody Carter still watched her. Michaela could feel the power of his gaze. Its heat. Its strength. And something that felt strangely like anger, though he had no reason to have any emotion toward her. Strangers from different worlds, brought together beneath the heavy silver moon on a night made for hell itself. That was their only connection.

The second she finished that thought, she knew it was a lie. But she couldn't deal with it now. Not tonight. Not when her whole world balanced on the edge of destruction.

Willing her backbone to keep her upright, Michaela Doucet focused on the towering blaze of a roaring bonfire that rose from the far side of the clearing, its orange flames burning with maniacal zeal against the inky black curtain of the night. Many of the Lycans had already shifted into their preternatural shapes, their fur-covered bodies standing like monstrous shadows at the edges of the forest as they waited with restless expectancy for her brother.

Her nineteen-year-old brother, Max, had been attacked by a rogue werewolf—a Lycan who preyed upon humans for food. Max had been bitten in the attack, which meant he was no longer human, but a breed of creature that existed between the two worlds of man and beast, much like the Bloodrunners themselves.

The Elders parted, and two hulking shapes emerged from the trees. In their wolf forms, the Lycans stood over seven feet tall, their legs bent at an odd angle as they stalked forward. They each held a thick chain that had been wound around their inside wrists, the twin lengths leading back into the shadows. The Lycans had taken no more than a few steps when they jerked on the chains, and her brother appeared.

Bound like an animal.

Biting at her trembling lower lip, she glanced left, then right, surprised to see that others had joined her. Now the Bloodrunners and their family and friends stood as a united force against the Silvercrest pack, which had yet to accept the fact that something sinister was eating away at its foundation—something that would rip down the protective walls that separated their world from the humans'. It occurred to Michaela that loyalties were being announced tonight—a separation made between those who would stand with the Runners in their fight against the rogues and those who blindly supported the pack's refusal to face reality. But all she could focus on was her brother. Max looked so hurt...so terrified.

"Leave him alone," she screamed, her soft-soled, black satin slip-ons struggling for purchase in the damp earth as she rushed toward Max, only to find herself lifted off the ground when a hard, heavily muscled arm clamped around her waist from behind, pulling her clear off her feet. "Damn it, let me down!" she snarled, unable to take her eyes off her brother as the golden-eyed Lycan kicked him.

Mindless with heartache and rage, Michaela clawed at the arm holding her, kicking her heels against whatever part of her captor's legs she could reach. "Stop it," a deep, husky voice grunted in her ear. "You're not helping him by losing it. I give you my word he'll survive the ceremony, but you have to keep it together."

"Nooooo!" she screamed, too hysterical to listen to reason. "You're monsters! All of you! Look what you've done to him! How dare you! *How dare you!*"

The arm tightened with a powerful flex of muscle, cinching her waist. Her breath sucked in on a sharp, wailing gasp.

"Shut up before you get both yourself and your brother killed. I will *not* let that happen. Do you understand me?" her captor growled, shaking her so hard that her teeth clicked together. "Do you understand me, Doucet?"

"Damn it," she cried, stricken as she watched one of the guards grab Max by his hair. Around them Lycans huffed and growled as they watched the spectacle, while others outright howled for the show to begin.

"That's enough!" the voice seethed in her ear. "They'll tear you apart before you even reach him, and I'll be damned if I'm going to stand here and watch you die."

Suddenly, through the haze of fear and agony and outrage in her mind, she finally recognized who'd caught her. *Brody.*

He held her in his arms, her body locked against his powerful form, her back to the burning heat of his chest. A low, keening sound of anguish tore through her, and her head dropped forward as hoarse sobs of pain ripped from her throat. "Let me go. I have to help him. *Please,*" she begged brokenly, knowing only that she needed to get to Max. "Let me go, Brody."

He muttered something against her hair, his breath warm against her scalp, and Michaela could have sworn it was a single word…. But she must have heard wrong. She was too upset. Too furious. Too terrified. She must be out of her mind.

Because it sounded as if he'd quietly snarled the word *never.*

Silhouette

nocturne™

THE FINAL INSTALLMENT OF
THE BLOODRUNNERS TRILOGY

Last Wolf Watching

Runner Brody Carter has found his match in Michaela Doucet, a human with unusual psychic powers. When Michaela's brother is threatened, Brody becomes her protector, and suddenly not only has to protect her from her enemies but also from himself....

LOOK FOR

LAST WOLF WATCHING

BY

RHYANNON BYRD

Available May 2008 wherever you buy books.

Dramatic and Sensual Tales of Paranormal Romance

www.eHarlequin.com

SN61786

REQUEST YOUR FREE BOOKS!

2 FREE NOVELS PLUS 2 FREE GIFTS!

HARLEQUIN®

Blaze™

Red-hot reads!

YES! Please send me 2 FREE Harlequin® Blaze™ novels and my 2 FREE gifts (gifts are worth about $10). After receiving them, if I don't wish to receive any more books, I can return the shipping statement marked "cancel". If I don't cancel, I will receive 6 brand-new novels every month and be billed just $4.24 per book in the U.S. or $4.71 per book in Canada, plus 25¢ shipping and handling per book and applicable taxes, if any*. That's a savings of 15% or more off the cover price! I understand that accepting the 2 free books and gifts places me under no obligation to buy anything. I can always return a shipment and cancel at any time. Even if I never buy another book, the two free books and gifts are mine to keep forever.

151 HDN ERVA 351 HDN ERUX

Name (PLEASE PRINT)

Address Apt. #

City State/Prov. Zip/Postal Code

Signature (if under 18, a parent or guardian must sign)

Mail to the **Harlequin Reader Service:**

IN U.S.A.: P.O. Box 1867, Buffalo, NY 14240-1867

IN CANADA: P.O. Box 609, Fort Erie, Ontario L2A 5X3

Not valid to current subscribers of Harlequin Blaze books.

Want to try two free books from another line?

Call 1-800-873-8635 or visit www.morefreebooks.com.

* Terms and prices subject to change without notice. N.Y. residents add applicable sales tax. Canadian residents will be charged applicable provincial taxes and GST. This offer is limited to one order per household. All orders subject to approval. Credit or debit balances in a customer's account(s) may be offset by any other outstanding balance owed by or to the customer. Please allow 4 to 6 weeks for delivery. Offer available while quantities last.

Your Privacy: Harlequin Books is committed to protecting your privacy. Our Privacy Policy is available online at www.eHarlequin.com or upon request from the Reader Service. From time to time we make our lists of customers available to reputable third parties who may have a product or service of interest to you. If you would prefer we not share your name and address, please check here. ☐

HB08

Silhouette®

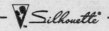

SPECIAL EDITION™

THE WILDER FAMILY

Healing Hearts in Walnut River

Social worker Isobel Suarez was proud to work at Walnut River General Hospital, so when Neil Kane showed up from the attorney general's office to investigate insurance fraud, she was up in arms. Until she melted in his arms, and things got very tricky...

Look for

HER MR. RIGHT?

by

KAREN ROSE SMITH

Available May wherever books are sold.

Visit Silhouette Books at www.eHarlequin.com SSE24897

Silhouette®

Romantic
SUSPENSE

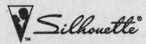

**Sparked by Danger,
Fueled by Passion.**

**Seduction Summer:
Seduction in the sand...and a killer on the beach.**

Silhouette Romantic Suspense invites you to the hottest summer yet with three connected stories from some of our steamiest storytellers! Get ready for...

Killer Temptation

by Nina Bruhns;

a millionaire this tempting is worth a little danger.

Killer Passion

by Sheri WhiteFeather;

an FBI profiler's forbidden passion incites a killer's rage,

and

Killer Affair

by Cindy Dees;

this affair with a mystery man is to die for.

Look for

KILLER TEMPTATION by Nina Bruhns in June 2008
KILLER PASSION by Sheri WhiteFeather in July 2008
and
KILLER AFFAIR by Cindy Dees in August 2008.

Available wherever you buy books!

Visit Silhouette Books at www.eHarlequin.com SRS27586

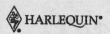

HARLEQUIN®

INTRIGUE®

Introducing

THE CURSE OF RAVEN'S CLIFF

A quaint seaside village's most chilling secrets are revealed for the first time in this new continuity!

Britta Jackobson disappeared from the witness protection program without a trace. But could Ryan Burton return Britta to safety—when the most dangerous thing in her life was him?

Look for

WITH THE MATERIAL WITNESS IN THE SAFEHOUSE

BY CARLA CASSIDY

Available May 2008 wherever you buy books.

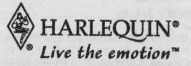

HARLEQUIN®

Live the emotion™

www.eHarlequin.com

HI69329

HARLEQUIN®

Blaze™

COMING NEXT MONTH

#393 INDULGE ME Isabel Sharpe
Forbidden Fantasies
Darcy Wolf has three wild fantasies she's going to fulfill before she leaves town. But after seducing her hottie housepainter Tyler Houston, she might just have to put Fantasy #2 and Fantasy #3 on hold!

#394 NIGHTCAP Kathleen O'Reilly
Those Sexy O'Sullivans, Bk. 3
Sean O'Sullivan—watch out! Three former college girlfriends have just hatched a revenge plot on the world's most lovable womanizer. Cleo Hollings, in particular, is anxious to get started on her make-life-difficult-for-Sean plan. Only, she never guesses how difficult it will be for her when she starts sleeping with the enemy.

#395 UP CLOSE AND PERSONAL Joanne Rock
Who's impersonating sizzling sensuality guru Jessica Winslow? Rocco Easton is going undercover to find out. And he has to do it soon, because the identity thief is getting braver, pretending to be Jessica everywhere—even in his bed!

#396 A SEXY TIME OF IT Cara Summers
Extreme
Bookstore owner Neely Rafferty can't believe it when she realizes that the time-traveling she does in her dreams is actually real. And so, she soon discovers, is the sexy time-cop who's come to stop her. Max Gale arrives in 2008 with a job to do. And he'll do it, too—if Neely ever lets him out of her bed....

#397 FIRE IN THE BLOOD Kelley St. John
The Sexth Sense, Bk. 4
Chantalle Bedeau is being haunted by a particularly nasty ghost, and the only person who can help her is medium Tristan Vicknair. Sure, she hasn't seen him since their incredible one-night stand but what's the worst he can do—give her the best sex of her life again?

#398 HAVE MERCY Jo Leigh
Do Not Disturb
Pet concierge Mercy Jones has seen it all working at the exclusive Hush Hotel in Manhattan. But when sexy Will Desmond saunters in with his pooch she's shocked by the fantasies he generates. This is one man who could unleash the animal in Mercy!

www.eHarlequin.com

HBCNM0408